The Bastard from Fairyland

This book is dedicated to numerous people who have been instrumental in its development. The good folk of Glastonbury who provided insights into the legends and informed so much of my research. To my daughter, Lauren, whose timely intervention with books on writing informed my creative processes. To Sarah Linley, another wonderful writer whose work I admire enormously and who provided honest feedback and encouragement when I needed it most.

You can find out more about Phil Parker and The Knights' Trilogy at:
https://philparkerwriter.wixsite.com/fantasy
My Twitter account is:
@PhilSpeculates

"Either I mistake your shape and making quite,
Or else you are that shrewd and knavish sprite
Called Robin Goodfellow."

A Midsummer Night's Dream, Act II, Scene 1.

Contents

Chapter 1

There were fairies at the bottom of my garden and they were torturing someone.

Technically they weren't Fae. My people didn't like to bloody their hands, not when they could use Spriggans, as an enslaved race they had the perfect skill-set for doing the fighting for them. Their seven-foot height and ape-like limbs, made them easy to spot through the spy-hole in my boarded windows. Whoever was out there now, whose screams had first drawn my attention, was another victim of Spriggan sadism that had become commonplace since the invasion. The difference this time, they were doing it in my back garden. It had to be deliberate provocation.

They'd come for me. Finally. After centuries of waiting, my people had demonstrated how long they could hold a grudge.

Dragging some hapless human to my door and doing unspeakable things to him would bring me running, sword in hand, into a trap no doubt. Screams turned into a high-pitched wail. It had to be a kid. They were trying to yank my heart strings, obviously no one had told them they'd been severed long ago. This wasn't my fight, whoever was screaming wasn't my responsibility, I'd be stupid to give up the safety of my cottage, booby-trapped for just this eventuality.

More screams. A plea for it to stop. Silence.

I waited. Listened.

A loud, protracted howl, like a wounded animal. A pause. Next, gibbering calls for help, designed to draw me out. They'd know I'd been a Trooping Fairy once, how the need to save others had been hard-wired into my brain.

Indoctrination I'd spent centuries in the human realm trying to repress.

Another plea for help, desperate and raw now. They'd keep it going, Spriggans knew how to make torture last, it was an art form to them. It all came down to how long I could hold out listening to its orchestration.

Whoever was in charge of fetching me home, knew what they were doing. It was the screams of a kid. I couldn't stand by and listen to the injustice of it any longer.

Well, never let it be said Robin Goodfellow didn't answer the call, no matter if it was from a bloody refugee's brat who was nothing more than bait. I grabbed my iron sword from where it hung, pride of place, on my kitchen wall. Unlocked the door, threw it open.

'All right, you Spriggan bastards. Want a fight, do you?'

Sword aloft, running for all I was worth, battle fury rediscovered after all this time.

'Come on then!'

Four Spriggans, built like enormous orang-utans, turned their attention from a teenage boy strung up between two apple trees in my orchard, the skin on his back striped red. He was a pathetic specimen of humanity, a bag of bones in rags plastered to his body by the freezing rain. Confident in their greater number, the four Spriggans lazily raised swords and cudgels, ignorant of what it meant to be a Trooping Fairy. I smiled. I'd enjoy teaching them never to underestimate an assailant, a lesson I'd learned painfully long ago.

One of them, the tallest, strode towards me, heavy footsteps squelching in the mud, cudgel raised over his bald head. He picked up speed as I got within striking distance, with a circular movement of his arm he swung his cudgel to drive my jaw into my brain. Except I wasn't where he expected me to be. I pivoted, turned through ninety degrees, heard the swish of the cudgel as it flew past me. It left his seven-foot frame exposed for a second, enough time to run my blade through a bloated stomach that brought him tumbling to the ground. I sliced the throat as I turned to face my next opponent who was rapidly reassessing the threat it faced.

Spriggans are good fighters but they're not quick. At moving or thinking. By the time it had decided I wasn't going to be a pushover, I'd sliced a bloody gash across its thighs so it fell to its knees, a better height from which to cut its throat. It fell next to its comrade, their blood forming red pools amidst the tussocks of long grass.

A strong wind, straight off the Bristol Channel, strafed us with pellets of ice. I was used to our new form of extreme British weather; my chums weren't. The next Spriggan roared its anger as it held its long blade aloft and ran towards me, wiping rainwater off its face. All you need is a distraction, a second where your opponent is focused on something else. I was trained to ignore all extraneous factors, schooled in ways so painful you never forgot the lesson, I allowed the rain and the ice to hit my face and kept my eyes fixed on my rangy and angry adversary.

The trouble with fighting Spriggans lies in their length of reach, they can slice your head off before you can inflict a scratch, the answer lies in getting inside their arms before your head hits the floor and rolls away. Wiping his eyes at just the right moment gave me that chance, I ducked my head and ran at him. I gambled on the mud allowing me to push him backwards while preventing his greater strength from getting the traction needed to stop me. My bet paid off, my head hit firm stomach muscle but I had enough momentum to cause him to lose his balance. His arms windmilled as he tried to remain upright, an action that made him commit the gravest sin any warrior could commit. He dropped his sword. I grinned as I remembered the beatings I'd suffered for doing the same thing, memories are fickle like that. As he toppled backwards, like a demolished chimney stack, I ran him through. He was dead before he hit the ground.

The fourth spriggan looked aghast at the carnage and then glanced at his knife, then at me. His fear was evident in the way his hand shook as he drew back the knife he'd used to get the sound effects he wanted from the boy. With a deft flick of its wrist, he flung it, I ducked and it struck the apple tree behind me, no more than an inch from my head.

I didn't take my eyes off him as I reached up and pulled it out of the wood, he stared back at me through the rain, rooted to the spot, unwilling to commit to any other reaction until he knew my intention. I flipped the knife so the handle fitted snugly in my hand, making it obvious what I intended to do.

'Who sent you?'

The Spriggan's eye focused on the knife, waiting for me to throw it. In the silence that followed the kid's snivelling sobs and gasps were the only answer I received. I deliberately looked at his body and allowed my face to show anger.

'I'm not going to kill you. Not straight away.' I pantomimed weighing the knife in my hand and looked into the creature's face. 'I'll stop you from running away first. You're going to get this in your groin. Then I'll string you up.'

Spriggans aren't cowards but I suspected this one had been brought along for his skill at torturing rather than his ability to fight, he was squat and lumpy in comparison to the rest. He swallowed heavily and did nothing to hide his panic.

'So, unless you want to answer my question in a high voice, who sent you?'

He looked beyond my garden fence, to the empty street, then to the pathway at the side of my cottage. He was expecting reinforcements.

So was I. It made no sense to send a handful of spriggans, they had to know I'd defeat them easily. None of this made any sense.

He must have thought he'd distracted me sufficiently to give him time to hide behind the spread-eagled boy, as though those scarecrow dimensions offered any protection. Before he'd moved two steps he screamed as the knife struck him squarely between his legs and he crumbled to the wet earth, holding what was left of his genitals, blood coursed through his fingers.

I strode over to him, he watched, petrified and blubbering.

'I told you. Next answer in a high voice. Who sent you?'

I yanked him up by the collar, exposing his throat, with my other hand I pressed my blade against it. He squealed loudly, like a stuck pig.

'Last chance...'

Amidst pleas for mercy, his snivelling delivered my answer, 'The High Lord.'

I sighed. Oberon had finally decided to punish me. There would be others arriving shortly, this little incident was no more than a calling card. They'd turn up in greater numbers, I doubted they'd care if they took me back dead or alive. I certainly wasn't bothered.

I ran the blade across soft flesh and let the body drop to the ground.

I was soaking wet and freezing cold, as the adrenalin from the fight faded, I felt empty and flat. I began to plan my resistance for when the rest arrived. I certainly wasn't going to cooperate and accompany them without taking as many out as I could. I had a reputation to uphold.

The boy's sobbing penetrated my deliberations. I ambled over, cut his ropes with my sword and watched him slump to the muddy ground. All he wore was a thin pair of trousers and shoes that were falling apart, his skin was blue with cold, where it wasn't streaked with his blood. In this weather, he'd die of hypothermia, it was common among refugees at this time of year. Bodies like his littered the countryside. He looked up at me as I turned to make my way back to the cottage, I needed to get ready.

'Please. Help me. Please. Mister Goodfellow.'

I froze. The kid knew my name. My mind raced with explanations, paranoia fed every one of them. I turned and looked into the desperate features of the lad, he had to be no more than fifteen though he was so thin it was difficult to tell. The kid tried to smile but the freezing rain washed it off.

It was his deep brown eyes and high cheek bones that reminded me of an older version of the youth staring up at me.

'Are you...?' I couldn't bring myself to finish the sentence.

The kid nodded, the smile appeared again. 'Mickey's brother. Yeah. I'm Simon.'

'Where is he?'

A flicker of eyes and snatched breath told me what to expect.

'Dead.' Eyes found the mud at his feet and stared at it. 'The Taunton gang. Two months ago.'

I stared at the kid as feelings, pushed down deep, found their way back to the surface. Mickey had always looked for the best in people, he was naïve in that way. He'd been the same with me, insisted I found a purpose to life again, laughed at my rants, dismissed my dark moods and made my bed a place of happiness. Qualities that had got him killed.

The kid looked up at me, red eyes full of tears, breath coming in spasms. He didn't need to repeat his plea for help, my expression probably showed the regret. I pulled my attention away from the kid, tried to remind myself of those severed heart strings but apparently, they'd regrown. I looked around the garden, at the street beyond, expectant. I still couldn't work out why the Fae had used this kid, unless it had just been some awful coincidence.

'Oh, fucking hell. Get inside.'

The lad struggled to stand, in the end it was quicker to pick him up and carry him indoors, he weighed so little it was like carrying an infant. I took him into the bathroom, cleaned his wounds and ran a bath.

'I'll find some clothes. There'll be food downstairs afterwards.'

11

'Mickey said you were a good man. He loved you, you know.'

I did. That was why I'd driven him away. Towards a murderous bunch of bastards who ruled like medieval warlords. I went downstairs, furious at myself for breaking my golden rule of not getting involved with humans. Like my rabbit casserole, my resentment simmered for the next fifteen minutes, until the kid turned up, wrapped in a towel.

I nodded to the pile of clothes on a chair, left behind by his brother. While he dressed, I ladled casserole into two bowls. I turned around and sighed at the scarecrow lost in the clothes of a man with a muscular body, one I'd savoured getting to know.

Those Taunton bastards had murdered a soldier, a man who'd fought at the Battle of Swindon to protect them from the Fae invasion, the injustice of it stirred resentment into anger. I stared at the kid as he wolfed down the casserole, at the features that summoned his brother's ghost. It had been good to spend time with another warrior, someone who understood what it meant to fight so others could live. The memory only made me aware of how lonely I was now, so I dismissed it. I filled the kid's bowl a second time, it was gone in no time. I filled our mugs with cider, the lad drank it thirstily, and thanked me.

'What happened to Mickey?' I ground my teeth, furious at myself for wanting to know the details. 'What were you doing getting caught by those Taunton bastards?'

The kid shuddered and, for a moment, he looked like he was going to blub again. He controlled himself with a few deep breaths.

'There was no work here in Glastonbury, except for those with boats brave enough to risk the storms at sea. There was supposed to be work picking apples...'

'He should have known better. There haven't been large orchards since the mega-storms destroyed them a decade ago. There isn't work anywhere. It's just stories of hope passed around by refugees. He shouldn't have gone. He should have stayed here.'

My tempest blew itself out the moment I uttered that final sentence. The kid looked at me, wide-eyed. Quieter now. So was my own voice.

'I told him not to trust people.'

Wind hurtled down the chimney, making sparks dance like hyperactive fireflies. Nothing I'd learned so far explained why the Fae had used this kid for bait. Or why they weren't already attacking me. With the meal finished I motioned for the lad to join me in front of the fire in the hope he could provide some answers.

'And why did you come back?'

He stared into the flames, jerked a thumb over his shoulder, indicating the landscape beyond my walls.

'I used to live here. Till the floods destroyed everything. I thought I stood a better chance in a place I knew. Except nothing's the same any more, is it?'

'And you travelled all this way without getting caught by slavers? Or by the Fae?'

He looked at me just a little too long before turning back to the fire, watching me out of the corners of his eyes. I growled a threat and it was enough. His words tumbled from his mouth, like he was desperate to spew them out.

'They found me. Near the coast. They were going to kill me.' He shuddered. 'Until they asked me if I knew this town, when I said I did, that was when they got interested.'

I held my breath.

'They asked me if I knew you.'

There we were. Finally.

'What did you say?' The kid had stopped, probably expecting me to vent my fury. I felt vaguely surprised there wasn't any fury to vent.

'I didn't want to tell them, Mister Goodfellow.'

'But you did.'

A tight nod. 'I'm not very good at lying. And I was scared. I told them everything I knew. All the stuff Mickey had told me about you.'

I wasn't angry at the kid, I'd got the answers I needed. I stood up, I had to get ready. I took my supply of salt from the cupboard, it has a painfully astringent effect on Spriggan skin. The kid watched, his question didn't disguise the hope in his voice.

'You're going to fight them, aren't you? Like you did the others.' He ignored my grunt of disinterest. 'Mickey said you used to be a soldier for them. You know, the fairies. Is that true?'

I ignored him and started to clean Spriggan blood from my sword.

'It's just that you don't look like a fairy. When I was a kid, you know, before the floods and stuff, I thought fairies were small, with wings and looked like flowers.'

'We have the Victorians to thank for that.'

'Who?' He scrutinised my face with a frown, when I didn't reply he continued. 'Mickey said you're really old too. But you look like a young man, there's no lines on your face or stuff like that. You look the same age as Mickey.'

'Yeah, it's all down to a healthy diet.'

He scowled, uncertain if I was being serious.

'Mickey said you could see how old you were by looking in your eyes but I can't, they're just really deep blue.'

'Yeah. Well. Mickey talked a load of shit.'

The lad blinked, realised he was treading on thin ice. His endless references to Mickey made my simmering anger return to the boil, I needed to bring this cosy situation to an end.

'Listen,' I said, 'I'm not a nice man. For a very long time, do you know how your people described me?' A shake of the head. 'A demon. A hobgoblin. They even wrote a play about me, I wasn't very nice in that either. I'm something more than a soldier. When they come for me, you need to be long gone. It won't be safe near me. Do you understand?'

We both heard the heavy footsteps outside, the kid looked at me, panic written across his face in capital letters. He wasn't going to escape and we both knew it. I ran to the spyholes in my boarded windows, there were Spriggans everywhere, standing like sentinels. They'd be waiting for whoever was in charge to give the order to attack. I grabbed my sword and turned to the kid.

'Get upstairs, quick. Find somewhere to hide.'

He didn't hesitate, he hauled up his clown trousers and hurried to the staircase.

An explosion rocked the cottage, dust fell from the ceiling beams. They'd tried to get in upstairs, it looked like my ancient booby-traps still worked. Outside urgent commands were bellowed. Another explosion and outside things landed heavily on the ground. More commands, growled and furious this time. They were going to make me suffer for this but I didn't care, I was a Trooping Fairy and we always ran towards a fight, never away. A loud thud smacked against the door and I held my sword ready.

Chapter 2

As a soldier, you often wonder where you'll die; in my youth I'd hoped it would be in battle, later in the bed of the man I loved. Reality was going be less glorious, the death of Robin Goodfellow in a kitchen wouldn't be a popular tavern tale. But then who would care?

Another explosion. More loud groans and muffled commands.

I wondered who was leading the attack. It wouldn't be Oberon; kings send minions for stuff like this. The big ugly bastards currently helping to demolish my home needed someone to issue the orders, I wondered which poor bugger had been given the responsibility. Probably some underling I'd never heard of.

Heavy footsteps outside. This was going to be like old times. I readied myself.

The door flew off its hinges and smashed heavily against the stone-slabbed floor. I hurled salt in the face of the first hulking spriggan to appear in the entrance, it clawed its skin and howled until I ran it through with my sword. The body fell like a huge tree over my threshold. A quick pivot, maintaining balance and momentum, blade slicing through the air and across the bulging belly of the second attacker as it stormed the doorway. It collapsed on its comrade in a tangle of over-long, ape-like limbs and steaming intestines.

A third rushed at me, roaring. This one was huge, I sprang to meet it, raising my sword at the same time, to bring it down on the arm carrying an enormous cudgel. The roar turned into a howl as, weapon-less but undeterred, it rushed me, relying on its mass to knock me to the floor. It tried to grab me with its one arm but I was too quick, a nifty dodge let me stick my sword up into a foul-smelling armpit. With a groan my latest victim joined the others in a rapidly-growing wall of corpses in the doorway.

The next one brandished a sword in hand and a grin on a misshapen face. He was fast and skilled with his weapon, we parried a few times but he made the mistake of using his strength to push me backwards. Swordplay needs dexterity, plus a few sly tricks I'd learned over time. A quick upward flick of my blade forced him into an upward parrying movement, with his eyes on our swords he didn't see me kick him between the legs, he felt it though and doubled up groaning, making it easy to ram my blade through his ribs. He sank atop the pile of stinking bodies.

The doorway had become a choke point, now it was half-filled with spriggan corpses I could defend it, they'd need to knock down the wall to reach me. It wouldn't take them long and I was probably moments from death, but I hadn't felt so alive, my body thrummed with battle energy, the drug I'd fought hard to resist as a youth.

'Robin!'

The voice brought me up sharp. With no adversaries left I froze.

'Robin? Can you hear me?'

I held my breath as ice coursed through my veins and time stopped. I was vulnerable to attack but my head buzzed with possibilities I couldn't begin to process. I stood in my kitchen, blankly staring beyond the doorway trying to work out what to do next. Oberon must have plumbed the depths of irony to achieve his revenge.

The voice hadn't changed in all this time, it still held the same mellow tone and lyrical lilt of the storyteller. A voice which had melted my heart a long time ago. I struggled to find my own voice amidst the lump in my throat.

'I can hear you Oisin.'

I pictured his reaction to me using his name, his pause satisfied me.

'We need to talk. Let's end this senseless bloodshed.'

'Since when do you care about the death of a few spriggans?'

'I wasn't thinking of their blood.'

There was something in his tone that intrigued me, a tinge of regret perhaps? Or was I just being an incurable romantic?

'Why does it matter if they kill me? You'll have done your duty by dragging my body back to the Dark Court. I'll just shoot my mouth off if you take me back alive.'

Silence.

The eventual reply had an unmistakeable tinge of curiosity.

'Why do you think we're here Robin?'

Now I was the one silenced. His question suggested a different scenario to the one I'd anticipated, I couldn't think of a reply but thankfully Oisin didn't wait.

'Let's meet and talk so we can clear up this misunderstanding.'

My home was a ruin, there were bodies everywhere and we'd only had a misunderstanding?

'All right.'

My whirling brain searched for explanations. A troop of spriggans had sought me out, used the boy hiding upstairs as bait and they were led by the man I'd once loved. Why had Oberon sent Oisin to capture me when I hadn't seen him in the lifespan of several human generations, a man who had no military experience. I knew every intonation Oisin used, any lie had always been instantly obvious to me, so much so we used to joke about it. Unless he'd changed significantly, Oisin was telling the truth, this was some sort of misunderstanding. I tried to think, be ready for every eventuality because that was what warriors were supposed to do. My brain could only focus on one thing.

I was about to see the man I'd once loved and had abandoned.

The morning sun cast Oisin's shadow over the stinking corpses and made me look up from staring at my feet where I'd hoped I'd find a smattering of inspiration.

'Hello Robin.'

I peered blindly at the dark silhouette standing in my doorway, desperate to see his face again. He stepped awkwardly over the bodies at his feet and I gazed into perfect beauty.

He'd always hated it when I described him that way, he'd rebuke me for assigning him perfection when he was nothing of the kind. He hadn't changed in all this time. Blonde curls framed a perfectly symmetrical face with a strong jaw, high and perfectly defined cheek bones and cornflower blue eyes. Despite everything, my heart lurched and the saliva in my throat evaporated.

'Hello Oisin,' I croaked.

Suddenly, catching me hopelessly distracted, another man appeared in the doorway.

'Well, isn't this awkward eh? How long is it since you two saw each other?'

Perfectly-formed features, the work of hours of careful shaving, rigorous skincare and styling of hair that contained almost as much oil as the conceited voice, dragged my attention away from Oisin. The smell of dead spriggan caused his fine aquiline nose to wrinkle, I expected a perfumed handkerchief to appear to cover the offended nostrils.

'Llyr.'

Astonishment and that dry throat I mentioned, robbed me of the disdain I tried to put into my reply. Either he didn't notice or didn't care, I suspected the latter. As he took a couple of steps towards me I had enough time to glance at Oisin's expression. What I saw didn't fill me with confidence. My brain abandoned its search for meaning and made subtle preparations to fight. Going by the wide and perfect smile I was awarded, nothing appeared further from this man's mind but I knew that meant nothing. He waggled perfect eyebrows suggestively.

'You're a handsome specimen of manhood Robin, you've still got those exciting bulges in all the right places.'

I rolled my eyes to let him know we'd moved beyond boyish humour. He peered at me harder.

'But those beautiful blue eyes seem to have lost their mischief, there's a sadness that wasn't there before.' He looked around my kitchen with thinly-disguised distaste. 'I'm beginning to see why. Have you lived in... this... for long?'

He drew a finger over my kitchen table and examined it with a curled lip.

'What do you want Llyr?'

The perfectly-formed smile widened, if that was possible.

'Always straight to the point, eh Robin? Not even an invitation to seat your guests.'

He reached out to take a chair and thought better of it as he withdrew his hand and brushed away atoms of dust.

'I said, what do you want?'

I turned it into enough of a growl to make my intent obvious. I still held my sword and he glanced at my hand as I shifted my grip.

Perfect teeth flashed at me. 'Relax Robin. We're here to talk. But I would like to be reassured of our safety. Would you mind if Oisin checked the other rooms? I'm sure in this hovel of yours, that won't take long?'

I shrugged. I had no choice in the matter. I hoped the lad upstairs was well hidden.

Oisin marched past, without looking in my direction. I caught his scent and felt my pulse quicken. The bastard standing in front of me noticed and grinned wickedly.

'I've missed you Robin. We used to have such good times.'

I wanted to smash those perfect teeth down his throat.

'Do you mean when you behaved like some love-struck dairy maid contriving ways for me to fuck you?'

The grin froze for an instant, when it returned there was an emptiness behind it. I'd hurt him. Good.

'In the early days, after your sudden departure, Oisin and I would speak often of your propensity to hurt other people, him more than anyone of course. I'm not surprised he never forgave you.'

The conceit in his smile wasn't just satisfaction at his retaliation, there was something else behind those dark eyes. He'd changed. There was no sign of the playful, rebellious kid eager to establish himself as the crown prince. Instead his narrowed eyes and lips displayed a feral quality I didn't like. It made me wonder why he was here, he ran enormous risks, if humans captured him it could end the war. It left me with one question: why was he risking so much by coming to find me?

'Why are you risking so much coming to find me Llyr?'

I was never one to beat about the bush.

The inevitable grin displayed whiter-than-white teeth but now I saw less of a toothpaste advert and more of the snarl of a hyena. It was the slightly manic giggle that went with it that made me think of the animal.

'I've missed your candour Robin. The Dark Court is full of fawning bootlickers; it's refreshing to hear someone speak their mind.'

'I'm sure. But to answer my question?'

The hyena grin widened. 'I seek your help Robin.'

'Is that why you arrived here with a battalion of spriggans and duped me into believing it was only Oisin I was inviting into my home?'

His eyes didn't leave mine, even as he picked up a wooden chair, spun it round and straddled it, laying his arms across the upright back and resting his chin on them. An act of ostentatious affectation and nothing like the boy I'd known.

'Would you have invited me in otherwise?'

'Of course. We used to be friends.'

He chuckled at my lie. 'Well, I didn't want to take the risk. We'd parted on such sour terms. I didn't know if you'd retained a grudge.'

Grudge? Me? Too fucking right, I retained a grudge. The bastard had wrecked my life for no other reason than his pride got hurt.

I smiled and shrugged. 'Harbouring grudges causes frown lines.'

It got a loud and unconvincing guffaw. 'Good. I want us to be friends again.'

'So, tell me why you're here.'

'I want you to tell me you where you've hidden the Knights.'

I maintained a complacent expression, Llyr would be watching every facial muscle for a clue, my mind raced as I fed him lies.

'The Knights? Why do they matter? You've all but destroyed humanity's opposition. Leave them a couple of years and they'll finish themselves off. Besides, this generation of Knights are still kids.' I snorted contempt and hoped I sounded believable. 'It's been so long since Gawain promised Arthur he and his descendants would defend mankind against the Fae, most of it has been forgotten anyway. These two kids have very limited grasp of their heritage and certainly no expertise with their special skills.'

I gave him by best smile.

'The Knights aren't a threat to you. Forget them.'

His smile remained but it was a lie too.

'You didn't tell me where they are.'

Llyr continued his scrutiny.

'You're right that they don't pose a threat, we made sure of that by eliminating the previous generation in readiness for the invasion.' I made sure not to show any reaction. 'They serve a different purpose Robin. A political one.'

'I don't understand.' I really didn't.

Upstairs loud thumps reverberated through the ceiling. He picked up on my concern. His top lip curled.

'Sounds like Oisin's found something.'

My mind whirled in desperation as options presented themselves as if I was flicking through pages of a manual. They all involved killing the bastard but I doubted he would leave himself so vulnerable, Llyr was too devious for that, suddenly an explanation formed out of the confusion in my head.

'You're facing opposition from the Dark Court aren't you? They've lost faith in you.'

The smile slid off his face and left only the snarl.

'Now I remember why I forced you out of my Court.'

'It's yours now is it?' I said, proud I was irking him into making mistakes.

'Tell me where the Knights are Robin.' The snarl had deepened.

I took a deep breath and hoped I could provoke him into reacting before events upstairs compromised me.

'Llyr, go fuck yourself.'

I raised my sword and launched at him. If I was fast, he was faster. He had something in his hand I realised, small and shiny. He hurled it at my feet and suddenly, I couldn't move. Icy cold permeated my feet in a second, coursed through my veins into my calves and up to my knee, my sprint turned into slow motion until I came to an abrupt halt. By the time my brain had caught up with my legs, they glistened with thousands of miniature diamonds, like frost had enveloped them.

I looked up at the bastard's face. Needless to say, it was grinning.

'I had the royal thaumaturgicians develop this clever little device for me. I've found it very useful. It rises just far enough up the leg that it immobilises the victim but ensures sensations elsewhere in the body remain unimpaired.'

'Llyr, I swear, you'd better release me...'

He stepped around me, out of view, suddenly he smacked my wrist so hard that I dropped my sword out of surprise. He allowed the same hand to caress my arse.

'When you saw fit to inform the Dark Court you'd been buggering their Crown Prince, my rivals chose to use it against me. When you incapacitate them in this way you can commit all kinds of ignominy on them.'

He stepped in front of me, just out of reach of my fists.

'Because of you I had to develop the strength to withstand their treason. I confess it introduced me to satisfaction I'd never encountered before.'

'You're sick Llyr.'

'Perhaps. It doesn't matter. I've replaced my feeble-minded father and now I'm the ruler of the Dark

Court, everyone does as I say. That includes you Robin. Oh, you might fight me initially. But you'll tell me what I want to know.'

The door opened, Oisin stood there, face pale and anxious. Behind him two spriggan soldiers held the boy who struggled and fought them impotently. The moment he saw me the kid begged for my help until he saw my own situation, then his face fell and he began to cry. Oisin glanced at me but said nothing as he gestured for the guards to stand the boy next to Llyr.

We all knew what was going to happen. The boy looked at me the whole time, his enormous, tear-filled eyes full of condemnation for not keeping him safe.

'Let the boy go Llyr. He's nothing.'

A red tongue licked narrow lips as a smirk formed on them.

'I disagree. It's significant that you brought him in to your home.'

'Let him go. He did his job, leading you to me. I'm the one you want to hurt.'

'True. But you can be so uncooperative Robin. No, the boy's purpose is more of a lever for negotiation. I knew you couldn't resist rescuing him.'

All the pieces of the jigsaw that had confused me until now, fell into place and I didn't like the picture it created. Llyr watched me process it all, when I looked at him again, he repeated his question. The edge in his voice was unmistakeable.

'Tell me where you've hidden the Knights.'

My mind hunted for some way to end my dilemma. I searched each face for an answer, focusing on Oisin's longest in the hope he'd do something to prevent the inevitable. He chose to stare at the floor.

'If I betray the Knights you'll parade them in front of both Courts, martial the political impetus to prove you've seized the initiative to end this war. If the Light Court join you, the human race will be annihilated. There would be carnage.'

The bastard nodded. 'I suppose I should be surprised by your assessment but you always were a political animal Robin. My question demands a simple decision: where do you pledge your loyalty? To the human vermin that infest this planet or to your own kind?'

'It isn't that simple.'

He looked at me. The grin remained in place but those brown eyes, filled with so much malice, darkened further. Slowly, to build the drama, Llyr took a highly polished and ostentatiously decorated knife from his belt and held it to the boy's throat. The kid gave a strangled scream and stopped wriggling against the implacable grasp of the two spriggans. Oisin continued staring at the floor.

'Tell me where the Knights are Robin.'

The boy looked at me, his eyes told me he knew his fate as enormous tears tumbled down his cheek. Eyes that reminded me of his brother.

I shook my head.

The knife slid across the white throat, a thin line quickly opened as bubbling red blood splashed onto the clown-size sweater. The spriggans released the boy to flop on the floor, to spasm and writhe at my feet, his clothes which had kept his brother warm once, absorbed his blood, its stench made me want to vomit. Eventually, in what felt like an eternity, the spasming stopped and the kid's eyes stared back at me with their hollow accusations.

I looked across at Llyr who watched me with that same sick smile. He pantomimed a coy finger to his mouth and flicked perfectly manicured eyebrows at me. I felt Puck rise up inside me. He was the last thing I needed.

Chapter 3

If Puck took control I had no idea what would happen. I wondered if he'd even care that my legs were frozen to the floor. With his anger-driven and obsessive need to kill, he'd probably rip our legs free to get to his victim and that scared the shit out of me. I tried to stay calm, keep him imprisoned in the subterranean recesses of my brain where he belonged. If I focused enough and shut the world out, I sometimes succeeded. The times I failed were when a part of me wanted revenge and I wanted to ram that fucking knife in Llyr's cold heart now more than anything.

Suddenly, in the ruined doorway, a spriggan, wild-eyed and anxious.

'My lord, the humans. They've found us. They're attacking.'

Llyr turned, snarling.

'Then fucking deal with them. Can't you see I'm busy?'

'I'm sorry my lord. But there are many and it appears more are on the way...'

Knife in hand, dripping the blood of an innocent, the murderous bastard roared his fury and provided the evidence, as if any was needed, that he was insane. He pointed the knife at me, eyes wide with fury.

'You will tell me where you've hidden the Knights, Robin. You think I'll stop at one of these creatures? I've killed hundreds of them. Thousands. And I'll kill thousands more until you cooperate.' He must have seen something in my expression. 'And you will cooperate. Because I will kill whatever I need to get my way. Know that Robin.'

He flicked his eyes at Oisin.

'Anything.'

He marched out of my kitchen bellowing orders, the two spriggans now spattered with the boy's blood remained outside, on sentry duty. As Llyr strode out of my home and away from my wrath, I felt Puck start to fade. I heaved a sigh of relief.

Oisin went to follow until I called his name. He paused in the doorway.

'You've changed Oisin. The man I knew would never support such a fucking lunatic.'

Torment wrote its name in the face that turned to me but I could tell it wasn't going to be enough. I needed to twist the knife. I pointed at the body where blood formed a dark red halo around the boy's head.

'You're just as responsible for that boy's death. Is that what you do now? Murder children?'

I could tell my words wounded the integrity he prized so highly, by the deepening lines on his forehead and the wide eyes so close to tears now. I hoped the man I knew couldn't change that much because he was my only means of freedom.

'You don't understand Robin.'

'No. I don't.'

He stood there in my doorway, looking indecisive. He needed one more push and if guilt wasn't going to work I needed to twist the knife further.

'But if you are the man I loved so long ago, you'll free me so I can stop this bastard before he kills others.'

He swallowed hard and shook his head. He was weakening.

'He'd kill me.'

'He's going to kill you anyway. When he's run out of bargaining tools, he'll use you.'

I jerked a thumb at the pathetic little body. He swallowed hard, he was genuinely scared I realised. This wasn't just indecision, he was fighting real terror.

'He told me to come along so I could prevent you from getting killed.'

Llyr's words started to sound like a lie. Oisin's reactions suggested he might still have some feelings for me. If that was true, I could use them to get out of this mess.

'He manipulated you, Oisin. You were his ultimate bargaining tool. He knew you were the one thing in this world, and Tir na nÓg, I would never sacrifice.'

Those impossibly blue eyes latched on to mine then glanced at the boy's body and returned to search my face. He sighed heavily.

'Do you have any salt?'

I pointed at the pantry as I gave the man my warmest smile, there I was accusing Llyr of manipulation. I was such a hypocrite.

Like salt works on a slug, it dissolved the stuff encasing my feet and legs into a foul-smelling white foam. I stumbled, blood hadn't discovered my feet but Oisin caught me and held me tightly. His scent intoxicated me, happy memories flooded my addled brain but I dismissed them.

Outside an explosion made the foundations of the cottage shiver.

'It won't take him long to deal with the human threat,' Oisin said quietly. 'He'll be back soon.'

I nodded. There'd be a few hundred citizens of Glastonbury, armed with axes, spades and pitchforks, sacrificing their lives for no other reason other than to repel the invader. The sooner I drew Llyr away, the more would survive. Beyond that I wasn't sure what I was going to do except guarantee the Knights remained safe. That was one pledge I would give my life to keep. I picked up my sword and collected the rucksack I kept for emergencies like this.

'Come on.'

I stumbled towards the doorway as the feeling slowly returned to my feet and toes.

'What do you mean?'

I turned and sighed. 'You can't stay here.'

'But, you don't trust me. Do you?'

'No. But I'm not leaving you to die either, so come on!'

His angelic features held a mixture of relief and panic, it made me smile.

Another explosion, louder than the one before, made the air itself shudder. It was followed by screams and panicked shouts. I knew how spriggans fought, I guessed their technology wouldn't have changed much in the time I'd been away, it meant the people of Glastonbury wouldn't stand a chance. It was a battle between David and Goliath, the equivalent of a sling shot against an enemy with bazookas.

The two spriggans outside were thankfully more involved in watching the battle so didn't immediately notice me stumble through the doorway. I finished them off with my sword and hoped my legs and feet could recover to aid my escape as I lurched over my soggy vegetable patch and through my abandoned orchard.

A rag-tag bunch of locals had barricaded either end of the street at the end of my garden with rusting cars so they could trap their enemy in the middle. The trouble was they couldn't capitalise on their advantage with their limited weaponry of bricks, lumps of concrete and swiftly made Molotov cocktails that often exploded while they were being thrown. Spriggans and certain other species of my people cannot bear to touch, or be near to, iron so the barricades were partially successful but Llyr was blasting them to pieces with a weapon I knew well; the marekanite sphere.

Like so much of Fae technology it was simple and efficient. I'd used them as a parlour trick to amaze the court of King Charles II, they'd called them Prince Rupert's Drops, after the King's cousin began using them. He was something of a show-off. They looked innocent enough, tadpole-shaped pieces of glass, formed by dropping a specially-formulated molten glass into cold water, when you broke the surface tension it exploded. Change the chemistry of the glass, build them bigger and you have a weapon with such an enormous percussive charge it can destroy objects ten times its size. Like rusting car bodies.

The locals didn't know any of this. All they could see were fairies hurling small shiny things through the air that shimmered briefly before exploding with the force of an armoured shell. For generations human beings believed my people capable of magic, the expressions of shock and awe on the faces of the local population hadn't changed in all that time. They'd retell these moments and describe how magic was used to defeat them, rather than the less exciting solution of basic chemistry.

'This way!' I called to Oisin and leapt into the middle of the street, making as much noise as possible. From one end of the street I heard Llyr's fury screamed at me so I lumbered in the opposite direction, where smoke from the remains of a car chassis hung lazily in the still morning air and created a gap in the barricade. We burst through it, surprising the handful of cowering young men who scuttled out of our way in panic. One of them recognised me and called out to the others not to attack, though to be honest, they were too busy hiding to offer any kind of threat.

'Let the fairies through!' I screamed at them, 'we'll lead them away from the town.'

The young man nodded in wide-eyed astonishment. Oisin and I made our way down the street as another explosion landed so close I could feel its heat on my skin. A quick glance over my shoulder told me I'd wasted my time giving any instructions. Bodies, at least parts of them, and the remains of the barricade, lay scattered across the street.

We turned a corner and zig-zagged our way through streets and alleyways, sensations were finally returning to my feet and legs. I needed a plan and keeping in front of Llyr's rampaging spriggans was as strategic as it got.

Oisin held my arm, turned me to face him. 'I couldn't have stopped Llyr from. You Know. I was too. Scared.'

I knew by his furtive looks, as we'd hurried along the street, he'd needed to unload his guilt. I'd never met anyone who cherished his principles so highly, they'd been the cause of so many of our arguments once. That he'd compromised them for Llyr intrigued me but I looked at him blankly. I wasn't going to let him off the hook so easily.

'What you saw Robin. It was just a glimpse of what he can do.'

'Why isn't anyone stopping him?' I panted, running with uncooperative legs was tiring.

I got a contemptuous snort. 'He's powerful Robin. As Oberon's insanity worsened more and more power was transferred to him as the only heir to the throne. Some questioned his ability to rule but they quickly disappeared, had accidents or died in mysterious circumstances. Everyone else learned to do as they were told.'

'I warned them. I told them Oberon's paranoia was real. But no one listened, they did nothing as he took away my money and my friends for no other reason than he believed I was committing treason against him. Serves them right.'

I stared angrily at the man who avoided eye contact. So he should, he'd been one of them. We hurried along a deserted street in silence. Eventually my resentment got the better of me.

'And now you're doing his bidding, like a good boy.'

It got the flare of indignation I hoped was still there.

'You don't know what it's been like. You ran away.'

'I didn't run away.' I gave my indignation free reign. 'Oberon's minions were out to kill me.' A vivid memory of a fight on London Bridge six centuries earlier sprang to mind. 'Did you ever hear of someone called Ankou?'

Oisin frowned and nodded.

'He was sent to kill me. Would have succeeded if I hadn't drowned him in the Thames. Oberon knew it would take somebody with his skill and determination to finish me off. We'd even trained and fought together, long ago.'

That earned me a look. I'd told Oisin some of those horror stories. I sniffed.

'Our training turned us both psychotic, the only difference was, Ankou liked it.'

We continued running as a loud explosion echoed up and down the street and a huge plume of smoke rose into the sky behind us, no doubt signifying the end to the human's resistance in Glastonbury. Oisin kept looking at me.

'Is that why you thought we'd returned for you?'

'Yeah. I thought he still held a grudge. You see…'

I felt stupid now.

'…around the same time, I shared a secret with someone, a human. A secret about Oberon and the stupid bastard wrote a play about it, even put me in it. I thought Oberon had found out about my… indiscretion.'

'I see. So Llyr's search for the Knights came as a shock?'

I just nodded, humiliated by my arrogance.

'What happened to Oberon?'

Oisin shook his head. 'Dead. Everyone suspects Llyr but there was no chance to examine the body, a mysterious fire in Oberon's bedroom prevented it. No one dared to suggest the death was anything other than a result of Oberon's insanity.'

'The Dark Court must be made up of a bunch of limp-dicked cowards if Llyr took control so easily.'

The grip on my arm tightened, Oisin's stare intensified.

'Robin, don't underestimate Llyr. You remember the members of the Trooping Fairies don't you?'

I nodded. I'd trained with them.

'They're dead.'

I stopped. The Trooping Fairies were the elite force of the Dark Court, they were the strongest, toughest, angriest fighters you could find. We prided ourselves on never being beaten, no matter what dangers we faced. Everyone trembled at the threat of the Trooping Fairies, how could they be dead?

'What do you mean? Belenus? Emer? Nisien?'

Oisin nodded, watching my reaction.

'But how? Emer could beat me with ease. At the Battle of Gabhra, when we were cornered in an old farmyard, he killed six of their finest warriors and saved our lives that day. What about Vosegus?'

'A riding accident.'

'But he taught me to ride, he was the best rider of all of us.'

'Do you see what I mean? Robin, if you hadn't escaped, you'd have been Llyr's first victim.'

I started to understand. The hardest enemy to defeat is fear, it's how dictators rule, opposition melts in the face of it. Llyr had done what all despots do, eliminate everyone who presented any kind of threat, it left no one to argue against him and no army to depose him. Oisin's anxiety made more sense, Llyr was hell-bent on regaining control of this world, to rule it and impose his own insane nightmare vision. If he captured the Knights it provided him with status and power to bring the Light Court into this war. In comparison, the Dark Court were rank amateurs. Together they would be unstoppable.

'You are going to stop him, aren't you Robin?'

I could hear the hope in Oisin's trembling voice. I could also hear the heavy thud of spriggan boots.

'I've vowed to keep the Knights safe, that's all. Now come on, we need to hurry.'

We sprinted through the alleyways of the old town until we arrived on Magdalene Street.

'This is where we arrived, in that ruin,' Oisin pointed at the remains of the Abbey.

I'd guessed as much. The Fae's invasion of the whole country had followed the same pattern, using portals from Tir na nÓg to transport spriggan armies into the middle of ancient towns and cities. Chester had been first to fall, and with it, the north-west within a day of their arrival. Lincoln cathedral was decimated as a battalion of spriggans interrupted a Sunday service by marching out of the crypt. The people of Bury St Edmunds put up a defence that cost thousands of lives and left the town a smoking ruin.

Pagan sites, with their mystical legends absorbed into Christianity, were the doorways to fairyland. The trouble was no one believed in fairies any longer. Not until they arrived bringing death and destruction and the cruelty Shakespeare understood. Much as I hated to admit anything good about that bastard.

We hurried down Benedict Street until we paused for breath in front of the square edifice of Saint Mary's church tower. Scrawled across its ancient stonework, graffiti complained about the London government's desertion while newer messages cursed the Fae and promised differing forms of retribution, frequently via the insertion of cold iron objects. Oisin gestured towards the daubing of a particularly graphic illustration.

'How do they tell the difference between human beings and Fae?'

'Quite often, they don't. All strangers are a threat. They steal food, murder people or abduct them to sell to slavers. The sadistic ones like to test newcomers to see how they react to iron, when it's placed on the skin. Or under it.'

Oisin swallowed hard. 'Nice.'

'Stay close.'

'Where are we going?'

'For help.'

Up ahead, at a street corner, a fleeting shadow coalesced and vanished in a second. Moments later, hurried footsteps echoed only to stop abruptly. A short and shrill whistle sounded a short distance away then a brick landed in the middle of the road in front of us, jagged pieces pinged off walls, boarded windows, rusting cars and the detritus of ten years of neglect.

We kept walking as nonchalantly as possible. Laughter echoed along the street, another brick smashed behind us.

'On the roof,' Oisin whispered.

I didn't need to look up at the flat-topped roofs of the houses, I'd known this route carried risks but our pursuers would be watching the main roads.

At the junction of Garvins Street a quick glance showed a line of dark human shapes standing like sentinels across its width. I deliberately ignored them and continued down Benedict Street. Houses with conventional roofs meant the bombing campaign fizzled out but as the end of the street drew closer and Wirrall Park came into view, another threat formed.

'Don't say anything, your accent will give you away. Understand?' I got a terse grunt.

The pock-marked remains of tennis courts indicated where the entrance to the park used to be. From under the stunted remains of an apple tree a figure strode confidently into the centre of the street. Behind him I could hear more footsteps, along with the murmur of satisfaction and amusement, the gang was growing. Behind the lone figure a half dozen more figures coalesced, dressed in filthy, baggy clothes.

Children.

The character in front of us pulled back a loose hood to reveal a shaved head and a face so pale and pinched it was almost skeletal, he couldn't have been any older than the dead boy on my kitchen floor. The thought made my stomach lurch.

'Out for a walk are you gents?' The lilting local accent couldn't hide the tension.

I didn't say anything, better to force the boy to show his hand. He nodded at my blade. The tension in his voice increased slightly.

'Armed too I see.'

Wings flapped above us and an owl hooted, it startled the silhouetted figures, even their leader who returned my smile with a flash of embarrassment. These groups were usually linked to local gangs, accountable to them too. This youth would need to deliver so many stolen items within any month or pay a forfeit that was always about teaching the rest a lesson. In the past, this kid would have hung around the tennis courts smoking weed and drinking cider and thought himself tough. Desperation made kids like these unpredictable, the last thing I wanted to do was harm any of them.

My lack of reply made the kid shift awkwardly, he glanced at his gang and flexed narrow shoulders.

'You know what we want,' he said gruffly. 'Empty your pockets and drop the sword.'

I stood completely still and said nothing.

'You fucking heard me.' The kid stood up straight but it was hardly an imposing stance. He beckoned his gang in closer, they obeyed immediately.

'Who are you two anyway?' he said as his provocation gained no response.

The owl hooted again but got ignored.

'I told you to fucking empty your pockets!' His voice cracked and behind him one of his gang chuckled briefly before being elbowed by the kid at his side. Embarrassment and the need to maintain his status caused the kid to get agitated, all I needed was a moment of distraction.

'We'll fucking slice you open if you don't do as I fucking say!' he screamed. He turned and gestured to the others and knives appeared in a few hands.

I rushed him, yanked him off his feet and pinned him to my body with my free arm and held my sword at his throat with the other. The kid screamed in terror, gurgled something incoherent. There was nothing to him, just bones and the sickly-sweet smell of an unwashed body. His gang stepped towards me hesitantly, I allowed my blade to draw a little blood, his struggling stopped immediately.

It halted the gang. Confusion reigned, they shouted abuse, bemoaned the unfairness of what had happened but looked on helplessly.

'Listen, you little bastards,' I growled, 'I've just left one kid with his throat cut, I don't want another.'

Silence. I could feel the kid tremble against me and he whimpered softly.

'Have you heard the explosions?'

A dozen heads nodded simultaneously.

'Well that's because the fucking fairies are trying to catch the Colonel here.' I nodded at a bemused Oisin. 'And if you little wankers slow us down any longer, they'll succeed. Is that what you want?'

Urgent shaking of shaved heads.

'What's your name kid?'

'Daz.' The voice came out as a shaky soprano.

Back to the assembled kids. 'I don't want to kill Daz, there's been enough brave lads lost their lives since Swindon, hasn't there?'

Nodding and murmured assent.

'We're going to need brave lads like you lot when you're a bit older. So, don't make me kill you now.'

The kid who'd giggled at his leader's voice earlier spoke up and addressed the others, his voice full of authority. 'We need to let the boss know, we can't let fucking fairies walk around Glastonbury like they own the fucking place.'

Heads nodded. A small twelve-year-old put up his hand, like he was in school. 'Shall I go tell him Turner?'

This story was unravelling too quickly.

'Look lads, no offence, but your friends will be helpless against these bastards. They don't have the manpower or the weaponry.'

Turner snorted and spat at his feet. 'Well the fucking government won't do anything. They're fighting to control the fucking capital, from what we've heard. The bastards have fucking deserted us.'

We didn't have time for storytelling.

'I need to get the Colonel to our forces quickly before we're overrun with fucking fairies, and you know what they like to do to boys, don't you?'

Vigorous nodding, the inevitable propaganda of war was like a virus.

It looked like Daz had been usurped as leader so I hurled him to the ground. A couple of his gang hurried to his side. Turner watched disinterestedly for a second before switching his eyes back to mine.

'I recognise you. You sell eggs and vegetables.'

Oh shit.

'There's stories about you.' The voice hardened. 'You fuck men.'

His words drew attention from the others who stared with renewed animosity.

Oisin didn't react but I noticed the subtle tensing of his muscles. I glared at the kid.

'There'll be stories about you too, you little wanker. About how you let the fairies capture this town because you wanted to believe fucking rumours. We're leaving and if any of you want to stop us, you'll find this in your guts.' I brandished my sword.

Daz struggled to his feet, stood in front of Turner and turned to Oisin.

'Sorry for causing you trouble Colonel.'

The gang's schism took shape as the two boys faced each other.

'You believe them do you Daz?'

Thin shoulders flexed, one hand reached up to smear the trickle of blood running down his neck.

'Doesn't fucking matter what we believe, does it?'

Like a tennis match the gang looked from one angry face to the other. I didn't wait to find who would win the day. We strode off down the street, past a few of the older youths, who turned to Daz then Turner, looking for instructions but didn't get any.

Sufficiently out of earshot Oisin spoke. 'Are they following?'

'No. They're having a leadership crisis.'

A chuckle. 'Colonel eh?'

'Don't let the promotion go to your head.'

Flapping wings above our heads made us both look up. The ghost-like form of a barn owl swooped over us. I grinned.

'Still not going to tell me where we going?' Oisin asked.

'No.'

We strode out of the town in silence. With little to halt its progress, strong gusts of wind met us as we made our way along the Old Beckery Road. Water lapped at its edges, sunshine flashed on waves that occasionally spread across the tarmac. I could see Oisin frown as he tried to

45

understand why humans would build a road that was washed by the sea.

'Celtic pilgrims once took this route to the Tor two thousand years ago. They landed their boats over there at Bride's Mound to make the rest of the way across a wooden causeway. Eventually the sea receded and people built the road you see now.'

'And now the sea has returned.'

'Yes. It began shortly after they murdered the previous generation of Knights. It rained for two months continuously. A lot of people lost their homes, their farms, their lives. Parts of England were flooded so badly transport routes disappeared so quickly it meant rescue became a series of strategic choices.'

'It must have been terrible.'

'It was. Until we redefined terrible when the Dark Court invaded.'

I stopped and looked hard at Oisin. 'Llyr told me they'd had the previous generation of Knights murdered. Did you know that?'

Oisin held my eye, he knew I was testing him. 'Like so many others, it was done secretly. If the Light Court knew about it, they've not said anything.'

'Without evidence they'd be helpless. Even Nimue.'

'I'm not on his side Robin. He's insane, just like his father. He's not just a huge danger to the humans but to my people too.'

I looked at him, waited for him to realise how he'd used the personal pronoun. He bit his lip, he always did that when he knew he'd made a mistake. It had once aroused me.

'You've changed so much Robin. You behave so...
human now. Sorry.'

'A long-lived life in exile does that to you. The
human life span is so short it means any kind of
relationship is...' I tried to find the right word. 'Futile. But I
had no alternative, did I? It certainly wasn't the life I had
anticipated.'

'I can imagine.' He raised a sympathetic hand but I
turned too quickly before he could give me the patronising
pat on the shoulder he'd planned.

He hurried to catch up as I marched along the road.

'We're about to meet someone with a lot of local
spies. She'll have information.'

'Spies?'

His puzzled expression caused me to smirk.

'You've just seen one of them. He watched our
encounter with the Lord of the Flies brigade back there.'

The puzzled expression deepened.

'We need to hurry before your friends find us.'

I didn't need to look to know I'd irked him.

'They're not my friends Robin.'

I shrugged. 'It's a human expression.'

I walked on, smirking.

Chapter 4

Tir na nÓg: The palace of the High Lord of the Dark Court

I stashed the wicker pannier in the furthest corner of the kitchen, nearest to the door to the courtyard, while Mistress Cera berated the butcher for his poor-quality meat. Her strident voice travelled the length of the corridor to the rear entrance of the palace. I had only a few minutes before the butcher retreated and the kitchen became a place where survival meant keeping out of the way, Mistress Cera's tempers were the stuff of legend. I had two, perhaps three, minutes from the moment her yelling stopped, while she stomped back along the corridor.

A good thief learns to take only those things that won't be missed. You leave solitary items and small quantities because their absence gets noticed. Good housekeepers like Mistress Cera ran her kitchen with iron discipline and kept visual catalogues of provisions in their heads. The secret was to target large quantities where one or two things wouldn't be missed.

In recent weeks I'd learned where best to filch. From the meat pantry I hurled a couple of chops and a leg of mutton, which had contributed to this week's argument with the butcher, into the pannier. From the bakery I snatched a handful of bread rolls that were starting to go stale and two apples from the store basket. A flask of milk caught my eye. A half dozen had only just come up from the dairy and I wasn't sure Mistress Cera had even seen them. The flask would make it a lot easier to carry, I'd spilled the last lot. I placed the flask in the pannier, stacked carefully between the mutton and the apples.

The tirade had ended I realised. I couldn't hear footsteps. I panicked.

I hauled the pannier outside into the courtyard and hid it behind a water butt and raced back to the kitchen just as a vision of red hair and red face stomped into the kitchen and hurled lumps of meat on to a table. I'd had enough time to pick up a drying cloth and a plate and pretended to be busy.

She looked at the empty sink and narrowed her eyes.

'Keir,' she always pronounced my name like it was a threat. 'You've cleaned those things bloody quickly, you little shit. They'd better be clean or I'll beat your arse raw.'

I gave her my best smile and looked suitably anxious. It wasn't difficult, I'd only rinsed them to save time. Now came the hardest part, convincing her of my need to escape.

'Please may I leave Mistress? I have finished all my jobs.'

She wiped a muscular forearm beneath her nose where a moustache was forming and sniffed suspiciously.

'To go where?'

I smiled again. 'Master Sidwell wanted me to help him Mistress.'

The two were rivals, so never spoke. At least I hoped they wouldn't.

'What does that old bastard want with you? You're kitchen staff, you're not part of his snooty palace retinue.'

It was best not to be specific in your lies, the woman tended to interrogate even more closely if she had solid information. Plus, there was a chance those details could get back to the Palace's chief steward and, since he was the only person who was kind to me, I didn't want to take advantage of him too much.

49

'I don't know Mistress. Sorry.'

'This is the third time you've helped him. I think I need to have words.'

'Oh, don't do that!'

Close-set eyes narrowed to scrutinise me. It was never wise to tell Mistress Cera not to do something, no matter how casually, I had the bruises to prove it. One hand inched its way to the ring around my thumb, a habit the woman had come to associate with my guilt. I snatched it back instantly and put both hands behind my back and looked suitably subservient.

I launched into a lie without knowing how it was going to develop.

'I offer to help him, Mistress, because... because I like to show him how much I've learned from you.'

Her eyes narrowed into pouchy slits.

'In fact, last time he said he was thinking of employing more of your discipline with his stewards and valets.'

Her thick lips curled upwards. I allowed myself the slightest of breaths. Lately I'd developed the ability to spin stories like Mistress Neala wove the clothes we wore. Every slave learns to lie, to cover mistakes or others' poor decisions, when you're a slave everything becomes your fault eventually. I didn't find it came naturally but, as the old saying goes, practice makes perfect. I'd learned that lies involve risk and the successful liar balances the right amount of risk against the possibility of discovery.

I thought of the pannier of food hidden in the courtyard and that the afternoon was drawing to an end, time was running out. My heart beat so loudly I felt sure she'd hear it and the need to feel the security of the cinnamon coloured crystal in my ring was almost unbearable.

'He'd do well to apply my rules to those jumped-up, nose-in-the-air types that float around the palace like they're the High Lord himself.'

She pounded a joint of beef with a meaty fist. 'Snooty bastards.'

She appeared lost in her simmering resentment of anyone who possessed good manners or who spoke correctly.

'May I go Mistress? To Master Sidwell?'

'All right.'

I turned to make a hasty departure.

'Keir?'

I held my breath.

'I want you back here by fifth bell. Understood?'

'Yes Mistress!' I said as I sprinted out of the kitchen before she changed her mind.

I scooped up the pannier and hurried across cobbles, slick with rain, careful to avoid piles of horseshit. Heavy clouds meant the afternoon was darkening faster than usual, I'd have even less time.

The passageway to the stables was dark and smelled of hay, I could cut through that way because the grooms would still be exercising the horses. I heard voices in the tack room and slowed down so as not to look suspicious, slaves didn't hurry anywhere. Once beyond the stables I had just the laundry to negotiate, beyond that the garden and freedom. I picked up the pace, satisfied I'd made it.

Fate had other plans.

'Where are you going in such a hurry?'

I mentally grimaced and instinctively slowed down to give myself time to invent a story.

'Well? Perhaps you're hurrying to the river to clean your dirty brown skin?'

I ground my teeth. I didn't have time for our usual routine but I had to be careful I didn't betray my urgency to escape either.

'Oh, but wait! That muck doesn't wash off, does it?'

Irvyn stepped out of the laundry room, grinning at his wit. Just beyond him was the outside door to the gardens but the route to it was blocked by the tall, muscular blockhead.

'Get out of my way, I'm busy.' Try as I may I couldn't stop my voice trembling. Irvyn's fists could inflict real damage.

'Busy doing what?' His eyes flicked to my pannier.

'An errand for Mistress Cera. If I tell her you delayed me, you know what she'll do to you?'

Thankfully the woman's reputation caused the boy's bravado to falter.

'I'm not delaying you,' he said, stepping into the doorway of the laundry.

I eased passed him suspiciously, the brute liked to trip or push his unsuspecting victims but nothing happened and I reached the door to the garden. Irvyn wasn't one to let opportunities to torment me escape him, I hurriedly constructed an alibi.

I sensed him following and tensed but he stepped in front of me to hold open the door into the garden. A cool breeze and faint drizzle reached my face. I should have brought something warm to wear I realised but that would have only prompted more questions. Irvyn peered into the pannier.

'If you're giving that to the pigs, why the milk? It looks fresh.'

I faltered, he'd used my alibi. I turned towards him to give myself time to think. Nothing occurred and so I resorted to the dangerous tactic of challenging him. It had worked with the threat of Mistress Cera, perhaps I could try a second time?

'What does it matter to you? Mistress Cera sent me to do a job. Or should I tell her you're questioning her instructions?'

Grey eyes zeroed in on mine. That wasn't a good sign. Neither was the slight curl of his top lip. I'd gone too far but it was too late to change now, I stood my ground. As Mister Sidwell kept telling me, 'Face your fear, Keir.'

So I looked up into those grey eyes.

'You're getting bold, shit stain.' The threat was evident in Irvyn's tone. 'Must be time to teach you another lesson.'

His fist hit my chin before I realised he'd moved. That was a result of his training with Gamesmaster Murtagh, who'd spotted a well-built moron who was perfect for fighting in the lists at the Belthane festival. I stumbled backwards, dropping the pannier as my arms windmilled to stop myself falling. I landed on my backside heavily with a loud, 'Oof!'

Irvyn laughed and dropped to his knees to straddle my chest, fists bunched ready to launch his attack.

'You're up to something shit stain. I've seen you carrying that fucking basket into the garden for weeks now. What are you up to?'

'Get off me!' I shouted as I tried to wriggle loose, only to find his legs tightened their grip on either side of my ribs until the discomfort made me lie still, defeated.

Irvyn wrinkled his nose as though he smelled something unpleasant, he got off me.

'Gladly. Your skin's the colour of shit and you fucking smell like it. You shat your drawers have you?'

He chuckled as he stood up but planted a booted foot on my chest.

'Tell me where you're going, you filthy hybrid bastard or I'll crush you like a fucking bug.'

He pressed his boot down hard on my chest, making it difficult to breathe, I felt tears sting my eyes and tried to hold them back.

'It's for the spriggan guards. Rations. They get overlooked. Here. At the rear of the palace.'

There were guards stationed everywhere these days, they'd increased their numbers because the High Lord had spotted another assassin a few days before. I had to hope Irvyn would find my lie believable.

He looked sceptical.

'Doesn't sound like Mistress Cera, to consider bloody spriggans.'

He was right, it didn't.

'I know.' I feigned a lack of interest. 'Just follow orders. Don't want. Beating.'

The boot on my chest was lifted and he stared at me with distaste.

54

'Why do you stay here, shit stain? Everybody despises your fucking hybrid blood. And with that shit brown colour, how are you ever going to fit in when the rest of us have white skin eh?'

It was a good question. I wished I had the answer.

'Do everyone a favour. Leave the palace and fuck off will you? I hear there's a gateway to the fucking human realm around here somewhere. Go see them, you might fit in there, because you fucking don't here!'

He kicked my backside hard. The pain triggered the tears I'd been struggling to hold back. He snorted his disdain and marched back through the doorway, slamming it behind him.

I was trapped on the outside of the palace grounds now. To get back in I'd have to enter through the main gate and get interrogated by the guards.

I stood up and cursed Irvyn with every form of bad luck possible but his final words refused to leave me. I'd considered running away lots of times. He was right, I didn't fit in. Not just because I was a hybrid but because of the colour of my skin, it made me stand out so that everyone looked at me with distaste. There were several hybrids in the Dark Court, some of them quite highly placed, it wasn't always easy to be sure who they were, they were like pure-bred Fae, pale skinned and blonde haired. The opposite of me.

When you were a slave, already worthless, and you looked so conspicuous, you drew attention for all the wrong reasons. I always got the blame because I was the first one everyone thought of when searching for a scapegoat.

For as long as I could remember I'd fantasised about finding the lost gateway to the human realm to set out on a quest to find others like me. It was the kind of tale which storytellers like Oisin would entertain lords, ladies and courtiers with on dark winter nights. Except I wasn't the kind of hero you found in such stories because I didn't have the courage, I saw disaster and terror everywhere. Knowing my luck, life in the human realm would be even worse than it was here.

The drizzle turned heavier and it made me shiver as I scooped up the things that had fallen out of the pannier, thankfully the flask of milk hadn't broken. I avoided the two spriggans shambling along the garden wall, disinterested in anything other than the end of their duty shift. I waited until they'd gone before climbing the branches of an old pear tree that reached up and over the garden wall. I jumped down the other side, carefully holding the pannier tight, and jogged along a cart track, over a meadow and into the wood that was no more than a dark smudge in the gathering twilight.

I felt my spirits lift the moment I saw the old barn. I whistled twice and heard the thin crooning noise that drifted back in reply. It made me smile. I pulled open the rotting door wide enough to squeeze through to be greeted by a snuffling sound that fluttered out of the darkness on soft wings as a shadowy form stepped out of the darkness.

'You can smell your dinner, can't you?'

The crooning noise grew louder from behind a stack of hay bales. I emptied the contents of the pannier onto the floor and stood back and kept very still.

From out of the darkness stretched the long, scaled neck and head of my wyvern. She dived on the food enthusiastically and ate noisily. I poured the milk into a battered bucket nearby then sat on a hay bale and watched the animal with fascination.

'I'm sorry I couldn't get here sooner. You're hungry, aren't you?'

The animal glanced at me briefly as it chewed on the mutton leg, as though she understood what I was saying to her. It had felt silly at the start, speaking to an animal. I'd only done it out of panic, but when she responded to my voice, I decided if it stopped her eating me, I'd happily chatter away for as long as needed. When she stuck her snout into the basket I'd been carrying on my foraging mission in the woods, she eaten everything I'd found without caring what it was.

'I've been reading about you. I found a book in the palace library. I'm not allowed in there but you are worth the risk.'

She plunged her snout into the bucket of milk and drank noisily.

'Did you know you're a wyvern? A smaller-than-average species of dragon? Your red colour is typical of your type apparently. The book said you're very intelligent and loyal. But I can see that for myself.'

She took her snout out of the bucket and snorted through wide nostrils, blowing milk all over me. I laughed. She twisted her head from one side to the other, behaviour I started to think showed she was trying to understand me.

She stepped closer, the rest of her body emerging from the shadows as she did so. She was bigger than a bull at the shoulders, perhaps half as big again with powerful legs and jaws that could easily rip me to shreds. Thankfully

I didn't appear to be on her menu, quite the opposite, she'd realised I brought her food and that action had caused a bond to form between us. She sat down in front of me and planted her scaly head on the hay bale. Gently, and very slowly, I reached over and stroked it, and got a low moan of satisfaction that made me smile. It was like a dog or cat you'd stroke and be rewarded for your affection.

The book I'd found was very old, covered in dust and on the shelves at the furthest corner of the library where no one went. Not that anyone used the library except me. The final chapter of the book had talked about how dragons were being hunted to the point of extinction. No one knew anything about them now, I'd made very careful enquiries of Master Sidwell and if anyone would have known, it would have been him.

The real mystery was why a wyvern would be roaming the woods on its own now.

My thigh got a gentle nudge and I laughed.

'I'm sorry, I forgot our after-dinner ritual.'

There was a point behind the frilled area at the back of its head that protected a small hole in its scales, the book told me it was the wyvern's ear. She liked me to massage her there so I pressed the heel of my palm on the muscle tissue around it and instantly got a low groan.

'You like this, don't you?'

Another grunt that made me laugh even more.

'I can't do it for long, I have to get back to the palace.'

My spirits nose-dived. I didn't know why I felt so happy in this animal's company but I did. Returning to the palace meant going back to drudgery, beatings and never-ending hardship. I was a slave; those things were my heritage and my future.

My thoughts spiralled around the reason for being born in the first place, I couldn't work out why any member of the Fae had conceived me. It wasn't uncommon for them to use human beings as sexual partners but they took great care to find one who was similar in appearance. I couldn't understand why my parents had gone out of their way to be so conspicuous about doing the opposite. The only conclusion I could reach wasn't nice to consider; I was an indiscretion, a mistake.

Irvyn's reprimand echoed in my head and that ever-present fantasy sprang to life of finding the forbidden gateway and running away to the human realm.

The wyvern nestled against me with a throaty moan, I stroked her tenderly and indulged in a new fantasy I'd started to develop recently; a future with my wyvern. I imagined myself training her to do things so that we could travel the land entertaining people. She was clever, she would frighten people but then they'd see her tricks and be amazed at my courage at handling this frightening animal. No one would mock me then, not with such a vicious friend to protect me.

I jerked awake.

Above me, though a hole in the roof, I could see stars. I'd be seeing a different kind when Mistress Cera punished me for being late. My brain searched frantically for an excuse as I ran out of the barn and back to the palace, leaving the pannier and my best friend behind.

Chapter 5

We were met by snarling dogs. Oisin moved nearer and looked at them nervously. They pushed muzzles through an ancient wooden gate and ran up and down a thick hedge yapping and barking. A half dozen cats surrounded us, backs arched in hostility, while dozens of birds eyed us suspiciously from gnarled fruit trees. We came to a halt on a tarmac track Nature was reclaiming with alarming speed outside a thatched cottage, its roof green with age and neglect.

'You can call off your welcoming committee!' I shouted over the din. 'You've made your point!'

Amelie de Leon appeared on the threshold to her home with an expression that matched the mutts at her gate. She was a lot thinner than when we'd last met, the denim overalls she wore emphasized her bony angles and her lined skin gripped her face with the kind of tenacity that prevented a smile. She brushed wiry white hair out of her eyes and smeared flour on her cheek in the process.

'What do you want, you queer bastard?'

'I've come for a fuck. You're the only woman who can tempt me, looking like that.'

Despite her efforts, it earned me half a smile. Oisin looked bewildered.

'Major, call them off.'

The fiercest of the dogs, muzzle covered with scars, one eye missing and ears that looked like bits of chewed leather gave a single bark, deep and resonant and instantly there was silence. Oisin raised blond eyebrows in surprise and I smiled. He was going to get better shocks than that one.

I pushed open the gate and walked up the garden path, Oisin half a step behind nervously watching the wildlife.

The old woman remained in the doorway, she hadn't taken her eyes off Oisin the whole time. I prepared myself for the worse. I leaned over and gave her a kiss on the cheek. She smiled, half turned to go in the cottage and swung her arm and gave me a stinging slap across the cheek. Oisin took a half dozen steps backwards and almost trod on Major, who gave him a deep growl. He froze in position and looked petrified.

'What was that for?' I asked, holding my cheek in a pantomime of hurt.

'For abandoning me. I haven't seen you in months, you bastard.'

'I've been busy.' It was an automatic response.

The old woman shook her head and gave me a loud snort of contempt but she moved inside. I glanced over my shoulder and smiled at Oisin and beckoned him in. He moved with caution, not taking his eyes off Major.

Amelie's kitchen always smelled good, there was usually food being cooked and from the ceiling hung bunches of every kind of herb you could mention. On the huge range saucepans bubbled away, emitting pillars of steam. She'd moved to an enormous wooden table in the middle of the kitchen and ladled soup into three bowls, it was full of vegetables and smelled delicious, as did the freshly made bread that had been carved into huge chunks in the centre of the table. I settled myself down to eat, motioned for Oisin to do the same though he took a while to notice, he was more concerned with the other features of the kitchen.

Wildlife inhabited the place in even greater abundance.

Cats dozed on shelves, armchairs and window sills, three goats were curled up on blankets in a corner and birds perched on rafters and amidst the dangling branches of herbs.

'No need to ask who this is.' She nodded at Oisin and gave him a gap-toothed grin. 'Those blond curls, the blue eyes and perfect bone structure. The perfect man.'

She plonked my soup bowl in front of me heavily.

'At least that's what he used to call you.'

Oisin blinked and looked at her, then at me and blushed.

'Ignore her Oisin. When she sees a man it arouses long-dormant hormones that addle her brain.'

She waggled bushy white eyebrows suggestively. 'And every inch a man. No doubt lots of inches too.'

Oisin gasped and flushed a perfect shade of scarlet, it made me laugh. She turned her attention to me and nodded her approval, as though she thought I needed it. It was time for introductions.

'Oisin, this Amelie de Leon. The locals think she's a witch, they use her name to scare their kids and her temper you've already witnessed. I don't need to tell you about Oisin apparently, nor how he got here I assume.'

That piqued the other man's interest and he frowned as he spooned his first mouthful of soup into his mouth, looked at it and smiled with satisfaction.

I nodded my head at the menagerie of creatures who stared at us. 'Amelie's spies told her.' It was enough to make him pause lifting his spoon a second time.

She tutted at me. 'They're not spies. They're my friends. They tell me what's happening now it's no longer safe to leave my home.'

Oisin still held a spoonful of soup half way to his mouth. 'Tell you, how?'

She looked to me to give the explanation, I shook my head and returned to my soup.

'I'm the descendent of Yvain, who Chretien de Troyes described in his stories as the Knight of the Lion.'

'Who is Chretien de Troyes?' Oisin's soup spoon finally reached his mouth.

Amelia's voice held the same pride as the expression on her face. 'In twelfth century France he was a storyteller responsible for the tales of King Arthur and his Round Table knights. A storyteller as successful as you, from what Robin tells me.'

Blue eyes flicked to me briefly but I kept eating my soup.

'Thomas Mallory stole the stories and turned Arthur into a Christian hero to pacify the authorities who'd imprisoned him for rape and theft.'

'Why Knight of the Lion?'

'The story goes that my ancestor rescued a lion and, with its help, killed two monsters. It appeared Yvain had an affinity with animals, which led Arthur to enlist him as one of his knights.'

Oisin clicked his fingers. 'The bird in the tree, when those youths surrounded us...'

The old woman smiled. 'I call him Solomon because he fits the archetype, he's a clever old bird, little escapes his attention.'

'So you can talk to them?'

She shook her head. 'Nothing so formal. We share… images, feelings. It takes a while to understand what is being said, you have to think of communication in different terms.'

'You must wield enormous power.'

Amelie shook her head. 'The creatures communicate with me. That's all.'

I chuckled at her modesty.

'Don't listen to her Oisin. Let me describe this woman's power. A legion of spriggans arrived in Glastonbury when they first invaded. It's a sight I'll never forget!'

I looked at the old woman with her skin covered in age spots, lined face framed by wild white hair and thought how her appearance hid a force of nature.

'You wouldn't think to look at her that she repelled the invasion single-handedly.'

She dismissed my claim with a wave of a bony hand.

'It wasn't me. Those bastards ran back to fairyland because of my friends.'

Oisin turned his attention back to me, eager to hear the story.

'She stood atop the Tor, black cape billowing in the wind, surrounded by every animal and bird in a five-mile radius. Dozens of seven foot spriggans flailing their arms against birds that pecked and shat on them while dogs, cats, foxes, badgers and even cows and bulls bit and trampled them into retreat.

I beamed at the old woman but her expression was bleak. I'd hoped time might have eased her pain.

'I lost lots of friends that day Robin. Those creatures gave their lives out of loyalty to me. It's guilt I still carry. Don't make it sound more than it is.'

Oisin lowered his eyes to his empty bowl and kept them there.

I suppose she knew me too well. She turned back, caught my expression, realisation dawned and turned her grey eyes to flint.

'No Robin. Not a second time.'

'Come on Amelie. You can do the same thing again, drive them all back, including that psychotic bastard, Llyr.'

'I told you. No. I will not risk the lives of my friends.'

'But if you don't a lot of people are going to die.'

She snatched up our bowls from the table and hurled them into the sink where they landed with a clatter. When she looked at me again there was an expression on her face I didn't like, I knew what was coming.

'Tell me Robin, in all the years since the Fae invasion, where were you?'

'It's different now. Llyr is here.'

'And who for? Eh? For you Robin.' Tears formed in her eyes, she brushed them away angrily. 'This fight has suddenly become personal and now you want help. What about when I told you to go to the authorities and explain everything to them?'

I'd hoped we weren't going to revisit this little spat. I tried to avoid the argument by affecting an upper class voice.

'Hello Prime Minister. I'm a member of the Fae race that are currently invading this country but I'm really on your side. Please let me be your advisor. Oh but wait Prime Minister, why are you putting me in prison?'

Oisin smiled politely but my mockery had made matters worse. She glared at me. Mainly because she knew I was right and she was wrong.

'Stop being ridiculous. The fact remains you hid in that cottage of yours and hoped the war would pass you by. It hasn't. It's come knocking at your door.'

A final attempt at levity. 'They knocked it down actually.'

Her expression, as a certain famous playwright was fond of saying, could freeze beer.

'Find someone else Robin.'

I knew better than to provoke her any further, not with a kitchen full of creatures who'd take her side. Major was already growling softly.

I attempted a smile. 'How are the twins?'

With the change of topic her shoulders relaxed and she glanced at Oisin.

'It's OK, you can talk in front of him.'

That earned me a look of gratitude.

'They're not having too good a time. A local group have started sniffing around the farm. It started with stealing, just the usual petty stuff, but Brea got annoyed and blasted some of them. Needless to say that's drawn a lot more attention. They've had several nights of sustained attacks.'

'Shit. Why can't she just…'

Her raised eyebrow told me not to finish that sentence. The tone of her voice told me this was going to be a lecture, one not to be interrupted.

'You've neglected those kids, just like you have me. They're lonely, they're kids without parents.'

'They're seventeen!' I said and got frowned at.

'They're kids. And they're trying to come to terms with being different to everyone else. It's not so bad for Finn in a way, he can hide his skill. But Brea is struggling. I mean, fuck it Robin, you've known the family a hell of a lot longer than I have. You know what she's going through. The energy she keeps pent up in her body affects her in so many ways. She's still learning to control it and it makes her cranky, which causes her to blast any sly buggers who steal things from her.'

I'd had enough of the guilt trip. 'I've given them a home haven't I? It's secluded enough to keep them safe, so long as Brea doesn't draw attention to herself.'

Amelie looked at me in the way she always did by the end of our conversations. She wore an expression of impatient antagonism. She took a deep breath, apparently the lecture wasn't over.

'It's not a home when you're lonely, isolated and afraid, certainly not when your family are all dead and everyone blames you for the situation the world's in. Plus, they are Gawain's descendants. To the rest of humanity, they are freaks Robin. They are teenagers, with all that entails, unable to fit in and they live like hermits, not by choice but by necessity. Your obligation to their father was more than keeping them safe in some isolated farmhouse. It was about being a surrogate parent.'

Her voice took on the tone of a military leader, it wasn't so much a suggestion, more a command. I felt my temper building, she'd bottled all this blame inside her and needed to express it, but I had other things to consider beyond parentcraft.

'You need to go there and help them.'

She flicked her eyes at Oisin, her question was obvious. Was I taking him with me?

Before I could reply a loud flapping of wings announced the arrival of a barn owl that swooped through the open window and landed lightly on the table in front of us. It turned its head to look at Oisin before switching its focus on to Amelie. She frowned as she stared into its unblinking eyes, exhaled loudly and glanced at me and shook her head sadly. Conversation finished, she stood up, moved to a shelf on the wall, reached into a bowl and took out a piece of meat. The owl watched her avidly and the instant the meat appeared in her hand it took off, snatched the meat from her fingers and flew back out through the window.

'We've got visitors.' Those flint-grey eyes turned on me, the accusation clear.

I hurriedly tried to think of a plan. Amelie's cottage was at the end of a narrow gully with no other way out, trapping us. She knew there was only one option.

'How did he find us?' Oisin asked, panic on his face now.

Amelie shook her head. 'The boys you met? Whatever you said to them must have made them curious. They followed you. Llyr caught them.'

Oisin's lack of experience of life in wartime Britain became apparent.

'Are they all right?'

Amelie's expression hid none of her contempt. 'Of course not. He tortured them.'

He looked at me the way he once did when I'd disappointed him. There was just sadness and disbelief. In his world, as the most celebrated storyteller in Tir na nÓg, he hadn't experienced such horrors. He had always possessed a light in his being which compensated for the darkness in mine, it was one reason for loving him as I had. If he stayed with me for much longer, that light was going to get snuffed out.

'You need to leave quickly.'

All the creatures in the kitchen reacted to her words, even though they were meant for me. The place became chaotic as cats, dogs and goats strutted to positions at windows, doors and outside the cottage. The birds swirled around the kitchen once before flying out of the window.

'But what about you?' I asked.

'Solomon's getting help. My friends will protect our home.'

I was responsible for the trouble I'd brought her and said as much, she only shrugged her shoulders.

'You need to get to the horses.'

We hurried outside, to the stable behind the cottage. She'd already got them saddled, she'd decided she was sending me to the twins before I'd arrived. I didn't like being manipulated but when you face imminent capture you shut up and show your gratitude for a quick escape.

From a pocket in her dress she took out some cubes of green stuff that smelled of summer meadows. Both horses' heads instantly swung in her direction. She made a point of handing them to us both, two pairs of dark brown eyes watched every movement.

'It's encouragement if they get spooked but these two will carry you to where you need to go.'

Her look made it clear we both knew where that was.

Oisin and I led the horses out of the stable and on to the narrow lane. I kissed her on the cheek and thanked her again and got an impatient and rude reply before she slapped the rump of my horse.

At the end of the narrow lane lines of spriggans waited, weapons ready.

They were wedged in tightly between the walls of the gulley so bursting through with the horses was never going to happen. The sight and sounds of angry spriggans made the horses nervous, it hadn't occurred to me to ask Amelie how to feed my animal its special cube when I was sat on its back. I looked behind me in the hope of help and in those couple of seconds a cacophony of high pitched shrieks almost deafened us. The spriggans turned their heads as birds of all descriptions, many of them huge gulls, dive bombed. In another few seconds the spriggan lines were broken as long arms flailed helplessly and the smarter spriggans knelt on the ground so the birds attacked the taller targets. The gulls were especially vicious. And agile. They swooped, changing direction in a fraction of a second, clawing and pecking their victims. There were a few raptors, buzzards and kestrels mainly, who preferred to strafe, clawing scalps and lacerating faces.

Oisin and I were completely ignored, Solomon had successfully identified who needed to be attacked and who had to be left alone. I had never been so grateful to an owl in my life. We galloped through the avian mayhem, trampling a couple of distracted spriggans in the process and arrived on the Old Beckery Road and straight into Llyr. He stood far enough away, watching in astonishment and free from attack, presumably because the birds judged his human appearance to mean he was an ally.

He grinned at me as our horses skidded to a halt in front of him, it wasn't until that point I understood why he wasn't hurrying to get out of the way. He reached into a pocket and prepared to throw what he took out. I launched myself at him, determined not to be frozen again when a strident screech and the noise of flapping wings distracted Llyr. He dropped the small crystal in a desperate effort to protect himself from the barn owl's raking claws. The ground instantly turned frosty white, forcing Llyr to dance on tiptoes around the expanding fingers of frost. He almost succeeded but one booted foot wasn't quite quick enough, it turned white and rooted him to the spot.

His grin froze as well when he saw me reach over my shoulder to snatch my sword from its scabbard on my back. He looked around in the hope of rescue but his spriggans were fighting battles of their own, preoccupied by the need to defend against squawking squadrons of birds plus dogs and cats now too.

'You mad bastard!' I yelled, grabbing Llyr by the flowery frills of his shirt. 'I'm going to slit your throat just like that kid you murdered.'

He babbled something, his widening eyes fixed on mine. Deep in my head I felt Puck cheer me on, which robbed me of some of the vengeance I felt but I dismissed it as I raised my sword arm.

'No Robin! Don't!

Oisin grabbed it, pulled it back with all his strength. I tried to shake it loose, angered so much I could feel Puck bristling with frustration, I yelled at him, tried to yank myself free, shook the man like a rag doll. Panic made him shake his head repeatedly until he suddenly let me go. When he spoke it was breathless but with authority, like he was delivering a performance.

'Kill Llyr and you will bring the Light Court into the war.'

That stopped me.

He pressed his advantage quickly.

'You'll make him a martyr. You will have committed treason and regicide. You will have done what he's been trying to do since he snatched the throne. Is that what you want?'

I lowered my sword, turned from Oisin to look at the grinning face of the bastard I wanted to kill so badly.

Behind us some of the spriggans had realised their monarch was in deadly peril and raced towards us, treading on the stricken bodies of animals and birds beneath their feet.

You choose where and when to fight your battles if you want to win them. It was a lesson I'd learned in the early days of my training, a painful one, as they all were. It didn't make the decision any easier to bear. The man I hated, whose death was what I wanted more than anything, stood in front of me, immobilised. I could kill him and risk the repercussions. That fucking grin of his tempted me even more. But Oisin was right, we all knew it, especially Llyr, and that made me even angrier.

I jumped on to my horse and galloped off down the Old Beckery Road, listening to Llyr's insults and threats to hunt us down until we were out of earshot.

We followed the pitted tarmac route that had once been the A39 out of Glastonbury. We rode hard and in silence, Oisin knew better than to say anything to me in my present mood.

Llyr had beaten me again, even when he was helpless and vulnerable. No wonder he grinned at me so much. I was a soldier, I didn't run away from a fight. I had to admit my training hadn't equipped me for thinking strategically, I was the type that dealt with danger rather than look for ways to avoid it, Oisin had known that. Though, if I was being honest with myself, I used to be like that. Amelie's words stuck in my head, I had hidden in my cottage and hoped the war wouldn't come knocking. Not out of fear but purely because it wasn't my battle, I was the queer guy trapped in the middle of it all. She'd been right about me failing in my obligations to the twins too, that was another instance of not having a strategy. I hated being blamed, especially when others were in the right. My brain spiralled with more and more regrets, guilt and disappointments that made life such a lump of shit. Spirals tend to go one way, you finish up at the bottom of a dark pit where your thoughts focus on the futility of everything.

My horse had slowed, she was breathless, I'd ridden her too hard for too long. I looked around, at the twilight countryside.

'Robin?'

The hesitancy in Oisin's voice was obvious. I let him draw level.

'Is it safe to travel at night?'

I shook my head. I felt him watching me but I kept my eyes straight ahead as though I was searching for the route. I should have been grateful to him but he was so fucking rational. After ten minutes of awkward silences we arrived at an old barn where I'd stayed on previous occasions when I'd ridden to see the twins. It was made of corrugated steel and sheltered by a wood on three sides so had survived the mega-storms without too much damage. It was filled with old hay bales which had provided fodder for animals long since gone.

'We'll stay here.'

We led the horses into the back of the barn where the hay kept them content. I closed the wooden doors to keep the cold and damp out as much as possible. Oisin remained with his horse, talking to it quietly and stroking its nose affectionately.

'I forgot how much you like horses.'

He glanced at me, his lips curling into the smallest of smiles. 'Any animal. Do you remember the mouse I rescued from that cat when we were boys?'

I did, it was stupid how such small events stayed with you over such a long life. He'd been broken hearted at the way the cat played with the little creature as it desperately tried to escape. In the end he chased the cat away and took the exhausted mouse, fed it and kept it safe until it was fully recovered. I'd tried to make him understand the frustration of the cat, having successfully hunted its prey and how its playful behaviour was actually about honing its reaction time. Oisin didn't care, to him, the cat was cruel.

It made me wonder if that was when I first saw Oisin's light and my darkness.

My recollection and the silence it brought meant the moment quickly passed. I lay on hay bales and stared up into the rafters of the barn. Some distance away I heard Oisin lie down too. We didn't say anything for a long time. Finally I heard him take a breath.

'Amelie was hard on you. You do what you can Robin but you're not the twins' father. You're just a man who made a vow to someone.'

I stared into the darkness and thought about how it mirrored what was inside me, how it hid the demons that lived there, Puck particularly. Here was this man trying to tell me otherwise.

'I make vows too readily. Always fucking doing it.'

I could hear his smile in his voice. 'Do you know why?'

'Because I'm a fucking idiot.'

'No Robin. You pledge to help people because you care for them. You try your hardest to protect them.'

'And I fuck that up too.'

A light laugh. 'You do sometimes. But it's because you're can't always prevent it. That boy, earlier, you couldn't have helped him. Sometimes bad things happen and you can't stop all of them Robin. The fact you try is what's important.'

'I should have woken up earlier, got him out of the house sooner.'

Suddenly I could just make out Oisin's outline in the darkness as he sat beside me.

'Robin,' the smile was in his voice still. 'We followed him and waited for dawn. You'd have sent him straight into Llyr's soldiers. He'd served his purpose. Llyr was going to kill him. I think he guessed you'd take him and try to protect him. Do you see? You couldn't have prevented that boy's death.'

'Still...'

It got an exasperated sigh. 'Stop blaming yourself for everything Robin. I don't know why you feel the need to protect others all the time.'

'Yes, you do.' This was a discussion we'd had a very long time ago and I wondered if he remembered.

'Because you were once part of an elite fighting unit committed to defending people with your lives. But that was a long time ago and in a different world. You can stop now.'

'That's my point. It's so ingrained in me that I can't stop. I wish I could.'

'Do you? Really?'

If he really knew me he'd have understood that my training and formative years were driven to one goal at the expense of everything else, nothing else made life meaningful. The one time I'd abandoned my purpose and become the Court clown, Fate shat on me.

'Amelie was right about one thing. I had hidden in my cottage and hoped I could avoid the war. I'd tried to stop being me, you see. That was my mistake.'

'So what are you going to do now?'

'Go back to being Robin Goodfellow, the Trooping Fairy. I'm going to see the twins, make sure I take better care of them, get them somewhere safe. Then I'm going to hunt Llyr down and find a way to kill the bastard that won't bring the entire Fae race through the portals.'

I took a breath.

'And get you home too.'

'I'm not leaving your side Robin. Do you remember how we used to talk about my light and your darkness?'

I smirked, knowing he couldn't see me. 'Vaguely.'

'You need me to show you the light when the darkness threatens to overwhelm you.'

'Can you do that?'

A soft snigger.

'Managed it this evening, haven't I?'

'I bet you feel smug, don't you?'

I felt him lie down, close enough to me that we almost touched.

'I do actually.'

We lay in silence, I listened to his steady breathing and found I'd missed it. I wanted him to be with me, he was right, he did complement my dark nature but I worried what lay ahead for us. I would never forgive myself if anything happened to this man. We seemed to be rekindling our friendship and I didn't want to lose it, not again.

I heard him stir. 'I remember another time when you and I spent time in a barn. And what we did there. Do you?'

I kept still and breathed in a regular rhythm to make him think I was asleep. He moved closer to me, placed an arm over my body. After a while his breathing slowed. I moved his arm off me and shuffled further away.

That was the trouble with kindling, it could start fires easily and I wasn't going to be responsible for burning this man. I wouldn't do it deliberately, I cared for him too much, but I couldn't say the same for the demons hiding in the darkness.

Chapter 6

I ran like a mad thing, lungs burning, legs aching.

I scrambled up the old pear tree, clambered over the palace wall and dropped to the other side. The sun-baked ground was hard and in my hurry I failed to land properly, I turned my ankle and screamed in pain. On the other side of the wall shouts and loud commands reminded me I didn't have time to worry about such irrelevances, I hobbled along the cart track to reach my destination as quickly as possible.

I would be whipped for my misdemeanours, slaves weren't allowed off the palace grounds for one thing. They certainly didn't disobey orders from their superiors.

It might have been the pain in my ankle that had me doubting the wisdom of my actions now. I wasn't certain why I had taken off, except I needed to check for myself. I knew Irvyn wasn't a liar. He was a bully and a moron but he didn't need to lie to me. The fact he knew my secret was enough.

More than that; Irvyn had acted out of vengeance and I only had myself to blame.

I entered the wood and whistled. With a heart heavier than I could bear, I waited for a reply.

Silence.

I reached the barn. The door was smashed beyond recognition. The place was empty. My tears fell, their wellspring rooted in grief like I'd never known.

There were signs of a scuffle amidst churned soil and leaf litter, broken branches gave me an easy-to-follow route out of the wood and into the meadow. Beyond there, nothing.

The sun beat down on me from a cloudless blue sky, I collapsed on to soft grass, the pain in my ankle was bad but couldn't compare to the pain in my heart.

I'd woven together a neat tapestry of lies to allow me freedom for the entire day so I could spend more time with my wyvern. I'd started training her and been astonished by my success. My fantasy of roving the land with a tame wyvern was fast becoming reality. The library book had been helpful but I found she actually enjoyed learning the things I taught her, she clearly wanted to please me. We'd started on basic things, to come when I called her and to turn in certain directions, just like you'd do with a dog. I taught her to attack and to stop so I could scare the audience and amaze them by my control. She looked so impressive when I took her into the sunshine, she relished the heat, her scales shone with a burnished crimson that made her look so impressive.

And now she was gone.

I stared up into the sky, surprised that I wasn't blaming Irvyn more. I had learned the lesson Master Sidwell had once been at pains to teach me; never give your enemies a motive for vengeance. Trouble with that philosophy is that it's easy to say but difficult to do when you're ridiculed, beaten and humiliated on a regular basis. Plus, it had started off as just a joke.

I found myself wondering what I should have done differently but I suppose the answer was a simple one. Stay silent and inconspicuous. Yet the opportunity was just too good to pass up.

The Belthane Festival was in full swing and I'd watched Irvyn parade around the lists after success in the early rounds of the mêlée, soaking up the praise that made him even more arrogant. It was during the final round when his opponent had kneed him between the legs, leaving him to writhe on the ground and squeal like a girl, that the idea occurred.

I stood in the crowd with Kerra, a dim scullery maid. I joked about why his screams were so high-pitched and she looked confused. I explained the purpose of a man's balls and what could happen when they were injured. Her eyes widened with astonishment and she turned back to watch Irvyn being helped up so he could stagger out of the arena holding his crotch while he cried.

'Will he not be able to satisfy a woman now then?' she'd asked.

I convinced the poor girl that Irvyn, who she thought was the most attractive young man on the palace staff, wouldn't be providing any girls with excitement from now on. By the end of the day the seed I'd sewn grew into a rich harvest of rumours, each one stating how poor Irvyn wouldn't be sewing any of his seed from now on. I was confident the story wouldn't be traced back to me, I doubted Kerra would even remember how the stories had started, I knew what a gossip she was.

I hadn't reckoned on Irvyn's need to preserve his masculinity.

He tracked me down but rather than administer the beating I'd expected, he told me he would do far worse than give me a bloody nose. I waited in fear for ten whole days.

Tears blurred my vision of the blue sky above me. I didn't bother to move when heavy footfalls gathered around me and I was manhandled back to the palace by a bunch of angry spriggans.

Master Sidwell met me in the courtyard. Any kindness he'd ever shown me had vanished, he was grim and prim in equal measure. I was admonished for dereliction of duty, assault of a palace worker and for my extensively devious conduct as all my lies collapsed around me. I'd be made to work even harder as punishment and given no freedom of any kind because I couldn't be trusted, in fact I would be supervised to ensure my work was of sufficient quality. If it wasn't, I'd be punished even more. I was officially the lowest of the low in the palace.

When Master Sidwell completed his verdict, he looked at me with an expression that hurt most, there was so much disappointment on his old face. I was escorted to the palace infirmary to be treated for my injured ankle. A physician wiped freezing cold blue gel on the swollen joint and strapped it up before handing me back to my guard so I could be set to work; I wasn't going to get time off to recover.

A palace-wide conspiracy made sure I didn't have a moment to myself. I was watched the entire time, always by people who enjoyed being the task master for once, people who savoured being able to get their own back on someone lower than they were. I washed and swept floors, polished furniture, washed greasy pots and pans and any time I paused, I received a beating. At the end of each day I'd collapse on the filthy mattress in the corner of a cupboard that I called home, to sleep solidly until dawn arrived and the cycle of misery would start again. Exhaustion drove away any thoughts of pursuing my wyvern, it was replaced by a seething resentment I aimed at everyone.

Until one day when, on hands and knees, I was washing flagstones in front of the library. Few people used this part of the palace and it had been overlooked for that reason, the floor was filthy and my whole body ached from cleaning it. My good behaviour had earned me a friendlier supervisor who dusted the nooks and crannies and paid me little attention. I had just rinsed my brush in a bucket of water and turned back to continue scrubbing, to find a pair of brown leather boots, covered in mud, on my clear floor. I swallowed my complaint as I looked up at the imperious figure standing over me. The corridor was dark, the figure wore brown leather riding breeches, tunic and cloak, bare arms showed impressive biceps, not someone I wanted to upset therefore. The quality of their clothes told me they must be important. As a slave you know not to look the aristocracy in the face, it suggests equality, a huge slur to the great and the good of the Dark Court. I turned my attention back to my work and hoped I wouldn't get a kicking.

'Are you Keir?'

The voice was refined, its tone full of authority but it was the pitch that confused me. It was almost a deep tenor yet there was something lighter in its timbre.

'Yes sire.'

I kept my eyes firmly on the floor but my heart started to pound in my chest. No one, especially the aristocracy, spoke to slaves by their names. You hardly ever heard your name mentioned by anyone; you certainly weren't asked for by name, not unless you were in serious trouble. My mouth felt dry and swallowing proved impossible.

One muddy boot was lifted off the floor and I tensed, ready for a kicking for whatever it was I'd done wrong. It reached my chin, tilting my head upwards, allowing me to see the face of the cloaked figure. Black

83

hair was cut short at the sides of the head, leaving a mane to drop down to muscular shoulders. The deep scar across one cheek, ruthlessly thin lips and eyes the colour of iron meant it could only be one person. Recognition came from one source; her reputation, one that almost caused me to wet myself.

'My lady Mab!' I gasped and bowed repeatedly as I hurried to my feet.

As I tried to gather my senses, she turned her attention to the woman repeatedly dusting the same part of a doorframe while trying to not look like she was watching everything.

'You!' The cleaning woman jumped and tried to curtsy at the same time. 'Fuck off!'

The poor thing kept curtsying while she backed away, colliding with a door at one point before turning and running to safety. I wanted to go with her.

The one-time commander-in-chief of the forces of the Dark Court looked around, noticed the library and nodded her head towards it.

'In there!'

I scuttled after her swirling black cloak.

Once inside the library I was instructed to shut the door while Mab looked about her, she'd obviously never been in this room before. If I hadn't been so frightened I might have wondered why the lords and ladies bothered with a facility they never used but my greater interest lay in the hope of leaving the place alive.

She grabbed a chair, swung it round on one leg to straddle it like a horse. I stood in front of her while she looked me up and down. There were so many stories about this woman, such as her valour and ruthlessness in battle, it was the stuff of legend. Amongst the male staff in the palace there was the story of her castrating two men because they hadn't satisfied her sexually, at the same time!

She beckoned me closer with an imperious finger and I tottered nearer, aware of how much I was sweating now and how rank I smelled. My fingers sought the ring on my thumb and I twisted it anxiously, I didn't try to stop either, the alternative was to scream hysterically. Her eyes bore into mine and caused my bladder to demand to be emptied, it took every bit of self-control to make sure it didn't.

'You raised a wyvern.'

I blinked repeatedly. I don't know what I'd expected her to accuse me of, but that was at the bottom of my list of options. Eventually, as she glared at me, waiting for a reply, I nodded. My throat was like a dry river bed and speech was beyond me.

'Tell me how. I want to know every detail. Leave anything out and I will visit enormous pain on you. Understand?'

I nodded again. The need to stop her from castrating me, relaxed my vocal chords enough that I could speak. I didn't just speak, I babbled. I told her everything, of my discovery of the animal, secretly feeding it, forming a bond that led to training it. Her eyes narrowed as I described the training we'd done, I even told her of my ambition to tour the land with the animal. I explained how it reacted out of loyalty, rather than for reward as you'd expect from a dog or a horse. She leaned forwards and stared at me when I said that. When I'd finished, she watched me closely without saying a word. The silence hung and I wondered if she was considering whether to kill me.

'Where did you learn all this?'

I swallowed hard. Slaves weren't allowed in the library, if I confessed she could have me whipped. Or even worse, punishments that involved my scrotum.

'Remember my threat. I want every detail.'

'In here!' I squeaked and felt tears prick the back of my eyes. 'I found a book.'

There was the faintest curl of her mouth, almost indistinguishable amidst the numerous lines there. It struck me that no other woman in the Dark Court wore their age so unashamedly, like it was her badge of honour.

'You're a slave, how did you learn to read?'

That was easy to answer. 'Master Sidwell taught me the basics, my lady. I've used the books here in the past to learn things.'

She looked about her and shook her head.

'You must be the only one who has.'

I waited, uncertain if I should reply.

'What did you learn about wyverns?'

Gradually I found myself relaxing. She seemed more curious about wyverns than the petty criminal activity of a palace slave and I savoured discussing our mutual interest.

'They're really intelligent. I mean, more than other dragon species. They're loyal, I know I said that, but they form a bond with certain people. I think they like anyone that treats them kindly. But they're also really fierce in battle too. The book was written a long time ago and it said how, when they fight, they develop strategies. They don't need to be told what to do, they can work it out for themselves. Mine was clever like that, she...'

Suddenly tears streaked down my cheeks, I couldn't help it. Talking about my time with her brought it all back. I'd tried hard not to think about her and now I was describing all the wonderful things we'd done together. Lady Mab watched me, but not with any scorn or recrimination, just casual interest.

'Where is the moron that released the animal into the human realm?'

'In the infirmary, recovering from an injury.'

She frowned. 'What injury?' She'd obviously not heard what I'd done.

'He fell down some steps during an... argument.'

Her lips formed the slightest of smiles as I chose the final word.

'Good for you.'

Now I was the one to smile. I wiped away my tears with the back of my hand and wondered where all this was taking us. Lady Mab didn't interrogate slaves unless there was a very good reason for it. She was clearly angry Irvyn had sent the animal through the forbidden gateway into the human realm. What worried me most was what might happen next because I had a sneaking suspicion what it might be and I didn't like the idea at all.

She looked up from examining her boots to focus on me.

'Could you find it? In the human realm?'

Oh crap. I'd been right. My mind raced with possibilities. Here was a chance to find the wyvern and bring her home, to rescue her. I wanted that so much. The question was, exactly how much? There was some kind of war going on in the human realm, what if I got caught up in it? Humans hated Fae, even hybrids, everyone knew that; what would they do to me if they caught me? And, not to be overlooked, my dark skin and black hair made me stand out, what if no one else looked like that over there?

Those iron-grey eyes watched me. Mab wasn't someone to displease, her two ex-lovers would agree, no doubt in high voices. She didn't understand fear either, she was a ruthless and brave warrior. She'd never understand my cowardice.

Then Master Sidwell's voice was in my head. 'Face your fear, Keir.'

'Travel to the human realm is banned.' It was an excuse but a genuine one.

'Only if you were caught.'

'Isn't there a battle being fought there?'

'Yes. One that could endanger your pet.'

I didn't like how she had answers to all my excuses and I especially didn't like guilt being used against me.

'Why do you care about the wyvern?'

The words escaped my mouth before my brain realised they'd been said. I looked at the woman, horror-struck, and held my breath. The moment lasted for an eternity.

'A reasonable question.'

It was? I let my breath out in a heavy sigh. She laid her muscular arms across the back of the chair and raised her hands so she could rest her chin on them. She took a deep breath, never taking her eyes off me for a second.

'If you repeat what I'm going to tell you, I will have you killed, precious as you are.'

I was precious? How had that happened?

'Our new High Lord launched an unsuccessful attack against the humans.'

'I thought they were savages?'

I got an impatient wave of a hand. 'They've made greater advances than we'd been led to believe. It doesn't matter. We believe our dragon breeding programme could offset the present stalemate.'

'Dragon breeding?'

Again, my question was dismissed with greater impatience, I needed to keep my mouth shut.

'The animals we have introduced into the conflict have not performed...' she eyed me carefully, '...intelligently. In fact they need to be controlled by riders, like you might with horses. Once the rider is removed from the beast it goes berserk, its unpredictability has cost us almost as many casualties as the other side.'

'I'm not surprised if you're using the big, slow animals. My book said that.'

That didn't go down well. Her expression darkened. I really did need to keep quiet.

'Unfortunately, no one thought to consult the library. Except you.'

I couldn't avoid asking my next question as I tried to understand what I was getting involved in. 'So why keep breeding them?'

An impatient shake of the head. 'We thought, if we found the correct training methods, we might capitalise on our investment. The problem has been finding that method. No one, so far,' and her gaze intensified, 'appears to know what they're doing.'

'Except me.'

She sat silently, watching me, waiting to see what I was going to say next. I let my eyes drop to the floor so I had chance to think without her intimidating me. She wasn't just asking me to find my wyvern, this was bigger than that. She wanted someone to train the dragons so they could become a war-winning weapon. I was unique. The only person in the entire Dark Court, perhaps the whole realm, who could do this work. I would no longer be a slave, condemned to spend my life on menial tasks, I would be someone others respected. I raised my eyes to look into hers.

'Give me permission to go to the human realm to find her.'

She shook her head.

'Our Light Court cousins will not allow it and if we flout the law our flimsy peace might end. It is too great a risk, no matter how tempting I find it.'

She stood up and began to pace in front of me.

'You are a hybrid and your skin colour makes you easy to identify. You would be easily traced. No, if you go, it must be secretly and without my support.'

Once again Master Sidwell's voice filled my head. 'Face your fear, Keir.'

I'd spent my life being afraid, I'd always seen danger, sometimes when it wasn't there. I always hesitated, waited until things were certain and never took a risk, just in case. Look where it had got me. It was why morons like Irvyn chose to abuse me.

'I'll go.'

She smiled. It looked like her facial muscles weren't familiar with those positions because it soon vanished. She stopped pacing but there was an energy about her now, a commander-in-chief giving instructions.

'I'll help you prepare. Are you familiar with the human style of speech?

I shook my head, I hadn't even considered it.

A brief nod, I assume she'd expected it and she was moving on.

'I'll have someone teach you. Now...'

'But I'm made to work every hour of the day. Master Sidwell...'

That impatient hand waved him away. 'I'm promoting you.' She rubbed her chin, such a masculine gesture. 'You will be my page. Come with me.'

She strode out of the library, her cloak catching the chair and knocking it over, she paid it no attention. My supervisor had returned and waited timidly in the corridor. My new employer paused, glared at her.

'Go tell Sidwell this young man is now my page.'

The woman's jaw dropped at my unexpected promotion.

'Why are you still here? Move your arse woman!'

The woman scuttled along the dark corridor like a frightened mouse. I smiled. It was good not to be the one getting reprimanded.

Chapter 7

I woke from my dream instantly, wide awake, ready for anything. Just one more habit forged in the white-heat of my training and which I hadn't been able to shake in the intervening centuries. Tendrils from the dream slithered from my waking mind but its more vivid moments remained behind briefly; memories of Oisin and I in a similar barn one summer evening where the smell of hay and sex merged as we held each other close.

A gentle nudge in my ribs.

'There's something outside.'

The rose-red light of dawn could be seen through the warped wooden slats of the barn door which creaked as pressure was applied to it. On the other side I could hear a snuffling sound, it had the depth and reverberation that told you it wasn't anything small either.

'Keep still. It'll go away,' I whispered.

Oisin's body was pressed against mine and it reignited the sensations from my dream. Despite what my brain might say on the subject, my cock had its own ideas of where this moment was going. I could feel Oisin's breath on my neck as he spoke.

'It can smell us. Or the horses.'

They decided to nicker just at that moment, softly pounding the ground with their hooves. Oisin hurried over to calm them, I suspected with the cubes Amelie had given him. With Oisin gone the pounding I was experiencing in my groin went with it.

Whatever was outside gave the barn door a hefty thump, it bent inwards and wood and rusty metal creaked ominously. I spotted Oisin tiptoe across the floor to the barn door.

'What are you doing, come back!' I said in my best stage whisper.

He ignored me and knelt so he could peek out of an empty knot-hole. I didn't intend cowering behind bales of hay so I joined him.

'What can you see?'

He looked at me with that expression that poses the question, do you really want to know? He gestured at the knot hole.

I couldn't see anything other than the clearing filled with pink light from the rising sun. Not until a leg appeared, covered in tightly packed scales. It moved away from the door so I got to see more of the leg, which thickened as it moved upwards to the thigh then it stepped out of sight.

My brain tried to process the sight, to place the creature into a category I understood. I confess it took me a few painful seconds to arrive at the conclusion Oisin had reached instantly.

'It's a fucking dragon!'

I didn't care for his patronising sigh and nod of his head.

'What's a fucking dragon doing in England?' I asked, my stage whisper turning a little hoarse.

'Llyr introduced a breeding programme. He's using them in battle.'

I wasn't interested in the history, my interests were more urgent.

'But why is it here?'

Several heavy stomps brought the creature back to the door, I could see its snout as it pressed against the door and inhaled deeply. It whined softly.

'I don't know. But something's wrong. Plus, I don't think it's a dragon.'

'Whatever it is, it looks big and scary and I don't want to be its breakfast.'

Oisin turned to me and shook his head. 'The heroic Robin Goodfellow, scared?.'

'Yes!' I turned down the volume of my confession as the creature butted the door hard and wood began to crack. We scuttled backwards, I scuttled a lot further. 'I'd say it's a good idea to be afraid of something huge and ferocious with enormous jaws.'

'This is why you need me around you see?'

Oisin held out his hand and whispered for me to give him my horse cubes, he stood up and, before I could say or do anything, opened the door of the barn and stepped outside. He held his hand out, palm flat, just like you do to a horse. The dragon was even bigger now I could see it properly, all jaws and sharp teeth. I held my breath and the animal looked Oisin up and down, clearly wondering how tasty he might be. The thing had to be nine feet high at its shoulders with big, powerful hind legs, smaller forearms that sprouted from a pair of wings, smaller than its body and so useless for flight. Its body was covered in crimson scales which caught the early morning light and made them gleam.

Over the head scaly ridges stretched from powerful jaws to the serpent-like neck, sharp enough to eviscerate Oisin if it chose to nudge him like it had the doors. He appeared to show no fear as he stood perfectly still, making soothing noises. Except they weren't noises I realised after a few seconds, he was speaking to the animal and it appeared to understand him as it flicked its head from side to side. It craned its neck further forward and with greater care than I'd thought capable, it snuffled the cubes from Oisin's hand, without chomping off his wrist.

'Get some of the animal feed from the back of the barn.'

Oisin issued the command without taking his eyes off the creature. I hurried to obey, in case the monster got peckish and decided to eat the hand that fed it. As I scurried into the barn to scoop up the brown-green pellets we'd fed to the horses earlier, I marvelled at Oisin's courage.

I stepped as nonchalantly as I could towards Oisin who was still cooing at it. I tipped some of the pellets into his waiting hand and instantly black lips snuffled them into its mouth with astonishing delicacy.

The creature kept emitting a quiet whining noise which I thought was satisfaction, it appeared hungry but I noticed Oisin stroke the animal's head and move his hand along its neck slowly, on the opposite side to where I stood.

'Keep feeding it,' he said. 'It's wounded. There's a knife stuck in its neck.'

'Don't!' I whispered with every bit of urgency I could muster. I was ignored.

Left with no alternative but risk letting the animal feast on my arm rather than kill Oisin, I held out my pellet-filled hand and hoped its shaking wouldn't affect the monster's delicate table manners. Oisin stood at its side now, stroking its sinuous neck, speaking soft reassurances. I kept feeding until my pockets and my hands were empty and got ready to run.

With a high-pitched shriek the animal craned its head round to Oisin. I wished I'd brought my sword, though I wasn't sure it would be much use against the scaly hide. It turned out there was no need to worry. The animal made a low groaning noise, like it was relieved. Oisin kept talking to it as he moved around it's body, stroking its scales the whole time.

I was instructed to get more pellets and returned to find Oisin stroking the creature's nose just like he had the horses. We kept feeding it until contentment meant the animal gave a deep-throated groan. Oisin kept stroking the thing, telling it how beautiful she was and how he'd look after her.

'So if it's not a dragon, what is it? It looks like a dragon to me.'

My apparent ignorance earned me a look of disdain. 'It's a female wyvern.'

It rang a few discordant bells in my memory. 'Didn't your sister do some research on dragons and stuff?'

Now I got a shake of the head. 'Sibeal is widely recognised as the foremost expert on the species. It's why Llyr went to her at the start. Most of them had been hunted to extinction but she managed the breeding programme until she realised what he was going to do with them and refused to cooperate any further.'

'I imagine that must have annoyed Llyr.'

Suddenly Oisin's eyes filled with his eyes. 'Sibeal is in prison. She was another lever Llyr used to force me to join him.'

His shoulders heaved as his sobs made his chest convulse. The animal looked at him, again twitching its head from side to side in bewilderment. I ignored it and grabbed hold of him and held him tightly against me. By helping me escape he'd sacrificed his sister's life if Llyr returned to Tir na nÓg.

'I'm sorry Oisin. You should have told me.'

For a while he didn't speak as he slowly regained his composure. We stood like that for a moment until he gave me the look I'd imagined he'd used during the night when he'd cuddled up to me. I let him go instantly. My need for escape registered on his face.

'I hoped you might be the person to stop him.'

I shrugged self-consciously and hurried back into the barn to feed and water the horses. I felt Oisin's eyes on me as he kept stroking the wyvern. We needed to get away from barns and all that they represented, besides, we didn't have time to reminisce. Time was against us. During the night I'd woken up when I realised Amelie knew the location of the Knights and Llyr wouldn't think twice about torturing the old bird to get the truth out of her. The bastard meant it when he'd screamed his intention to hunt us down, he needed the Knights and she was the only other person with that knowledge.

I needed to find somewhere else to hide them, except I was running out of locations, these days newcomers got treated with suspicion and hostility and discreet hideaways were hard to find. All the same, Oisin's earlier comment rankled, I was running away from a fight and Robin Goodfellow didn't do that kind of thing. It had me kicking inanimate objects in frustration. That dark pit at the bottom of the spiral had returned and Oisin's discreet glances in my direction told me he'd realised it too. I resented those looks and the overtures he kept making. Anger bubbled away inside me.

'We need to leave. Get your horse.'

'Of course.' He saddled his animal but kept watching me. 'Why not tell me why the darkness has descended again.'

I explained how Amelie could lead Llyr to the twins in fairly terse statements and the urgent need to get to them quickly. Oisin had his horse saddled and ready before me, he was more familiar with the process while mine kept glancing outside at the red monster and nervously dancing about, hindering me even further. It only made me angrier, Oisin walked over and calmed the animal with a rub of its nose.

'Llyr will need to find horses and he wouldn't travel at night. We're still in front of him. Don't worry.'

That fucking rationality again. I nodded and calmed myself until I couldn't fasten the billet straps. He abandoned the horse's nose, bent down to take the leather straps from me, giving me a warm smile in the process.

Bloody horses.

'But that's not the issue, is it?'

If I was to climb out of my pit I needed help. He was the only with a ladder. I held his eyes that were still directed at mine.

'I don't know what to do with the twins. They can't stay where they are. I don't know where to keep them that's safe. It's all so fucking unfair.'

With the billet straps fastened he straightened up and patted the horse affectionately.

'Unfair how?'

'People. They didn't know how, for centuries, the Knights had led secret crusades into Tir na nÓg as mankind's champions. When they found out, after the invasion, the kids faced a barrage of resentment and hostility.'

'But why? They've maintained the peace since Gawain was humanity's first champion and, beyond that, because of the Knights' Protocol. That's admirable courage and devotion. Why would anyone criticise it, just because they didn't know about it?'

'For that reason. The government said they had a right to know, the secrecy led to humanity being completely unprepared.'

The nod and shrug of shoulders didn't help my temper, I didn't want rational arguments about the rights or wrongs.

'You can see their point.'

'Of course I fucking can! What's so unfair is that the ones who faced the fallout were teenage orphans. Their appearance makes them stand out, you can't hide them. Every time people saw them they knew instantly who they were and the blame would get recycled.'

'I see.'

'That's it?' I bellowed at him. 'How's that going to bring light into the darkness?'

Perhaps if he'd got angry with me that would have helped but all he did was nod and smile at me, I wanted to punch his smug face.

'There's one solution, I don't understand why you've not used it.'

I threw my hands into the air. 'Then do please enlighten me!'

He'd returned to the horse's nose, my animated behaviour was making the thing nervous.

'Keep the twins with you. That way you can protect them, be more of the guardian Amelie talked about.'

'Are you serious?' I shouted the words in disbelief. There spoke a man who'd never had kids. So much for the ladder out of the pit. 'We need to get moving.'

I led my horse nervously past the wyvern. The sun poked its yellow disc just above the trees, making the creature's scales shine. Oisin nodded at the wyvern that watched our imminent departure with interest as he led his own steed past it.

'What do we do with her?'

'Leave her here. I don't give a fuck.'

I mounted and took off.

The noise of Oisin's horse told me he was following not far behind but a minute later it was obvious we weren't on our own. Heavy thuds and loud cracks from breaking branches left us in no doubt the wyvern had no intention of being left behind. She spooked our horses who thought the monster was chasing them, their jittery behaviour quickly exhausted me and did nothing to diminish my bad mood. I halted at a bend in the road where a swollen river gave the horses a chance to drink, albeit very nervously.

The wyvern, oblivious of the chaos it was creating, chose to do the same thing. Somehow, as the creature dunked its head in the swirling waters and paid them no attention, the horses relaxed a little.

'You need to get rid it,' I snapped. The bloody thing provided a trail for Llyr to follow he couldn't miss.

'How do I do that?' The reply just as bad tempered now.

'I don't know. Perhaps if you hadn't fed the fucking thing.'

'Yeah. I should have let it eat you, shouldn't I?'

I pulled my horse's rein, spoiling its enjoyment as it tugged at lush grass, and took off again, quickly followed by a horse and a red menace.

A long time ago, when the land had last been flooded, our route had been called Arthur's Hunting Causeway, defined by a narrow ridgeway that remained above the water level. Except now human habitation had complicated everything.

We arrived at a small village which had grown up on either side of a narrow bridge which stretched over a river swollen now to a torrent of brown flood water that fed a lake half a mile away.

'What have we stopped for?' Oisin asked. 'It looks empty'

'Looks are deceiving.'

I pointed to the edge of the village where poles protruded out of a swamp, on two of them dangled the remains of bodies. I explained how these remote places survived on one thing, travellers that were made to pay a toll.

'Is that what we're going to do?' Oisin's expression told me he doubted it.

'Often the ones who stay to negotiate, if they happen to have things the locals want, decorate those poles as well. Horsemeat is scarce these days.'

Oisin frowned and patted his horse's neck. Behind us the distinctive snort of the wyvern made us both look over our shoulders, Oisin tried a smile with me.

'Our travelling companion might ease our passage through their toll.'

'True.' I dug my heels into my horse's flanks and galloped towards the village.

Four men and a fat woman in greasy overalls, wielding hoes, axes and a rusty sword, hurried to their positions in front of an array of furniture, branches and general rubbish stretched across the road. I lashed out with my sword at the man with the pitchfork, forcing him to stagger backwards into the others. One of them reacted fast enough to grab the reins of my horse, he realised his mistake when I booted him hard in the face and heard bones break. He screamed and fell to the ground. My horse leapt the barrier and I waited for Oisin to follow. Two of the men, recognising the mistake of their colleague, attacked on both sides while the fat woman hurled objects with alarming accuracy at Oisin. His horse reared up, if he hadn't been such a good rider he'd have been unseated, I readied myself to go back and help but the fat woman's screams halted everything.

Stupefied beyond disbelief, the villagers stared at the sight of the wyvern barrelling towards them, roaring its fury. They immediately gave up their attack in a desperate bid to get out of its way. Oisin's horse, still nervous and skittish, cleared the barrier but the wyvern made no such attempt, she demolished it and roared her defiance in the process.

The villagers screamed their fury as we cantered along the road on the other side of the river. When we were far enough from the village Oisin dismounted and patted the wyvern on its neck and fed it some of the pellets he'd brought with him. The animal appeared to recognise it had done something good and made a noise like a cat purring; only about three octaves lower.

'She's proving useful isn't she?' He attempted another smile in my direction.

I glowered. 'Come on. We're taking too long.'

We reached South Cadbury as the afternoon sun turned to a dusky orange ball low in the sky. Flood waters lapped at the side of a narrow road, reflecting the flaming colours of the setting sun. I pointed at the small cottage up a narrow farm track. We led the horses along to an ancient barn, it had a small amount of hay for them and an old bath was filled with water. The horses appeared to have become accustomed to the wyvern so when it joined them and started snacking on the hay, they paid it little attention.

'The horses look like they've got used to her.'

Oisin patted the wyvern fondly and tried to smile at me. It died the moment he saw my expression. I looked up at the cottage that was in a dreadful state of repair. The boarded windows had unmistakeable marks from shotguns and even a few arrows. The local Neighbourhood Watch had paid them a visit.

'Listen. You need to be careful what you say as well as what you think.'

I knew he understood the Knights' talents but knowing something and acting on it all the time is something else.

'They're teenagers. They've got a lot of resentment and anger and it tends to get voiced when I'm around. Especially by Brea. She's explosive in more ways than one. They're going to be suspicious of you. This isn't going to be easy.'

Oisin nodded his head sadly. I knew he understood all this but I wasn't saying it for his benefit.

I turned to walk up to the cottage but Oisin took my arm.

'Can I ask you a question first?'

I shrugged.

'I don't understand why you're protecting the Knights. Don't misunderstand me, you know I admire what you're trying to do. But this family have always fought the Fae and, well, I don't understand why you risk so much to help them.'

It was a fair question and I had to admire him for asking it. I stared at the cottage and, beyond it, the enormous earthwork which human historians believed were the foundations of Arthur's Camelot. It was that reason why I'd bought the place long ago, why it made an appropriate home.

'When I fled Tir na nÓg, there were a few attempts on my life by Oberon's forces. The Knights didn't like any Fae on their territory. They tolerated me because I'd chosen humanity over my own race. Plus I was a soldier and that helped them understand me I suppose. Eventually the attacks fizzled out but there was always the danger they might resume so one generation passed on their responsibility for me to the next. Then, eight years ago, the Knights discovered that the Dark Court had plans to murder them. I made a promise that I would look after the twins if anything happened. Eighteen months later the kids you're about to meet were made orphans and became my responsibility to defend against the Fae.'

'Not all Fae, Robin.'

'Perhaps not. But convincing these two of that distinction may not be so easy. Good luck.'

Chapter 8

Tir na nÓg: The palace of the High Lord of the Light Court

'I'm nothing more than a mobile baby incubator to you!' I screamed.

I took a deep breath, I sounded hysterical. I wasn't helping myself by displaying my emotions so readily, we didn't do that as a family, as the blank expression on my grandmother's face proved now. I could see the condemnation in her eyes, I was the youngest of her offspring and, in her view, spoiled beyond redemption.

She didn't speak but waited for me to apologise for my outburst. I wasn't going to give her that satisfaction. I made a point of smoothing my dress, I hated wearing the kind of frilly meringues protocol dictated whenever I was summoned to her palace chambers, they were utterly impractical and made women look frivolous and shallow.

I looked up and met the kind of scrutiny a butcher probably gives the animal it's about to slaughter. Well, this one wasn't going without a fight.

'I'd like to know, grandmother, precisely when you authorised the medical violation of my body to establish the certainty of my fertility.'

Her reply came without a moment's hesitation and in that tone she used to defend all of her actions, it was for the good of the Light Court.

'When you caught the chill last month, the royal physician gave you a sleeping draught and performed an examination. There was no inconvenience to you, I don't understand why you're being hysterical.'

There it was, the word. I knew she'd use it. I felt my jaw clench.

'And tell me, grandmother, why was it necessary for you to wait until I was too ill to object before carrying out this assault?'

The slightest of shrugs.

'You would have become emotional and overwrought and tried to refuse.'

I felt my fists clench, restraining my outrage was all but impossible.

'And had I refused? What then? Would your guards have strapped me to a table?'

Another shrug. She hadn't taken her eyes off me the whole time, those cold grey orbs were like ice. Like her heart no doubt.

'If it proved necessary, yes.'

I wanted to scream at her, to accuse her of treating her family as assets rather than people, of lacking any emotional depth of character, but I didn't. That wasn't what we did as a family. We reined it all in, repressed our fury so that it became part of our collective dysfunctionality.

'I see.' I took another deep breath and unclenched my fists, I even managed to smile. 'And now you are assured of my fertility, what plans do you have for me? I only ask because it would be nice to know how my life will be spent and what further physical abuses I can anticipate.'

The old woman turned, glided across the polished marble floor to a large window which looked out over her orchard, the one thing in the world which obsessed her, apart from clinging on to power. A cool breeze, heralding the approach of winter, wafted into the Silver Reception Room and it made me shiver, though my grandmother appeared not to notice. She was making me wait, one of her usual methods of pointing out who was in charge, it was humiliating that she did the same thing to my father, who was High Lord. I knew if I said anything she'd only make me wait even longer, so as I'd done so many times, I stared at the crystal walls and marvelled at the carvings that refracted the light so the room was filled with rainbows. I'd been fascinated by the room as a child, it had been the place which inspired me to find out what caused such a beautiful effect and so fuel my love of all learning.

Her reply came after a deep sigh, which meant this wasn't going to be good news. I prepared for the worst.

'You must understand Filidea, your body holds our only hope for the continuity of our family, of this Court, even our entire race. If you had proved incapable of producing offspring, then you and your brother would be the last of our line.'

I bet my brother hadn't had to undertake such a humiliating exercise to establish his fertility credentials. He spent all of his time sewing his seed in almost every woman in the Court. I should have known my grandmother would know what I was thinking.

'Sadly, if you brother had been fertile things would have been so much easier, he has always been so willing to impregnate. It is unfortunate his seed is barren.'

I grimaced, had they knocked him out to conduct an exploration of his nether regions too?

'Which leaves this heavy burden of responsibility to be carried by you, and you alone.' The old woman turned and fixed me with those cold eyes again. 'So yes, you are a mobile baby incubator, if you choose to label yourself in such a theatrical way. It is your responsibility, there can be none greater Filidea. You would do well to recognise just how enormous that obligation is to everyone in this realm.'

Her eyes narrowed.

'Or are you so utterly self-centred that you believe, as you put it, that *your* life and *your* body is more important?' She spat out the possessive pronouns as though they were dirt.

She'd done it again. The old woman had an inestimable ability to make you feel guilty for something that wasn't your fault, to turn the situation around so you were left defending yourself. When we'd been children, Midir and I used to call it 'weather-cocking', because no matter from what direction you approached any topic, grandmother always had the ability to turn the debate in her direction, like the wind turns a weathervane.

In an attempt to win back my self-esteem, I tried one more time.

'Of course I'm not reneging on my responsibility grandmother...'

And, before I could finish, her voice overpowered mine, contradicting the apparent weakness she displayed most of the time.

'Good. That's agreed. Now, as to your husband. I've given the matter considerable thought.'

'Husband?' The word came out as a strangled cry, making me sound helpless. She'd somehow assumed my acceptance to her plans and was about to marry me off.

With a frown she spoke as though she was talking to an idiot. 'Obviously. A royal princess does not give birth to bastards.'

'But...'

The world had suddenly twisted on its axis and spun me around so I didn't know if I was coming or going. One minute I was objecting to the discovery of a medical procedure and the next I'm being told who I'm going to marry. Events were running away without me. I needed to apply the brakes.

'I'm not getting married yet grandmother and when I do, I shall choose the man. Not you.'

I made sure my voice carried the same determined authority that she'd used. She wasn't going to treat me like the rest of the family.

I could see her calculating how best to deal with this latest act of rebellion. I didn't care what kind of guilt she dumped on me, I wasn't going to meekly obey her when it came to choosing a husband.

Then she did something that genuinely scared me. I think I might have gasped.

She smiled.

'Of course, you must have a say, Filidea, such a match must be agreed by all parties. This is not some business transaction. It is the means from which the next generation of this family will be created.'

'Oh. Good.' I felt like a ship suddenly robbed of a strong sea breeze, my rebellion had vanished and I was left becalmed.

Grandmother stepped forward and took my hands in hers, they were ice cold unsurprisingly. She pulled them towards her, into the diaphanous layers of grey silk that hung off her bony body. I half wondered if she was about to inject my wrists with something, to put me in a trance so I would sign a marital agreement, but I felt her pat my hands and continue to smile at me.

'We will arrange for suitable candidates to present themselves to you, my dear. We shall have such fun, selecting them, looking at which ones possess the relevant intelligence, good health, wealth and, of course, validated records of their fertility.'

'Oh. Good.'

I left the room in a daze. I had been entirely out manoeuvred by an expert. I knew how short the betrothal list would be. There were plenty of men with sufficient wealth, which automatically guaranteed good health. As for intelligence, well, that was in almost as short supply as guaranteed fertility. The search criteria hadn't included age or appearance I realised. I tried to tell myself such things didn't matter but then an image of Lord Aed sprang to mind, shrivelled, preoccupied with breeding pigs and with a face that looked like one. It made me shudder at the possibility.

My feet took me automatically towards the library, I kept going over and over the conversation wondering how I might have ended it with a different outcome. It was the smile that had swung it, disorientating me and leaving me vulnerable.

I was going to be married. I just didn't know who would be sharing my bed.

Clodagh greeted me but her expression quickly changed.

'What's happened? What did Lay Nimue want with you?'

I sat in my usual place at the reference table and stared emptily at the pile of books we'd planned to work through that afternoon. It felt so irrelevant suddenly, spending hours poring over ancient books no one else cared about, looking for information no one would want to hear. I glanced up at the dirty window no one ever thought to clean and looked at the woman staring back at me with her heavy-rimmed glasses, straight hair tied back in a loose pony tail and the long, flat face that no one had ever called pretty.

There I was, dismissing suitors who might be ugly and dull when I was no portrait either. There might be men who, at the sound of my name, would be changing the details in their fertility certificate to 'barren'.

I felt tears form and trickle down my cheeks. My pale cheeks, because I didn't spend any time outside, only in the dark and dusty environment of the library. Even Midir struggled to find a complimentary description, my brother's attempt had sounded less hurtful but had an indisputable accuracy: bookish.

Clodagh pulled up a chair beside me and took my hands in hers, they were warm. I looked up into her anxious face.

'What did that old witch say to you this time?'

I chuckled. 'If my grandmother heard you speak of her that way...'

Clodagh shrugged hunched shoulders. 'As if she, or any of her coven, would ever visit such a lonely place as the library. And it's no worse than how you describe her, so tell me what the old crone has done to upset you so badly.'

She listened as I described the whole sorry episode, she hadn't let go of my hands the whole time and now she squeezed them affectionately.

'You never know, you might find someone handsome and sexy. Like Bradon.'

He was Clodagh's latest obsession; ever since she'd seen him swimming in the river with his friends she'd marvelled at what a wonderful specimen of manhood he was. She seemed to possess no self-awareness where men were concerned. She lived a life of fantasy, where such men would be excited by someone who was so tiny she was mistaken for a little girl, flat-chested and with mousy-brown hair that hung to her bony shoulders, hunched by years of leaning over books. Neither of us were attractive, it was why we'd become such friends, both rejected by all the other girls in the Court.

'Yeah. Perhaps.'

She smiled at me but didn't try to build on the fantasy. I wasn't in the mood for it, life had turned serious.

'Do you know the worst thing, of all the bad things running through my mind just now?'

She shook her head.

'I won't be able to keep coming here. Not once I'm married.'

'Why not?'

The girl really did live in a fantasy world.

'Because I'll have a home and servants to manage. There'll be entertaining and dinner parties for other members of the Light Court. And pregnancy no doubt.'

Now I'd said it out loud the prospect filled me with so much despair I felt sick. It was a life I'd never wanted, one for which I was entirely unsuited. I would never have time for books ever again.

'I'll be his slave Clodagh.'

'No you won't!'

Clodagh's eyes burned fiercely as though I'd threatened to take my life. She shook her head repeatedly.

'Filidea, you are the most independent woman I know. There isn't a man who can equal your determination and strength. You have that old witch's blood in your veins, you're like her more than you know.'

'Thanks!'

'And for that reason you're not going to let any man tell you what to do.'

'But it's not just him. It's the customs and obligations of being a princess. There will be the expectations of parties and stuff. And, whoever I marry, he'll have a huge house that will need to be managed. I just have my rooms in the palace grounds now. Life is going to be so different.'

I watched her shoulders slump and felt mine do the same. We sat in silence for some time until I reached for the pile of books.

'Well. Until then we can keep researching. Perhaps after I'm married you can bring some books to me?'

She nodded unenthusiastically.

'Come on. We have to be positive. Now how far had we got in confirming what we know about genetic abnormalities? Did you find that work referenced by Finn Eces on the continuity of abnormities over generations?'

Our studies quickly absorbed us and crowded out any negative thoughts about marriage. Suddenly Clodagh grabbed my hand, we'd been so engrossed it made me jump and I squealed, we both giggled.

'With all the talk of your impending nuptials, I forgot to tell you what I found out this morning. The High Lord of the Dark Court has put Sibeal in prison.'

I stared wide-eyed.

'That mad bastard. Why?'

I could guess but I wanted to be sure.

'Do you know why Llyr has been breeding dragons? Because he's using them in the war with the humans. Sibeal wasn't aware, when she found it, she refused to have any further part in it. She even released the wyverns she'd bred so he couldn't use them. '

'Good for her,' I said.

My guess had been right. I was already planning how I could persuade my grandmother to intercede. If she wanted me to cooperate then she had to do the same. Besides, the old woman was a big fan of Sibeal's brother, Oisin. I was fairly certain it wasn't just his physical attributes that attracted her, though the idea of the old woman having such urges made me feel ill. Anyway, he was attracted to men. Sadly.

'What are you thinking?' Clodagh asked, watching me intently.

'We have to help her. That woman has a brilliant mind, she could help us make real strides in our discoveries.'

That got a puzzled frown. 'She works with dragons.'

I dismissed it with an impatient wave of a hand. 'Breeding is about genetic lines Clodagh! Dragons, people, it's the same principle.'

'Right.'

We were silent for a moment, no doubt pursuing the same line of thought. Clodagh was the one to actually say it out loud.

'How do we get her released from prison though? I'm surprised Oisin hasn't already taken action over it. He's supposed to be friends with Llyr.'

I wasn't certain how many people knew the truth, I'd only discovered it after a little eavesdropping. It was a practice you developed early in our family, a good way to keep up to date with what grandmother was up to. I swore Clodagh to secrecy first.

'He's gone with Llyr into the human realm. They're looking for someone.'

After the inevitable questions of when and where and who and how, Clodagh gave me chance to finish what I was saying.

'It's someone who protects the Knights I think. Llyr wants to bring them here.'

Clodagh frowned. 'I thought they were dead?'

'That was the adults. These are kids.'

The frown lines on Clodagh's face deepened. 'But what's all this got to do with Sibeal?'

I grinned. Clodagh had been right, I was like my grandmother. The Lady of the Lake hadn't survived for as long as she had, and maintained control of the Light Court against every disaster to befall it, without the ability to find ways to achieve her ambitions. I was starting to see a way forward for me, just the smallest glimpse, but it was enough. It began by gathering people around me, I couldn't do this on my own.

And sometimes, just sometimes, you manipulated people to get what you wanted when they wouldn't cooperate.

My grin widened as I looked at my friend's bewildered expression.

'There's an old saying, while the cat's away, the mice will play.'

Bewilderment turned into outright confusion.

'We're little mice, Clodagh. We're about to go and play.'

Chapter 9

They stood in the doorway of the farmhouse like bookends. The Yin and Yang that represented the Knights, each expressing identical suspicion and hostility as they stared at Oisin.

'What have you brought him for?'

Inevitably Brea was the one to make her feelings known. She scrutinised Oisin with her distinctive jade-green eyes, the frown making no secret that she didn't like what she saw. She'd got thinner, her physique had always been boyish but now it was lean with toned muscle. She'd cut her hair very short, like her brother, so it made her features sharp and even more masculine. It didn't suit her but I wasn't planning on commenting on it.

'He's hoping to fuck him, that's why.'

I glared at Finn who merely raised white eyebrows and glowered back at me. His face was softer, slightly more rounded than his sister's, almost feminine. He'd also lost weight and it made him look unnaturally paler than usual, like a vampire. No wonder the locals had got nervous about them living on their doorstep. Their almost albino-like complexion and silver hair meant they looked like they deliberately avoided the sun, something superstitious types readily attributed to the supernatural. These days, where any difference made you a victim, the safest way to keep the kids alive meant keeping them out of sight. Oisin obviously hadn't understood that fact.

'And it's good to see you too,' I said and attempted a smile.

Brea stood in the doorway, blocking our entrance.

'Is he right?' she nodded at her brother. 'Because you haven't answered my question.'

'Call me old fashioned,' I replied determined to maintain my smile, 'but I thought we could discuss it in the house. We've been travelling for hours, we're knackered and hungry.'

She didn't react but walked into the kitchen, her brother followed with a similarly blank expression though that meant nothing where he was concerned.

Oisin went to speak but I silenced him with quick shake of the head, things were delicate enough as it was.

We sat at a rickety wooden table while Finn poured boiling water from a large kettle on the ancient Aga into a teapot. Chunks of bread and cheese were already waiting for us on the table. Brae leaned against the wall, eyes fixed on Oisin who looked very uncomfortable. No one spoke. I knew better than to try polite conversation with these two.

Large mugs of a steaming concoction that smelled like it was made from acorns were dumped on the table in front of us. The twins sat down at the table, Brea rotated the chair so she could straddle it to continue glaring at Oisin.

'Right. Niceties over. Answer my question.'

Her stern expression told me she hadn't considered her words ironic in any way.

I told them what had happened, there was no point in omitting any detail or skimming over events, not with Finn present. When I'd finished, he frowned.

'Why the dragon?'

'She's a wyvern. Not a dragon.'

Two pairs of cold eyes zeroed their animosity towards Oisin.

'Wyverns are far more intelligent than dragons. They are also fiercely loyal. Dragons in comparison are stupid, unpredictable and lumbering creatures that serve little purpose.'

'That's why Llyr's breeding them is it?'

Brea flicked a quick glance at her brother before turning back to scowl at Oisin. We hadn't mentioned Llyr's plans but Finn had already trawled that part of Oisin's mind. The poor guy blinked as he realised its implications. It silenced his defence of wyverns.

'So he wants to parade us as his vassals. Persuade the Light Court he has what it takes to unify the Fae into attacking humankind so he can wipe everyone out.'

I hadn't mentioned any of this either but Finn's summary displayed how clever the kid was, for someone with no education in battle strategy. I didn't bother to reply, he'd know I agreed. He looked at me a little harder, somewhere deep in my brain I could feel a slight tickling sensation.

'Why don't you just ask me instead?' I snapped.

It got the slightest of grins on his thin lips.

'I can't find out what your part is in all this.'

I sipped my drink then stuffed my mouth with a lump of hard cheese and crusty bread. I'd make the sods wait. Oisin, sensing tension mounting, did the same. Eventually, after taking a leisurely sip of my acorn tea, I shrugged.

'I don't know what to do.'

They all looked quizzically at me, Oisin especially.

'I can try to hide you two again.'

'Why? What's wrong with here?' Brea asked.

'Llyr is probably on his way already. Is he?'

I turned to Finn who closed his eyes and frowned. When he opened them again he shook his head.

'I can't sense him. But moving from here might not be a bad idea.'

'Fuck it Finn, I told you I'll blast those bastards to buggery if they try again.'

They looked across the table at one another and for a few seconds nothing was spoken, not out loud anyway so I shared the only conclusion I'd drawn so far. It wouldn't be long until the angry locals returned and caused real problems.

'Llyr will be here soon. Staying isn't an option,' I said.

They turned their attention back to me.

'The question is whether we find another place to hide or whether we do something else.'

'Like what?' Brea asked, bristling before she'd heard what I had to say.

'That's what I don't know.' I smiled at Finn. 'I truly don't. But I can't help but think we're running out of places to hide. And Llyr's desperate need to capture you two makes him vulnerable.'

The slightest of smiles formed on Brea's firm mouth. 'We kill him?'

'That's no use.' Finn was shaking his head but clearly concentrating on something. 'It would bring the Light Court into the war, it puts us in the same situation as before. Unless your fuck-buddy here was lying when he told you to spare Llyr's life?'

Oisin's face flushed dark pink. I pitched in before he said anything we'd regret.

'He wasn't lying, he has reasons for wanting Llyr dead too.'

'So if we don't kill him, what then?' Brea asked.

'We capture him.' I hoped ideas would form as I spoke because apart from that ambition, I had little else to offer.

Finn picked at a piece of bread thoughtfully. 'That robs him of his status, especially if we ransom him back to the Dark Court.'

'Exactly,' I said.

'So how do we capture him?' Brea asked.

Finn grinned. 'Yeah. How Robin?'

I assumed he knew I was empty of ideas but then Oisin rescued me.

'Llyr faces a major problem. He's here with a small force, his plan was to snatch Robin, force him to betray you two and return before the humans realised he was here. Now that plan is ruined. If he's going to capture you two, he needs to do it fast, before the humans can assemble a significant force. Time is running out for him, he can bring more of his spriggan forces through the portal but he knows that will only escalate the conflict. He needs to get back before that happens.'

I nodded. I could see where Oisin was going.

'So we destroy the portal and trap him here,' I said.

When Brea spoke her tone dripped suspicion.

'Unless that idea is part of Llyr's plan?'

She stared unforgivingly at Oisin.

'This one delivers us to him where he can abduct us easily and quickly.'

Finn started to nod as he frowned and focused his attention of Oisin.

I'd held myself in check until that moment. I was prepared to suffer their jibes and accusations but I felt defensive where Oisin was concerned. I couldn't be certain his sister was in prison but I knew Oisin to be a terrible liar. When we'd tried to keep our relationship secret he'd been the one who'd struggled with even the whitest of lies. I might have changed in the intervening years but he hadn't. Not in the slightest. It meant listening to the twins' accusations pushed the wrong button.

'Do you know the trouble with you two?' I snarled. 'You've stopped trusting anyone. You suspect everyone of everything. I understand why, but there has to come a point where you rely on someone else's judgement and I am telling you now, with absolute certainty, Oisin is not leading you into a trap.'

Both kids looked at me with astonishment. Admittedly, I didn't make speeches like that very often. If at all.

Finn snorted. 'You would say that. You want to fuck him.'

My blood pressure rose and I was on my feet, so was Oisin as he stuck an arm in front of me to stop me from punching the lad. He looked directly into Finn's eyes.

'If you think I'm working for Llyr, go into my head and find out for yourself. Have a good root around. Go where you like.'

The lad didn't waste any time, he grabbed hold of Oisin's shoulder and closed his eyes. We remained in that position as we watched a montage of expressions cross Finn's face until eventually he opened his eyes and shrugged. That gesture didn't do my anger any favours.

'No apology? No thanks for allowing that kind of intrusion?'

Oisin, still with his hand against my chest, shook his head. 'Robin, it's all right.'

'No it's not.' I turned back to Finn. 'It's a fucking violation! Have you two become so paranoid that you need to do that to everyone you meet? Perhaps you need to dig into my head as well Finn. Perhaps you don't trust me either these days?'

Both kids glared back at me. We stood around the old table, not moving, making unspoken accusations with our eyes. Eventually Finn muttered an apology of sorts and we all sat down again, no one knowing where to look.

I let my blood pressure ease back to normal by breaking off a piece of bread and chewing on it for want of something to do. If I was honest with myself, it was my fault these kids were as paranoid as they were. If I'd been a better guardian, if they'd been older and better able to understand what was happening. If, if, if.

I found myself thinking of Alec, their father, who'd grown into a young man with enormous sensitivity and a sense of fun. I'd started off as his favourite uncle, the crazy guy who always got him into trouble. Then as he grew into an adult, our relationship evolved into a genuine friendship. I'd promised Alec I'd take care of his children, help them grow into the next generation of Knights who would not only protect humanity but would avenge his, and his sister's, death.

I only had to look at the two resentful teenagers to know I'd well and truly fucked up on that promise.

'The problem as I see it, is getting Llyr alone.'

I wanted to smile at Oisin's indefatigable attempt to keep us on track.

'No plan is going to work with just the four of us.'

Brea's usual ability to poor cold water on anything was what we didn't need at this point. She gave a casual sniff of disinterest as a follow up.

'So we need to find others,' I said, trying to keep things positive.

That got another sniff, louder this time. 'Good luck doing that. Everyone thinks we're freaks and traitors who ought to be punished for causing this mess. And as for you two finding allies, good luck when they find out what you really are.'

I persisted with the lightness of touch I was so well known for.

'When they find out we're Fae or queer?'

Sniff. 'Either.'

I hated to admit it but she was right.

We spent the next couple of hours trying to find answers until the rabbit casserole Finn had cooking in the oven wrecked our concentration. We'd just finished eating and started to wash up when Finn went quiet and closed his eyes. Brea tensed instantly, as did I. When he opened them again his expression told us everything we needed to know. It showed fear.

'They're coming back,' he said.

'The same ones?' Brea's voice, in comparison held a note of excitement.

The lad frowned. 'Some. But this time it's different. There are others. It's organised. There's someone giving orders.'

Now I really was worried. Our trashing of the barrier in the village would have caused a stir, our route easy to follow. That was one option. The second one, that scared me more, Llyr had found us. Yet when I suggested this to Finn he said our night-time visitors were definitely human.

'How does he know?' Oisin asked as the twins hurried around the house to check its security. 'Can he read all their minds from a distance?'

'Not really. The male Knight has always been psychic but it comes in different forms. Finn's unusual. He can also receive mental images. When his skill became apparent his dad told me how the American army had already done some research into it. They call it remote viewing.'

Three gunshots cracked in the stillness of the night and the back door reverberated.

'How many are there Finn?' I asked.

The lad shook his head, frowning hard. 'Can't tell. Too dark. Chaotic.'

'All right, don't worry. I'm here.'

He swallowed hard and nodded at me. If I hadn't been so worried I'd have felt pleased. Brea on the other hand paced up and down in the kitchen flexing her fists.

More gun shots. Upstairs somewhere a boarded window rattled.

'Who are these people?' I asked. 'Do you know what they want?'

126

Finn shook his head. Brea sniffed. 'They're crazy local bastards.'

'But why attack in such force? This doesn't sound like a bunch of thugs having fun.'

There was the briefest of glances from brother to sister.

'What did you do Brea?'

A loud sniff. Then a second as she turned to glare at me.

'The bastards tried to steal the vegetables we'd spent all summer growing. Fucking lazy bastards. So I blasted them.'

'Did you kill them?' If so, we were dead too.

'No. I'm not stupid. I just shot a bolt or two over their heads. Scared them so much one of them pissed himself.' She giggled.

'Great.' We were in all kinds of shit. They'd have the kids labelled as demons and outside a mob would be getting ready with their pitchforks to make sacrifices. I'd seen more than my fair share of what happened to demons, suffered it too. Trouble was, to these people the Knights weren't just different, their special talents made them monsters and when bigots perceive anyone that way, it brought shitloads of suffering.

To make matters worse, the locals were about to meet a couple of gay guys who were also their enemy.

Yeah, all kinds of shit.

Gun shots hammered at the door three times in quick succession, upstairs more rattling boards. Then the sound I'd expected; the voice of authority.

'You've got one minute to get out of the house, then we set fire to it.'

'Fucking bastards!' Brea screamed as she ran to the door. I caught her just in time. She struggled in my arms, fought against me with such strength it surprised me but I was stronger and pushed her against the wall and pinned her there.

'Listen.' I stared hard into her face. 'Blasting everybody isn't the answer.'

'Fucking is!' she snapped back at me. 'I can zap bolts of different sizes and even strafe now. I can fucking light up the place like firework night.'

'She can.' Finn joined in but he hung back and spoke with less conviction.

'Good. But while you're doing that, they'll be shooting you. There's one of you and lots of them. The odds aren't good Brea.'

The logic got through to her and she stopped fighting.

'What then?'

Outside the voice of authority announced we had thirty seconds.

'We go outside and try to negotiate.'

Her eyes widened with astonishment. It surprised me too.

I opened the door slightly and yelled into the night. 'We're coming out!'

The same voice called for everyone to hold their fire but I waited a few seconds to make sure there weren't any trigger-happy types before I opened the door wider. I took a few steps beyond the threshold of the door.

'Let's talk!' I called. 'I think there's been a misunderstanding.'

I'm not known for diplomacy, finding the right words wasn't easy. My words provoked laughter.

'You don't say!' came the terse reply. 'Let's see all of you.'

The twins stepped out and stood on either side of me. I'd told Oisin to stand behind me and keep quiet so his accent didn't give him away.

'Is that all of you?'

'You know it is!' I called. 'You watched us arrive.'

That didn't get a reply so it suggested they had been watching the cottage.

'I'd prefer to talk to a man's face rather than call into the night. Last time I did that I was madly in love!'

A little humour I hoped would ease the tension. I hoped someone in the darkness would be smiling. I felt Finn's hand on my elbow as he whispered. 'They're moving closer. Three I think.'

From a short distance a lantern bobbed from side to side and got steadily nearer. I felt Brea tense.

'Don't you dare!' I whispered.

Eventually the outlines of dark shapes against the darker night formed then suddenly the man holding the lantern appeared in front of us, his face a ruin. A thin white diagonal line of scar tissue ran across his face; one eye socket was a mess of burned tissue like puckered plastic. I heard Finn gasp. The guy smirked, when he spoke I recognised this was who'd called out to us.

'I know. People always react like that. Handsome, aren't I?' he spoke with a mixture of humour and bitterness. There was a refined quality to his speech, certainly not a local, or if he was, he was well educated.

Two other men joined him. One was big, beefy and bearded with muscle turned to flab. He watched me in a way I recognised, he was sizing me up as a fighter. The other was younger, his hair a tangled mass and a beard struggling to make any impact and succeeding only in patches. It was his eyes that concerned me, there was a wild unpredictability there. A loose cannon.

Their leader, having made his own assessments, glared at Brea for a few seconds before turning his attention back to me. I needed to take the initiative.

'She's angered you. I understand that. She made your men think she meant to kill them but that wasn't the case at all.'

One eye narrowed as he watched me and a slight curl formed on narrow lips.

'You're a smart one, aren't you Mister...?'

'Fellows. Robin Fellows.' I stuck out a hand for him to shake just to stop him getting the measure of me. He looked at my hand and the smile curled a little more. 'And you are?'

'Joe Purdy,' he said. 'So you know why we're here.' It wasn't said as a question.

'Brea will make a full and complete apology to your men and you are invited to help yourself to the vegetables and any other food you need to improve your men's rations.'

I watched him closely as I made the military reference and sure enough, even with one eye, there was the briefest expression of surprise. This guy had held a military command, his two sidekicks had been his subordinates most likely, the beefy guy probably his sergeant major. He realised what I was doing and fixed me with that single orb.

'Yeah. Smart. Too smart.'

I didn't like that at all. Was I overplaying my hand? He shrugged broad shoulders, this guy would know how to handle himself in a fight, a fact I considered exploring if it meant we needed to play testosterone-fuelled games.

Suddenly, from out of the darkness, another figure appeared, tall and thin and brandishing a battered Bible. I knew this type well, I'd faced more than my fair share of religious nutcases.

'We're wasting time Joe Purdy. Bring these demons to face their punishment!'

He scowled at Brea, who bristled in return, I grabbed one of her hands to stop her from releasing the energy building in her body.

'These kids are not demons,' I said to the one-eyed man. I knew he'd be the one making decisions. 'They are soldiers with special talents designed to fight the fairies.'

'Lies! Lies!' screamed the Bible-grasping maniac whose eyes virtually rolled in his head as he screamed at us. 'God identifies our sins and punish us for them too! Take the demons for trial!'

From out of the night stepped reinforcements. An assortment of men who shared the same qualities, shaved heads, straggly beards and a hollow-eyed look that comes from staying alive by the simple quality of following orders no matter how crazy they are. You don't argue in situations like that, it gets you beaten to a pulp. Or killed by people who've abandoned the luxury of a conscience.

It's a lesson learned from a great deal of experience. Youth rarely acknowledges the value of that commodity though, it knows better, or its prepared to try a different approach that might work even better. I assume these were Brea's conclusions for behaving like she did. Her actions went a long way to proving Oisin and Amelie wrong when it came to me being a guardian. Brea called me a fucking coward and blasted two of the men who were about to grab her arms. They leapt out of the way, she'd telegraphed her intentions and provided enough warning that it saved their lives.

It did nothing to help our situation. Quite the reverse.

Seeing a young woman emit bolts of bright, white energy from her fingertips, for the uninitiated, is quite a sight. Even Oisin, who knew what the female Knight could do, gasped and looked at her in awe.

Sadly, Joe Purdey's gang was less inclined to react that way. Certainly, their zealous religious leader, who'd presumably only heard stories of her ability, launched into impassioned fire-and-brimstone exhortation, screaming for the salvation of his flock, who responded to his orders to capture the demons before they killed everyone.

Power shifted. Joe Purdey watched it with barely constrained fury but didn't interfere, it was the classic schism between religion and the military. The church, I'd learned, always won in such situations because they could galvanise fear, it was down to the military to defend against those who were the focus of that fear. With a lunatic in charge who could inspire people to acts of barbarism, we'd degenerated into something out of the Middle Ages.

Chaos followed. The men piled onto Brea to incapacitate her demonic power, throwing themselves on her like you would a grenade. I tried to stop them, so did Oisin. Men came at us, too many to stop. I saw someone knock Oisin to the ground while others grabbed a startled Finn and pinned him against the wall. I felt Puck rise up and worried his arrival would only make matters worse but then pain exploded at the back of my head and the ground came up to meet me with frightening speed.

I had just enough time to conclude we were in all kinds of shit now.

Chapter 10

Master Darragh's fury could be measured by the red marks on my cheeks. Each one represented a mistake in my phraseology of the human tongue. Our language may have been similar but there were too many idiosyncrasies. It depended on who you spoke to, the content of the conversation, even the time of day, it proved impossible to remember them all. A fact Master Darragh didn't appreciate, all his other pupils managed the differences without any problems, so I was supposed to believe.

It didn't help that the old man, with his milk-white hair and parchment-like skin, considered teaching a servant to be a huge insult. Somehow he ignored the distinction between slave and servant, servants were supposed to be treated with some respect, I was apparently too stupid to qualify. He made it very clear he'd taught royalty and now he'd been instructed to spend his time in the dusty library trying to turn shit into something useful. As I failed to use the correct greeting to a familiar and well-respected friend, he launched into familiar bellyaching.

'I'm wasting my time! Nothing stays in that head of yours, you stupid little shit. I do not understand why I should be forced to waste my time on ignorant hybrids.'

Tears weren't far away but I was determined not to give him the satisfaction of seeing how he upset me. It earned me another stinging slap. His insults were circular, starting with my hybrid ancestry, followed by my ignorance and then my gutter-like manners, my irrelevance to the world at large and finally, unsurprisingly, the colour of my skin before linking this back to my ancestry.

'If I knew who'd commanded me to undertake this humiliation I could tell them of the futility of teaching a cretin such as you. Who was it, wretch?'

This was how each session always ended, with a concerted effort by Master Darragh to force me to name names. No matter how desperate the old man's interrogation, it couldn't compare to the ocean of dread that swept over me at the thought of betraying my secret connection with Mab. Since our meeting in the library I'd been left in no doubt as to the implications of anyone discovering what she planned. My meteoric rise from devious slave to page had everyone gossiping, confronting me with all kinds of scenarios, some of them wildly offensive. It was made harder by not being able to say anything to deny them, which only made the gossip grow.

There was one good thing to counterpoint the repercussions in my rise to power.

Irvyn suffered a significant loss of status. He'd been ejected from the infirmary suddenly and lost his relative luxury in the laundry to be demoted to mucking out the horses. Stories abounded of his resentment, which others were quick to fuel, after all I was a brown-skinned hybrid and shouldn't be allowed such opportunities. It meant Master Darragh wasn't the only one in the palace who resented me. The world, according to some, had gone mad when hard-working, obedient and respectful individuals were ignored and jumped-up types with dubious parentage were promoted in their stead.

If I'd felt lonely before it was nothing compared to the isolation I experienced now.

I sat at our study table, in front of a red-faced Master Darragh, silently denying him an answer to his question. He stormed out of the library, cursing me for my lack of respect and my deceit.

I slumped in my chair and sighed at the unfairness of life, which had grown a lot more complicated. These moments were growing in number and I had to keep reminding myself why I'd chosen this new life.

There was never a day went by when I didn't think about my wyvern and my need to rescue her. Once I had her at my side, things would be clearer to everyone, I would have a purpose finally, I might even get to enjoy what I did every day.

That was the fantasy. In my darker moments, and there were a lot of them, I couldn't stop imagining horrific scenarios that would befall me on my quest. My dreams were full of them. As the date of my departure drew nearer, more and more details of my dreams infiltrated my daytime thoughts. I'd visited the infirmary twice, convinced I'd caught some terrible disease; I trembled constantly, felt sick and dizzy all the time and couldn't eat. The second time the impatient medic told me to go away, the symptoms I described had one simple cause: cowardice.

No one understood my fear of leaving the only place I knew. I'd spent the whole of my life in the palace, a place so big there were parts I'd never visited, yet its scale didn't compare to my destination. I was to travel to another world, a place where I was an alien and even more of an outsider than I was here.

Lady Mab had tried to explain what happened when I went through the gateway. I was going to travel to a world that lay a hair's breadth away but couldn't be reached without a gateway that connected the two worlds. It didn't make any sense to me, how could a world be so near, yet not be seen? Why did you need gateways to reach something so close?

According to Lady Mab our two worlds existed in exactly the same space and time, they were called dimensions apparently. She'd pointed to the stars in the sky, as we stood in a quiet courtyard after our latest planning session, and said they would exist in the human realm in the same way. For someone who'd known only the palace grounds, we were dealing with a scale I couldn't understand, and she gave up trying to teach me. At least she didn't beat me for my stupidity.

With my lesson over, Master Sidwell would expect me to return to my duties, like any other page. He'd been cold and distant since my reprimand, he wasn't happy about my promotion either but he knew better than to argue with Lady Mab, he was the only other person who knew about our arrangements.

I looked around, I was rapidly growing to love the library, despite Master Darragh. At this time in the afternoon, sunlight streamed through a window with coloured leaden panes that projected patterns on to the floor. Above me, the ceiling was a huge dome, painted dark blue with yellow stars in the patterns Mab had pointed out to me. Dust was everywhere, on every shelf of every bookcase that filled the room. There must be so much knowledge contained in the books and folded manuscripts, a whole world of learning that had to be as big as Tir na nÓg. People must have valued that information at some point, to go to all the trouble of writing it down and printing it. Even Lady Mab had recognised that they should have consulted the library about training dragons before they'd introduced their programme of breeding the beasts.

That thought process set me off thinking. I had, stuffed in my pocket, a document from Master Sidwell, giving me permission to be in this room. There was no time or date displayed so I could be here officially, should the unlikely event happen that someone asked, no one ever came here though so that seemed unlikely.

I felt a smile grow on my lips at the delight of finding out things about dragons without the fear of being discovered. I'd certainly never get a better opportunity.

I sprinted to the furthest corners, amidst rows of musty books on dusty shelves to find the section on dragons. My search brought me the single ancient tome I'd seen before, bound in cracked leather, at least this time I could take time to read it properly. With great care I flicked through its vellum pages. There were beautiful drawings of all kinds of dragons, detailing their behaviour, diet, mating habits and even training methods. This book held everything we needed to know.

Correction: everything I needed to know.

I settled myself into a comfortable seat in the stained glass window, placed the book on my knees and started reading.

It seemed the only occasions when Time got the better of me, was when dragons were involved. I realised how late it was when the lack of light caused me to squint. The sun had set and the library was gloomy and full of shadows. I'd be in trouble for evading my duties for so long but I was confident I'd learned enough about dragon training to convince Lady Mab to defend me against Master Sidwell.

I was returning the book to the shelf when I heard voices. My permission document would have little relevance at this time of day, when all servants should be with their masters and mistresses. I panicked. I tiptoed along the length of the bookshelf and dodged from the end of one row of shelves to another until I could see the space near the door where I had my lessons, beyond that the corridor. I weighed up the chance of risking a quick dash to the door but I waited too long.

The door closed with an ominous thud, to be followed by a voice I knew well and made my bowels quiver.

'Be wary. My patience wears thin.'

If Lady Mab knew I was eavesdropping on her, my value as a dragon trainer would have no bearing on the scale of my punishment. My stomach and my bowels churned.

Someone said something but they spoke so softly it was only a murmur.

Footsteps drew closer to my position and I froze. Hiding was my only option. The bookshelves stood on wooden legs, there was just enough space for me to squeeze under them so I wouldn't be discovered, I doubted anyone would look for anything at floor level.

I couldn't see much, only Mab's distinctive riding boots. The other pair of feet belonged to a man, he wore stylist shoes and green twill trousers, the garments of a high ranking member of the Dark Court.

When you've lived in a royal court all your life, with all of its intrigue and gossip, you know there is only one reason why two powerful people would meet in such an isolated place. They weren't interested in the books, they wanted to talk privately, Mab must have chosen the location for that reason.

The man's voice was easier to hear from my position, he must be nearer. He was softly spoken but his tone was firm, full of authority.

'Latest reports have him trapped, cornered by the humans.'

I didn't need to see his face to work out he was smiling, I could hear it in his voice. The same was true for Mab's reply.

'I told you what he'd do, didn't I? Now will you listen to my plan?'

I could tell from the position of their feet that they were facing each other. From the tone of her voice, Mab was negotiating, almost pleading for the man to listen to her. The thought of being discovered frightened me so much I thought they'd hear the noises made by my churning stomach, especially when the man asked his next question.

'We're not going to be discovered here, are we?'

The impatience in Mab's reply caused her to almost snarl.

'Don't change the subject. I want an answer.'

The man sighed heavily. 'I'm listening.'

'I have undertaken certain measures to ensure things deteriorate for him even though he's obtained reinforcements beyond his spriggan contingent.'

'Who?'

'Clíodna.' Mab spoke the name like it was poison.

The man cursed. 'How has he persuaded the Queen of the Bean Sidhe to join him?'

'He's promised to help her regain power. It doesn't matter. They won't prevail.'

There was scepticism in the man's voice now. 'How can you be so sure?'

The stone floor was making me cold and I started to shiver. I wondered how much longer they'd keep talking, I hoped it wasn't long. Mab's voice took on a lighter tone, as though she was smiling again.

'I am a skilled tactician, my lord.' She giggled, as though she was flirting with the man. 'Or have you forgotten how well I led the forces of the Dark Court before you chose to relieve me of the position?'

The man sighed heavily and with a tinge of impatience.

'Your wit has not diminished with age, my lady.'

They both laughed briefly but it wasn't genuine, it ended too suddenly. When the man spoke again the tone of his voice sounded like he was being promised something he wanted very much.

'And you guarantee he will be killed in this battle?'

I held my breath. They were planning someone's death, a person already in the human realm. That worried me, I had to hope that my journey wasn't connected to such a dreadful thing. It disappointed me that my first reaction was to consider my situation rather than the poor victim's, but I was dealing with Lady Mab and protecting myself always had to come first. When she spoke it was just as light-hearted, as though she was planning a party.

'Oh he will die. You see, I manipulated him into making a gross error of judgement. He went looking for someone in the human realm. Stirred a sleeping lion you might say.'

'Who?'

Mab sniggered. I found it impossible to picture her making such a sound, it couldn't come from the severe, humourless woman I knew.

'So, my lord, when the sad news of his death is announced, and you are hailed High Lord, will you return me to my rightful position as Commander in Chief?'

I had to put my hand over my mouth to stifle my horror. They were talking about the current High Lord being murdered by someone Mab knew, an act she had arranged. Now my bowels really did present a problem, what if I got drawn in to this treason? I felt trapped in more ways than my position beneath the bookshelf.

My movement disturbed layers of dust, it tickled my nose, the need to sneeze suddenly became all-consuming. I concentrated on the man's reply to distract myself.

'I do not make promises I cannot keep, my lady. Until the crown is placed on my head...'

Mab's voice was tight with exasperation.

'Very well. But if...' and she emphasized the last word and then repeated it, '... if you're crowned, you will grant my request?'

My nose was twitching like a rabbit's, I held my nostrils tight and tried to breathe through my mouth.

'We make a good team, you and I. Between us we will change the fortunes of the Dark Court, for this you have my guarantee. That idiot has weakened us but we will rebuild. Having removed the adult generation of Knights, I foresee no difficulty in killing their spawn. Then, with the Knights' Protocol equally as dead, we can invade in force without offending the sensitivities of Nimue and our Light Cousins.'

I was going to sneeze, I couldn't stop myself. The man turned and made his way to the door. I hoped with all my heart Mab would follow quickly because I was about to be discovered by two traitors who wouldn't hesitate in killing me too.

'Let me know when the deed is done.'

Mab joined him, I heard their footsteps tap along the stone floor of the library and then onto the corridor floor, the sound quickly receding.

My sneeze, held back for so long, exploded and echoed around the library, it was quickly followed by another and another. I kept perfectly still in the horrific expectation the two conspirators would return but after a minute of holding my breath, there were no footsteps to be heard.

I crawled out from beneath the bookcase and stretched my cold and aching muscles. I had to do something. I had to report the crime I'd just overheard. Except that wasn't so easy. I was Mab's page, a lowly servant. No one would take my word against hers, not after my history of devious behaviour. What was even worse, Mab wouldn't hesitate in using her clever, strategic brain to find a way to have me killed. If she could plan the death of the High Lord then mine would be easy.

I hurried along the corridor, away from the library, I didn't want to visit the place ever again. I'd find a way for my lessons with Master Darragh to happen somewhere else. Which was when I realised I'd forgotten my study texts. I needed them to memorise the sayings he'd insisted I learned for our next lesson.

With my heart in my mouth and pounding like a drum, I sprinted back to the library, collected my book from off the table and ran back out.

Straight into Mab.

It was so sudden, so unexpected I let out a strangled yelp as I staggered backwards to fall on my arse. She watched me with an unreadable expression but I noticed how she looked from me, to the library and back again. I knew what she was thinking.

'What are you doing here?'

I held up Master Darragh's book like a trophy, hoping it provided a strong enough alibi.

'I forgot my book. I left it in the library. I study there with Master Darragh.'

Her eyes bore into mine, searching them for lies.

'How long were you in the library?'

I tried to look bewildered by her question. 'Seconds. Just seconds. Not long.'

I was blabbing. I should have just answered her question simply. I sat on the floor, aware I was sweating and shaking. There was a very real danger I'd shit myself where I sat. I tried to smile nonchalantly but it only made me look more suspicious, my mouth froze in a rictus of regret.

'Then why are you so nervous?'

She reached her hand out to help me up. My palm was hot and sweaty, it would make me look even more frightened. I wasn't certain she intended to help me up, there were stories of her wrenching limbs off people. My hand went to meet hers, shaking like it was in a high wind. She helped me to my feet.

'Because you scare me, my lady.'

She grinned and looked vaguely satisfied by my answer.

'Fear keeps you sharp. You will need all your wits about you when you travel to the human realm to rescue your wyvern.'

Her eyes stayed riveted on mine, they hadn't shifted the whole time.

'You won't let me down, will you? I don't tolerate failure. Too much rests on your mission young man. Lives depend on your success. Do you understand?'

I nodded and, with black leather cloak swirling behind her, swept down the corridor like a huge bat.

I hurried to find a toilet, urgently.

Chapter 11

Another night spent in a barn, this time tied to a wooden pillar which held up the leaking roof. Oisin and I quickly learned not to tug too hard at our bonds, the wooden pillar held up the roof, we ran the risking of bringing the whole place down on our heads. Had I been on my own I'd have taken the gamble but I wasn't going to try my luck with the twins' lives. I felt sure we could escape these idiots.

Things inevitably got worse when Brea woke up. They'd tied her hands behind her back so if she tried to blast herself free it would be at the cost of her brother, who was bound behind her.

'Happy now!' Her voice edged towards hysteria. 'This is fucking diplomacy, is it? You should have let me blast them like I wanted. We wouldn't be in this fucking mess then.'

'That's right,' I said, trying to stay calm. 'We'd be dead.'

'Like we're not going to be any time soon?'

I could just make out her face as the first rays of dawn tentatively entered the barn. The bluster was only a thin disguise; I could see real terror on her face. I had a go at doing the reassuring uncle routine, it was rusty but I hoped it might work.

'We'll be OK. The one-eyed guy is the real power here. I'll get him to listen. Persuade him he can help us. He's a military man. He'll understand.'

'Are you fucking listening to yourself?' she screamed.

The routine was rustier than I'd thought. I tried a different approach.

'You said you'd made progress with releasing your energy, that's good news. Moya would be proud of you.'

I knew how much Brea had worshipped her aunt and I wasn't above using emotional distraction to calm the girl down.

'Fuck off Robin. I don't fall for that kid stuff anymore.'

I gave up. This was why I kept these kids at a distance. Finn cleared his throat, there was a huskiness to it that told me he was near to tears, even though I couldn't see him.

'You think we can escape, don't you?'

'Of course I do. I've been in far worse situations than this.'

I'd deliberately screened my thoughts. I didn't find it easy, it usually gave me a headache but I knew he'd be inside my head.

'Really?'

I kept my voice light. 'Yeah. Have I told you the time I was captured by a seventeenth century Balkan chieftain who caught me with his son? I'd had to leave Venice rather urgently and finished up in Croatia...'

'Someone's coming,' Finn said in a husky stage whisper.

Moments later, as the sun's rays entered the barn with more vigour, so did a deputation of pathetic, filthy and half-starved men. They were probably the same ones who'd brought us here but the light didn't do them any favours. Nor did it improve Joe Purdy's features either. His injury hadn't just taken out one eye but also one side of his nose and gouged out a part of his cheek so his mouth looked like it was set in a permanent sickly grin. Behind him were his two comrades, like minders.

At his side, with a manic smile so wide it looked like he'd dislocated his jaw, was the religious nutter. His grip on his Bible hadn't lessened any but now his wild eyes gleamed with the kind of joy that told me he wasn't going to be open to rational debate.

Standing with Joe Purdey, his face and clothes spattered with mud, was a man I vaguely recognised. Tombstone-like teeth protruded from a thin face with an abnormally narrow jaw and chin, he reminded me of a rat. The image triggered my memory into action.

At some point in the past I must have offended Trevor Ratner because the guy did everything he could to cause me trouble. He hadn't been religious before the war but since then he'd embraced it with enthusiasm, becoming a vocal member of The Morality League, no doubt abusing the power it gave him. He glanced at me, realised I'd recognised him and gave me a buck-toothed grin.

We were so deep in the shit now it was piling up around our eyes and ears.

Purdey might only have one eye but he noticed my recognition too.

'Mister Ratner's visit couldn't have been more timely it would appear Mister Fellows. You two are familiar with one another I understand.'

'I found him in a rat's nest, where he'd been abandoned.'

The buck-tooth grin vanished while Purdey's lop-sided mouth formed half a smile.

'So you're not friends?'

The man with a badly-crafted crucifix around his neck stepped forwards.

'God waits for us to purify this place Joe Purdey, enough of this pantomime.'

The manic face glowered at Oisin and I as he raised a hand to heaven, his voice doing the same.

'Lord, we purge this world of the scourge that caused you to bring us such calamity. We know you love us and want us to cleanse our world of the heathen, those who seek to forget thy existence and especially those degenerates whose lewd practices abase the institution of love and marriage.'

Around him the senseless morons chanted 'Amen'.

Brother Whelan, so deep into the throes of worship he appeared to stand a foot taller, strode towards the edge of the farm buildings, beckoning in the process. While some of the men unfastened our ropes, the rest stood with knives and guns ready for any attempt at escape. Oisin's face was white, he looked terrified as he looked at me with the expression of someone who expects a miracle to be performed. With guns levelled at my head I was fresh out of miracles.

Joe Purdey stepped closer to me, his voice a whisper.

'Don't worry, the kids are safe. I persuaded the villagers that your sins were greater than young demons. When Mister Ratner told them how you'd invited the fairies into your house, I convinced everyone we were doing the kids a favour by rescuing them.'

'But I didn't invite...'

He placed a finger over twisted lips.

'They're going to come in handy. We can use them to pay our tithe to Chief ColdIron. We're late and don't have the money so your arrival was well timed.'

Brea was screaming hysterically now and I struggled to hear what he said.

'The Taunton Gang control everywhere around here now. Things get unpleasant when a village doesn't pay its dues. I think he'll appreciate how powerful these two kids will make him. Me too perhaps.'

Half a dozen of the strongest men grabbed me and frog-marched me out of the barn, the remainder doing the same with Oisin.

'You're stopping us from beating the fairies!' I screamed as I fought and kicked my security guards. 'We can end this war! Don't you understand? Don't let these morons wreck humanity's chances!'

I heard Brea's screams, Finn's calls for help and felt Puck stir. For once I was glad of that feeling until, as I thrashed arms and legs wildly, something heavy hit the back of my head and everything went black. Again.

I woke with a marching band in my head and every muscle in my body complaining about their mistreatment. Somewhere nearby a discordant rendition of a hymn was waking God from his slumbers. I opened my eyes and the morning light encouraged the percussion section of the marching band to join in. The sun's rays also showed me how branches, bits of wood and assorted rubbish lay piled at my feet. It took my addled brain a few seconds to realise where I was, a discovery helped by my arms being tied to a wooden pole which pressed into my back, making my shoulders ache.

We were going to be burned at the stake like witches.

I'd seen enough ritual burnings in my time to know that a quick death was down to the quantity and quality of fuel. It all depended on the faggots, an ironic term given our crime. In medieval times there was an art to their construction so they burned quickly and fiercely. The few items that barely covered my feet proved it was a lost art, though I doubted they probably had a shortage of things to burn. The result would be the same; a very slow, painful death.

That realisation tempered the pounding in my head so that I became aware of Oisin's voice, he was tied to the same pole, his back against mine.

'If you're calling for help I don't think anyone is available.'

I heard him let out a deep sigh.

'I thought you were never going to wake up.'

'You know me, never a morning person. What are you doing?'

'Trying to stop us from dying. I'm calling the wyvern.'

I surveyed the farmyard, a place that was so badly neglected it looked like a strong wind would blow it down. The only building that looked reasonably well maintained was the huge wooden barn filled with hymn-singing maniacs. We were positioned on the edge of the farmyard, far enough away so flames wouldn't reach rotting timbers. Across the square farmyard were the tottering remains of the old barn where we'd spent the night, leaning drunkenly against it was a stable where they'd tied the wyvern to a pillar. It nodded its head from side to side at Oisin's call.

'How can the wyvern help?'

'Their saliva is an acid. If she licked our ropes she could burn through them.'

'Right. And does she understand the words for 'lick' and 'ropes' then?'

I could hear his exasperation. 'No, but she's clever.'

As the hymn ended I heard the voice of Brother Whelan rise up to instil in his flock the need to purge their community of evil and to seek God's forgiveness. Everyone from the nearby hamlets had to be in the large barn, no doubt seeking permission from a greater power than their religious leader to commit acts of murder.

'She needs to be fast then. From experience of these kind of community get-togethers, we've probably got one more hymn.'

'Help me call her then, unless you've got a better idea?'

I whistled, I used to have a horse that came when I did that, I didn't know if it worked on wyverns.

With a loud cracking noise and a huge amount of dust, the wyvern galloped out of the stable dragging the pillar behind it. The stable and adjacent barn, folded in on itself in a loud crash. It took her only a few strides to stand in front of us, head once again turning from side to side to understand why the strangers had tied themselves to a tree without branches.

In the huge barn the congregation began to sing Nearer my God to Thee.

Oisin, using a series of pantomime-like gestures, drew her attention to the rope sufficiently that the creature lowered its head and sniffed it. He praised her, encouraging me to join in. I reverted to distant memories of training my horse, repeating 'Good girl!' with as much enthusiasm as I could muster.

Reptiles use scent to help make sense of the world around them, Oisin explained at one point. They have narrow nostrils but much of their olfaction is derived from their tongues so, to understand our bonds, she needed to touch them. Thin wisps of smoke formed as her snake-like tongue came into contact with rope fibres, to rise into the air, our encouragement rising with them. Soon she was licking more energetically as we provided the motivation and the wisps turned from white to grey as the smoke thickened.

I couldn't help but feel we were wasting our time, the ropes were thick but when I mentioned this I was told to tug at them as hard as I could.

In the big barn, God was uncovering his ears as the hymn ended.

'We're running out of time!' I gasped as my arm muscles shrieked their complaints as I pushed and strained against our bonds.

Our calls to the wyvern moved up the encouragement scale quickly, from motivational to desperate. Even I began to think the animal appeared to understand what we wanted her to do, as her snake-like tongue wrapped around the ropes, in places I could see some of the fibres turned dark red and small sparks appear.

Across the farmyard, the large wooden doors of the barn were flung open with evangelical zeal by Brother Whelan, he took one look at the situation and screamed for God to smite the sinners with his holy wrath. Clearly

God was too busy, or ethically opposed to the murder of two men whose only crime was to enjoy other men, and chose not to smite anyone. This disinterest didn't deter Brother Whelan, he raised his arm like a general leading his men into battle and marched across the farmyard, Bible held aloft and with his villagers behind him, somewhat awestruck by the spectacle.

Our own chanting increased as we begged the wyvern to lick the rope for all she was worth. Then, as heat in the rope reached my wrists, I felt them give enough for my weary arms to slide out. I dropped to untie the ropes around my ankles and realised that I wasn't going to have time to free both of us and get away.

Oisin had other plans.

I heard his voice change. He called to the wyvern, using a tone he used in his storytelling performances, when he wanted to convey the urgent actions of the hero. The wyvern lifted her head, forgot the rope and turned to look at him. If wyverns had facial expressions, hers suddenly turned ultra-serious and he praised her for shifting her focus onto him. Next, Oisin pointed at the striding figure at the head of the column of angry villagers, the man's strident voice screaming to God for vengeance.

I knew the command he gave the animal. I'd heard it in battle many times.

'Attack!'

Deep in its chest the wyvern gave a rumbling sound so deep it felt like the ground trembled, she followed with a roar which echoed around the farmyard and made all but the evangelical maniac at the front of the column come to a sudden halt. I'm not sure he even heard it as he gazed rapturously up to the heavens, he appeared to be so close to his god that all his senses had shut down. He was certainly oblivious of his army coming to an abrupt stop behind him.

The wyvern stretched her serpentine neck to its full extent, opened powerful jaws and roared a second time, this time, even louder. The noise successfully penetrated Brother Whelan's heaven-sent euphoria, he looked up in time to realise the wyvern's attention was focused on him. She pounded towards him on her powerful hind legs, covering the distance with astonishing speed, this animal was fast.

The villagers panicked. Pathetic specimens of men, women and children ran, hid, climbed, trampled on some of their own and deliberately felled others, in their desperate attempts to escape a more tangible form of wrath than God's.

Brother Whelan stood his ground. Whether he believed God would protect him or he'd slipped into a state of shock wasn't clear, the result was the same. The wyvern powered towards him, lowered its head and, like a bull, flung Brother Whelan up into the air. The man screamed as, like an athlete, he tumbled over the wyvern's head and landed on its neck. The scream rose in pitch. The animal lifted its head, causing Whelan to ride down it and over the scaly ridged crest. The screams rose even higher until the long neck jerked, flinging the man upwards a second time, to sprawl heavily across its scaly body with a sickening thud. The screams ended abruptly, to be replaced by wet slurping noises as parts of Brother Whelan slithered to the ground on either side of the wyvern. It turned its head, sniffed the bloody remains and lifted its head up to roar its victory. Screams from the nearest villagers, still trying to find places of safety, drew its attention and its head turned in their direction.

Oisin shouted, his impressive stentorian voice filling the farmyard, 'Cease attack!'

He had to shout his command twice and, even then, the animal craned her head to glare at him. She was obviously having too good a time to stop now but, with a snort at her intended prey, she turned and stalked towards Oisin as though it was what she'd intended to do all along.

Slowly, hesitantly, faces appeared from behind walls and doors, haystacks and farm implements. I finished untying my ropes and freed Oisin, then strode over to three men who stared in stark terror at the wyvern, it watched them through merciless eyes.

'Tell me where Joe Purdey has taken the children.'

They looked from me, to the wyvern and back again. I featured much lower down the scale of frightening prospects so I grabbed one by his greasy hair and dragged him towards the wyvern. She lifted her head and I swear she smiled.

'Tell me where Joe Purdey took the children or she eats you.'

After a lot of gibbering and sobbing, the guy eventually started to talk but the information didn't help much. No one knew much beyond Purdey had gone to a hill fortification owned by the Taunton Gang. These people lived in a state of perpetual terror, I hoped the removal of one source, which lay eviscerated on the farmyard where crows were already pecking at body parts, might ease that fear. They milled around in confusion, like they'd awoken from a hypnotic trance, and gazed at the wyvern in case it decided to attack again.

Oisin arrived with our horses. 'Do you know where they've gone?'

'Only two places I can think of. Do you remember me mentioning Arthur's Hunting Path?'

He nodded.

'It forms a diamond shape. Glastonbury Tor is the northern tip, this the eastern one. There are fortifications on the other two points. Like Glastonbury, they're earthworks which protrude out of the flood waters, the two strategic locations on the Somerset Levels.'

He nodded again. There was a tension in his face that drew my attention. He took a deep breath when he realised I'd spotted it.

'That man you knew, the rat-like one. One of the villagers said he set off for Glastonbury the first chance he got. You don't think he...?'

'Works for Llyr? I wouldn't put it past the bastard.'

'But if Llyr knows where...'

I jumped on my horse and set off. I had to hope the twins had enough tricks up their sleeves to slow Purdy down so we could catch up. I didn't dare think what would happen if they were placed in the hands of the gang who'd murdered Mickey.

Or if Llyr got his perfectly manicured hands on them first.

Chapter 12

Master Sidwell's office lay at the top of a narrow staircase, close to the High Lord's suite, as befitted the highest office in the palace. As I climbed each step my level of uncertainty grew. I stopped at each window in the turret, to look out at the courtyard below. The irony wasn't lost on me, my rise in status in the palace had reached similar dizzy heights and now I was about to do something that would send me plummeting to the ground, perhaps literally.

What I was about to do, apart from risk my life, was an ethical necessity. There was no escape, I had to keep climbing. Once in Master Sidwell's office I knew all too well, if he summoned the guards there was no other escape than out of his window. It offered a swifter death, dashed on the cobbled courtyard at the base of the tower, than the one Mab would have in store.

I'd known fear lots of times. A slave is the butt of other people's anger, resentment and fear. Sometimes their joy of inflicting pain too. That was true of Llyr, he'd taken immense joy in making me suffer because of my dark skin. He'd once made me stand in front of a roaring fire in his room because it made him too hot; his reason for choosing me was simply because my brown skin already looked burned.

I hated the man. For a while, after hearing Mab and her mysterious partner discuss his death, I felt the same joy. He deserved to die I told myself, I might know their plans but I had no responsibility for what happened to him, I was no one. A nobody who had suffered at this man's sadistic whims.

I didn't get any sleep that night as my conscience grappled with my indignation.

By morning I'd decided I couldn't face myself if I didn't act. This wasn't about him, I kept telling myself, it was about my integrity. Every day I watched palace servants, and even their betters, commit deceitful acts purely to promote themselves at the expense of others. I always found it degrading and vowed I wouldn't be like that. Not on things that mattered anyway.

And here was my test. This mattered. A man's life depended on my reaction.

Which wasn't to say I was doing any of this happily or with any sense of hope it would turn out right for me. I was a servant, you don't hope for anything other than the inevitable punishments aren't too harsh.

I arrived at the top of the staircase, at the large oak door and knocked. I was told to come in. I opened the door and stepped inside, wondering if I'd feel quite so good about myself in a few minutes.

'Ah, Keir. I was about to send for you. Lady Mab spoke to me this morning.'

That was it, I was a dead man. I looked at the large window behind his desk, my last-ditch escape route. I gripped the ring on my thumb and twisted it urgently.

'Are you all right Keir?'

I turned my attention to the old man, sat behind a desk covered in folders, letters, orders and invoices stacked in tidy piles. It was a mammoth job running a royal palace and he did it single-handedly, late at night it was common to see a light in this office. Narrowed rheumy eyes watched me and I felt self-conscious suddenly. Master Sidwell could read me like a book, knew me better than I knew myself and he'd sense my unease. Knowing he'd already spoken to Mab posed a dilemma, if she had guessed about my eavesdropping in the library, or was sufficiently suspicious, Master Sidwell was about to deliver my death warrant. My declaration would seem like the desperate act of a guilty man.

'Keir?'

I had no way to know. All I could do was speak the truth and hope for the best.

I inhaled deeply to calm myself and told him everything. Words tumbled out of my mouth like they were desperate to escape, by the time I'd finished I'd run out of breath and gulped in air hungrily.

For a long time he just looked at me. There was no reaction, it was like I'd told him the latest piece of palace gossip.

'Have you told anyone else?'

I shook my head. My legs felt weak, I had to grip a chair for support. Why had he asked that question first? I knew the answer; if I died suddenly no one else would know about the treason. I began to panic, what if Master Sidwell was part of the treachery? It was well known he didn't like the new High Lord, they'd never got on. I could have just blabbed my way to a swift and accidental death, there had been a lot of them lately.

'And the man. Tell me again what clothes you saw.'

I did as I was told. The old man nodded, his expression hard and without emotion. He leaned against his high-backed chair and stroked his bald head, a gesture I'd seen dozens of times, one that showed he was making decisions.

'Do you know who the man is? I asked.

It was a devious question. If the old man was really a traitor, he'd deny knowing anyone so as to appear innocent of the treachery. I thought I knew him quite well, he'd been something of a guardian to me, I couldn't believe he could be part of a plot to murder another person. The thing was, you could never tell in the palace who was a friend, who was an enemy. All my experiences told me that anyone with any power wanted more of it and would do anything to get it, I had to hope Master Sidwell was the exception to that rule. I had no one else to turn to and when you're without friends you assume everyone else is an enemy.

'Yes. I know who he is.'

But that was as much as I got from the old man. He walked to the window and stared out of it, apparently lost in thought. I waited, uncertain what to do or even if I should speak. The old man had aged recently, he looked frail, slightly hunched but he still could surprise me by delivering a slap across my head that hurt. He continued to stare out of the window when he spoke.

'We are servants Keir. We must never forget that. We exist to serve our masters. We do not involve ourselves in their business. We cannot guess their reasons and supplant our ethics upon their actions.'

I was appalled. He was condoning not just murder, but treason.

'But...'

With surprising speed the old man spun round and fixed me with his stare, the same one he'd worn when he'd reprimanded me for injuring Irvyn and not being open about the wyvern.

'You will say and do nothing. Is that understood?'

I nodded like a little boy denied his favourite toy. His expression softened slightly.

'There are many things that happen in this palace which are wrong Keir. We are part of a world driven by the need for power. If we involve ourselves in that world we risk its dangers, far wiser to remain aloof.'

His wisdom doused the fire of indignation that had ignited in me, admittedly more of a spark than an actual flame. I reminded myself I wasn't a hero who could intervene to stop events. I was one of those people who suffer, even die, and are just a footnote in history if they are lucky. More likely, my life would be instantly forgotten. I was a one-time slave, now a servant. With luck I might become a dragon trainer. It was ridiculous to think I had a more important role to play.

I looked across at his lined face and smiled. He nodded and sighed.

'What did Lady Mab say?' I asked, curiosity getting the better of me.

He turned serious again and leaned heavily on the large desk.

'You are to travel to the human realm today.'

'But...'

My mind raced. Knowing you were going to travel to another world was one thing, while it was in the future I could deal with the possibility, but to suddenly face up to the imminent reality was something else. My heart pounded in my chest and my spine felt like jelly.

'Master Darragh hasn't finished...'

The old man held up the palm of his hand. 'Yes he has. He refuses to do anything more. I'm sure you know why.'

The old man ambled over to me, placed his hands on my shoulders, fixed his eyes on mine. They were amazingly blue, I'd never noticed that before but I'd never been this close to him, at any point in my life. I searched them for answers until I found the strength to ask.

'So why the rush?'

The old man went to speak and paused. He was close enough for me to see uncertainty in his eyes, perhaps it was anxiety. He sighed and went back to leaning against his desk. He didn't speak for a few seconds.

'Now you have shared with me the conversation you overheard, certain things are beginning to make sense. The war has gone badly for us, The High Lord sought to implement a strategy that could end it. But now with Lady Mab's subtle involvement I fear events are speeding towards a terrible climax, I worry it will affect us equally as much as the humans.'

'There will be a race to become the next High Lord, won't there?'

Master Sidwell nodded heavily. We both knew such times were dangerous for everyone, aristocrats and servants alike.

'Keir, you will have little time over there. If the High Lord is killed then our forces will need to withdraw. The gateways will be closed. If you're not careful, you could be trapped on the other side. Speed will be essential. You must remember that.'

Nobody had mentioned speed. That hadn't been part of the deal. I had a wyvern to find in the middle of a war and in a land I didn't know. How was that going to be quick? For a moment I thought about backing out. Only for a moment, I couldn't leave her in the middle of such a strange place.

'Are you listening lad?'

I glanced up at a face where lines of old age mixed with frowning anxiety.

I'd focused on my own fears and not given enough consideration to what my pet must be going through. She was still young, facing dangers on her own. Lost. I felt a rush of love for her that suddenly formed a lump in my throat. I had to find her and bring her back. She was my one friend. Sad perhaps, but true all the same.

'Yes sir.'

He smiled, a little sadly. 'You're a brave lad.'

I shook my head hard. 'I'm not, sir. Not at all. I just need to rescue her.'

'But it's a dragon, lad. Only a dragon.'

'She's a wyvern. I call her Cochrann.'

He gave me a smile I recognised all too well. The reaction you give to the simple-minded when they think they've done something wonderful but is average at best.

'Red girl.' He nodded, still smiling. 'That's nice.'

He didn't understand. He probably had friends, he was respected, he had a position in the court. He wasn't a lonely, isolated dark-skinned hybrid.

His smile faded and we returned to business out of awkwardness.

'You know where to find the portal? You know the route?'

'Yes sir.'

He returned to his desk and sat heavily in his huge chair and didn't look up again.

'Good luck young man. I trust you will return unharmed.'

I left the office and hurried down the staircase. I'd been told not to take anything with me, any items could betray me. I had no one else to wish me well, no one else knew what I was doing. This was it.

I marched along corridors where people hurried about their business, doing the things they did every day and would continue doing until they died. They weren't travelling to another world. It felt strange. I wanted to scream what I was about to do. For the first time in my life I felt slightly superior to all of them, it was an unusual sensation.

The stables on the far side of the courtyard were empty, the grooms would be out exercising in the brilliant sunshine, it was a beautiful day. I heard my name called softly and I looked about me, puzzled who might be calling.

Irvyn stepped out from a stable, with a shovel. He wore old clothes covered in straw. For a moment I tensed, ready for another beating. I thought about running away but he was faster and stronger than I was, he'd easily catch me and I didn't have time to waste.

He looked about nervously and beckoned me closer. I drew nearer cautiously, waiting for his fists or his shit-covered boots, to strike.

'Are you going now?'

It took me a second to work out what he meant but then I realised he had to know what I was doing. Mab would have extracted the information out of him, no doubt impatiently. I nodded curtly.

He looked around the stables nervously. It was so unlike him that I stared, amazed.

'Listen.' He dropped his voice to a whisper so I had to crane my neck to hear him. 'I didn't tell Lady Mab the truth. Please don't tell her. Please? Only I wanted to get my own back on you.'

'What do you mean?' Now he'd got me worried.

Another quick look around. 'I described a different gateway, not the one I sent the little dragon through.'

'What?'

Suddenly our plans were in tatters. I'd been told what to expect on the other side, the best places in the hill fort to hide until it turned dark and I could make my escape. And now all that information was meaningless. I glared at him with impotent fury.

He raised dirty hands in surrender.

'I know. I know. I'm sure you've made plans. I didn't know your mission was about saving the High Lord. If anyone finds out what I did…!'

'Which gateway do I need then?' I felt liked grabbing hold of his filthy clothes and shaking the idiot.

'Promise not to tell anyone what I've done. Lady Mab especially?'

His fear was obvious, he swallowed hard before even saying her name.

'Yes, yes,' I replied impatiently. 'Just tell me which route to take.'

He nodded, clearly relieved.

'The gateway is where you've been told to find it. Inside the gateway there are three portals. Yes?'

I nodded.

'Which one did they tell you to take?' he asked.

Now I was the one looking around suspiciously.

'The one on the left.'

He sighed. 'I told them a lie. I sent the little dragon through the middle one.'

He swallowed hard again and looked at me, his face pale.

'How do I know you're not misleading me now?'

He frowned as though my question was ridiculous.

'Because you're rescuing the High Lord. Why would I mislead you? It could cause all kinds of problems and you'd tell them I was responsible. I dread to think what Lady Mab would do to me.' He paused and blinked repeatedly. 'You've heard the stories?'

'So, the middle archway?'

Irvyn nodded and as I turned to go, he held my arm. I turned, expecting trouble.

'You're very brave, what you're doing. I couldn't do it.' He took a breath. 'I'm sorry for, you know, what I did. OK?'

I shook his arm loose and turned away and marched off. How our fortunes had changed, now he was apologising to me. Despite my nervousness, I smiled to myself.

The gateway was on the other side of the wood where I'd found the wyvern originally. A stone archway, partly covered in ivy, some of which was badly scorched, stood in the corner where the wood gave way to a meadow. It looked rather out of place and certainly not a device which catapulted you from one world and into another.

The two crystals, large enough for me to stagger under their weight, were where I'd been told to find them, in a recess at the feet of the archway, hidden by long grass. I positioned them next to the inside surface of the archway, on a copper plate that needed to be cleaned of mud and leaves and grass. The instant I placed the second crystal in position the air began to vibrate and the stone archway hummed, scraps of loose stone and mortar fell away. I stood back and waited.

Less than a minute later energy descended from the keystone like a bright yellow waterfall. I gasped at its beauty. It fizzed like the sparkling wine served in the palace at Belthane. I marvelled at it, I had never seen anything so wonderful. Time was against me though, I couldn't stand around admiring such things.

I stepped through the waterfall, felt my skin tingle and my hair drift around me like it was being blown by a summer breeze. Two steps took me to a point where I could see the other side, the dark space I'd been told to expect. After five steps I was on the other side of the waterfall of energy in a small space no bigger than Mistress Cera's pantry. It was a circular room made of a highly-polished wood, carved into the wall were three archways, in the keystones were crystals that provided the only illumination. The one on the left, which had been my original destination was green, the one in the middle yellow, the one on the right a delicate pink.

I stepped in front of the middle gateway and, as if it recognised my presence, more cascading energy fell from the keystone of the arch, a subtle shade of yellow that was more primrose than lemon. I took a deep breath and summoned a mental image of Cochrann, of how she'd react when I found her and I shut out the other thoughts trying to crowd in to stop me from going any further.

I walked into the light.

Chapter 13

'We'd better let the animals get a drink, beyond here the water will be too salty for them.'

I led my horse to a small stream by the side of a tarmac road that nature was busy reclaiming. Oisin dismounted and did the same; inevitably, the wyvern followed suit. I let them munch grass, they needed to maintain their energy for the journey ahead. In the distance, I could just make out a dark pimple on the horizon. Our destination would only be reached by a slightly higher finger of land which bisected the grey flood waters of the Bristol Channel and merged with a leaden sky.

'None of this is your fault Robin.'

It was the first words we'd spoken since leaving the village.

A sudden gust of wind robbed me of my breath, cold and unforgiving, buffeting waves across the roadway. Small flecks of sleet appeared, with only jacket and trousers I shivered. Winter appeared to be gearing up to destroy whatever humanity had hoped might survive for a little longer.

I said nothing and mounted my horse, hurried it across the roadway before seawater covered it completely and we were trapped. This was a land of flood, a drowned world where houses and farms were half-submerged, their roofs pitted and holed by the relentless barrage of waves. Washed up on the edges of the road were bleached skeletons of animals, their flesh removed by the winged scavengers that still flew above our heads in the hope of a meal. The predominant tones were grey, they were in the water and in the sky, as though colour had disappeared forever. It was a landscape that matched my bleak mood.

Hours later, when dark clouds had blotted out light and bullets of hail burned skin, we arrived at the earthworks that rose up out of the water. I pointed up at wooden sentry posts towering over the narrow gulley in front of us.

'Something's wrong. We shouldn't have reached this point without getting stopped.'

We dismounted and walked up to large wooden gate, the only access through a continuous high wooden fence that stretched around the island. The place looked impregnable, as it had over a thousand years ago when it served as a defensive position. From its raised location you could see for miles.

We strode along a track made from red clay, rain water was already turning it slick as it hurried to join the flood water around the island. As we drew nearer the fence we could see it was made of dozens of wooden stakes, twice the size of a man and sharpened to dangerous points. We approached partially open gates, another sign something was wrong. As we entered the compound I realised the colour of the draining water wasn't caused by the clay.

The first bodies lay at the top of the gulley, slaughtered as they tried to escape, women and children mostly, wounds in their backs as they ran from whatever had attacked. The horses nickered at the sight and we left them at the entrance to the fort.

In front of us lay carnage.

I'd only visited this place once before, on a sunny day with Alec, his wife Sarah and his sister Moya. We'd come for a day out, a chance for Finn and Brea to have fun, we'd even brought a picnic, like so many others. The twins ran up and down the small hillocks, hiding and jumping out at each other, soon they'd made friends with other kids and created miniature battles with two fingered guns, sniping and attacking with raucous disregard for the numbers of times anyone got killed. Before the environment went into meltdown and the Fae attacked, the ancient fortification had been a place of leisure and enjoyment. Now it had returned to its original purpose.

Except the dozens of bodies hadn't died fighting an enemy from beyond its wooden walls. They were trying to escape an enemy from within the compound. Oisin stood, face ashen, hair plastered to his skull by the rain, shaking his head repeatedly.

I'd seen enough battlefields to allow me to examine this one as a detective.

Most of the men had died fighting, slash wounds across stomachs and faces told me they'd confronted large swords, occasionally some had heads caved in. Women invariably were hacked down as they ran, legs cut from under them and then run through as they grovelled on the ground. The Taunton Gang had been criminals, murderers and rapists but they'd also been a community, I guessed around fifty. A secure location for the strong and powerful to live with their families and yet there wasn't a single child to be found. Boys and girls nearing adulthood certainly, but no youngster below the age of ten.

I realised Oisin stood next to me.

'No children,' he said quietly.

'Yeah. The attack came from within the compound.'

'But how did they got in?'

An idea struck me. I strode between burned shacks extinguished by the rain where people had struggled to make a living; overturned pots spilled out meagre rations of food, lines of washing lay trampled in the mud. I vaguely remembered one end of the fortification from before, a feature that Alec and I had discussed at some length.

Sure enough, at the end of the little township I found a lot more than I'd bargained for. Oisin and I ran towards it, recognising what we saw at the same time.

'The twins were here!' I shouted.

Two spriggan bodies, blackened holes the size of footballs in their backs, lay sprawled in the mud. A little further we found another, head little more than a black mass of pulp.

'She didn't mess about.' For the first time, I allowed myself to hope.

A short distance away my search proved successful. Admittedly it was a ruin now, some of the blocks of stones were splintered and covered in carbon. Brea had been busy.

'The fools.'

Oisin looked puzzled, I explained my theory.

'I suppose they must have rebuilt it as an altar.'

I clambered over some of the blocks and found another spriggan cut cleanly in half as though by careful surgery.

'Bree blasted it as the last of them escaped.'

The penny dropped for Oisin.

'It was a portal?'

I sat on a large angular block, the keystone of the whole archway I suspected.

'Why have our people always built portals on high places?'

Oisin shrugged. 'For strategic reasons, you can defend large areas easily.'

I nodded, it was something you learned as a child.

'When we abandoned this realm, mankind adopted these places for the same reason. They didn't understand their purpose, how could they? Later, when their new religion arrived, they built their places of worship in the same locations, perhaps as a sign of compromise for those who opposed the changes and didn't want to worship the new god.'

Oisin was nodding now. 'These people were like the ones in the other village. They see religion as a form of rescue and hope. They rebuilt the archway so they had somewhere to pray, to express their faith in a higher power saving them from death.'

'It allowed Llyr to send a handful of spriggans here to see if they could find the twins. And they did, but there weren't enough to capture them.'

'They must have arrived as the spriggan attack was ending. A shame the Knights didn't arrive a little sooner for these people.'

I looked around at the destruction. Night was arriving quickly and the pellets of hail were thickening into flakes of snow. I stood up, we needed to find cover for the night. One question remained to be asked.

'Oisin? The children. Has the situation at home changed?'

He looked at me, sadness written indelibly on his face.

'Worse. No children have been born for many years now. Not one. Only hybrids.' I suppose he must have seen my expression and tried to provide me with some reassurance. 'The children taken from here will live good lives Robin. They'll be valued.'

They wouldn't be with their parents though. They'd be alone and I knew what that was like.

While I stabled the horses and gathered things to feed us, Oisin found dry kindling and soon had a fire roaring in front of one of the few shacks that remained upright. Despite my attempts to dissuade it, the wyvern insisted on curling up in front of the fire, like a huge cat. The two of us stared into the flames as we waited for our food to cook. Silence hung over us like the smoke from the fire until Oisin shifted position so he sat directly in front of me.

'You have to speak to me now. Or do you want more protracted silences?'

I'd have preferred a bunch of spriggans to launch a surprise attack at that moment but only the snow fell on us.

'Don't know what you mean.'

A pathetic reply, it opened me up to ridicule and I waited. Silence. I filled it with something that had preoccupied me since we'd last spoken.

'The invasion. It's connected to the Fae's sterility, isn't it?'

His face, painted orange by the flames, gave away little for a few seconds.

'Even the Light Court are worried. Nimue talked of our problems arising out of the disappearance of a sacred object, a crime linked to the Knights' Protocol I think. I don't know how true that is but, with no pure blood, our long lives will come to an end and the race will die. Only hybrids will survive. There was a time when such offspring were treated with disdain but now they are the norm.'

I could see what he wasn't telling me.

'A successful invasion will provide a gene pool of beautiful, athletic adults and, in the interim, a rich selection of children to coddle and spoil. The rest will face the same fate as the other species the Fae encounters, slavery.'

Those beautiful blue eyes returned to watch the flames.

'So the Light Court have a vested interest in Llyr's successful acquisition of this realm. If they enter this war then mankind's future will be sealed.'

It was a statement that put a dampener on any further conversation.

We ate. The wyvern woke from its slumber and stared hungrily until Oisin began feeding it his own meal.

'You treat the bloody thing like a pet.'

Despite everything, he grinned. 'I'm going to call her Scáthach.'

I choked on my food as I chuckled loud enough to cause the wyvern look at me and nod its head from side to side as usual. I looked into Oisin's face, mischief sat there and I couldn't help but smile.

'I'd love to be the one tell the Dark Court how you've compared one of their female warriors to a bloody dragon.'

Oisin shrugged. 'Why not? They're both fierce in battle. She has red hair and the wyvern red scales.'

'And they both think the sun shines out of your arse.'

Another shrug but now it came with genuine laughter. 'They have similar teeth too.'

He managed to make me laugh as I remembered how the large, muscular woman, saw me as her love rival and used every chance she got to humiliate me. It quickly led us to recounting all the times I'd got my own back, making her the laughing stock of the palace. Each story made us laugh even harder as it triggered more memories.

'Do you remember when you gave her that basket of fruit as a gesture of reconciliation?'

I burst out laughing even harder as I described what happened next.

'She bit into that apple, do you remember? With those enormous teeth of hers? The apple was wax and it stuck to her teeth and turned them green.'

'Wasn't that when she persuaded that arrogant idiot, Eagan, to fight you?' Oisin furrowed his forehead suddenly. 'What happened about that?'

'Eagan's dick.'

'Oh you didn't?'

'Only in my mouth. He only lasted a couple of minutes.'

We burst out laughing even harder until exhaustion found us. The wyvern had curled up and fallen asleep. There were some smelly blankets in the shack and we wrapped ourselves in them after building up the fire and settled down to sleep. Outside huge pillows of feathery snow drifted downwards, we'd have a lousy journey in the morning and we'd need to get started early. There was a good chance we could catch them now.

We'd built the fire in the entrance to the shack, keeping warm meant getting as close as possible but the wyvern had taken up most of the space. I wasn't going to argue with it. I think that was why Oisin and I found ourselves lying side by side. I'm sure it was.

'Do you remember the last time we lay like this?'

I smiled at the memory. 'You'd asked me to join you in Mag Mell.'

Darkness crowded in at the sudden recollection. Oisin didn't reply.

I felt a need to unburden myself. 'It was my greatest mistake, saying no.'

I heard him change position.'

'Really?'

Weight left my shoulders, the weight I'd carried on them for most of my lifetime.

'Instead I chose a life of privilege as Oberon's confidant, with the prestige and influence and money it brought with it. Things I thought mattered more than living on a quiet little farm in the middle of nowhere.'

'It is quiet there. You'd soon have got bored.' He sounded like he was apologising and didn't see the irony, the remainder of my life had become quiet and boring. Anger festered inside me.

'Look where it got me. Exiled. Alone. Wishing death could find me.'

I felt a hand on my shoulder, it pulled me over to face him. I could just make out his features in the light from the fire.

'You don't mean that?'

I held his stare. 'I do. I'm going to kill Llyr somehow. You'll get your sister out of prison and the Knights will be free from danger.'

'But Rob…'

He hadn't called me that for the longest time.

'Think about it Oisin.' I wasn't on any sort of pity crusade, I'd thought all this through and he needed to know. 'Killing the crowned High Lord of the Dark Court is treason. They'll hunt me down, regardless of the impact on this realm. I should have killed him when I had the chance but I thought there might be another way. I realise there isn't now.'

'But Rob, you're wrong…'

I didn't give him chance to say another word.

'I should have killed Llyr when I had the chance Oisin. But, because I didn't, I put the twins' lives in danger, I might even be responsible for their deaths if I can't rescue them now. I vowed to protect them and look what's happened. I'm desperate to find somewhere to keep them safe from the Fae, that means constantly uprooting them to find another location and every time I do that, I risk the same fate as we faced earlier. I can't keep risking their lives like that. The only way to keep the twins safe, is to kill Llyr.'

I felt better for unburdening myself, I felt lighter somehow.

'And Oisin, now you've seen what's happening first hand, you can use your powerful talent as a storyteller to persuade the Light Court to remain neutral.'

'Please, Rob, there has to be another way. They'll kill you.'

'I'm still a Trooping Fairy. My life is worth nothing.'

His eyes darted across my face as though searching for something.

'You're serious aren't you?'

Now I'd shared with him what had been lingering in my head for so long I looked at his anxious, beautiful face and smiled, took one hand and squeezed it.

'I've had enough Oisin. I live amongst people with the lifespan of a fruit fly. I have little in common with them, they judge me for who I am. I'm an outcast in both realms.'

Suddenly his lips were on mine, hot and exciting. His arms held me tightly and for a moment I wanted to give in to the sensations flooding my body.

Instead I pushed him away.

'We've got an early start in the morning.'

I turned over and waited to hear his breathing slow. It didn't, not for the longest time. I stared into the darkness of the shack where a family had lived, a family now dead or, at best, their children would now be in another world.

Oisin was a poet and storyteller. He couldn't understand what it meant to be a soldier and, despite everything, that was what I still was. I'd tried to run away from facing that truth. There was so much darkness in this world, if I could remove its immediate threat, in the form of Llyr, then I might be able to bring a little light into it. I smiled at the irony. Mankind had always portrayed me as a demon, and they weren't so wrong about that label. I needed to kill, it was what I'd been trained to do. Llyr would be my last victim. It was fitting because by removing him, others could live. I was a Trooping Fairy, an elite warrior of the Fae, pledged to protect others and obliged to die in the process.

It was an obligation I'd avoided for far too long.

Chapter 14

Adrenalin thrummed through my veins, I had never felt so alive. We crouched behind a large rhododendron bush and peeked out to examine the comings and goings of the manor house in front of us. It wasn't palatial, despite Lord Taranis' wealth, he used it mainly as a hunting lodge I'd been told. It was probably why security was so lax, a fact that made our rescue so tempting. I was a princess of the Light Court, breaking into the home of someone so powerful risked not just imprisonment but political embarrassment for my family, their punishment would be even worse.

A couple of boggarts had stomped past the front entrance a few minutes before and now lounged against a garden wall, rather than continue their designated path of duty.

'Why aren't they moving?' Clodagh hissed impatiently. 'The guards on the inside will be monitoring the front entrance if they hang around much longer.'

She fidgeted with the strap of her hat constantly, a nervous habit she'd adopted the moment she put on her disguise. She looked ludicrous, though she'd been quick to point out I didn't look any better. We wore the overalls of laundry servants, which I'd acquired the day before, they were dirty and smelled of sweat but that made them all the more realistic. We'd decided to wear large brimmed hats to hide our faces, laundry girls were known for such affectations, anything to retain some degree of femininity with the overalls.

'Give them a minute, they'll move.'

I spoke like I had a detailed knowledge of boggart behaviour, it was more of an expression of hope.

180

Midir rolled his eyes and shook his head, a gesture I chose to let slip. My big brother's willingness to join in our adventure had been difficult to obtain, I'd only achieved it by threatening to tell two young women in the Court that he was screwing both of them. I'd hoped to avoid needing to use any man but I had to concede that if things went wrong, we might need some muscle and Midir had plenty of that.

Seconds later the boggarts proved me right, they picked up their spears, stretched their short arms and ambled off on their stumpy little legs. They didn't possess a serious threat to anyone who could handle a weapon, which discounted Clodagh and me, though I'd noticed Midir had a knife sheathed in his belt.

We sprinted across the drive, feet crunching on the gravel and pushed open the heavy main doors. Inside was a surprisingly small hall, thankfully unsupervised, a corridor led deeper into the house.

'In here!' I hissed at the others.

A thick curtain hid a small cloakroom and we concealed ourselves behind it briefly and listened for the thud of approaching boggart boots. The place was exactly as my source had told me, a young steward called Tighe who'd worked here and who, I knew, was attracted to me. I pitied the poor man if his taste in women meant he thought me pretty, I'd decided his charm was probably more a reflection of his ambition.

The lack of any patrolling boggarts allowed us to slip out from our hidey-hole and sprint down the corridor. The place appeared deserted. According to my reliable informant Tighe, Taranis was at home in his castle and had no plans for hunting today so his retinue would be with him. Nonetheless, we silently ran along the stone-slabbed corridor with its oak panels that made the place look dreary and dark, this really was a depressing place to live and it triggered even more sympathy for the woman we were hoping to rescue.

We arrived at two staircases. One led down, to the servants' quarters and the cellar, the other was wider and grander, lined with portraits of Taranis' stern-looking ancestors. Clodagh glanced at me nervously as she hurried towards the narrow staircase with her pannier filled with old shirts and crystals which looked like soap powder but had a very different purpose. Midir and I scurried upstairs to the first-floor suites.

We reached the top, paused to listen for any guards and, reassured we were safe, made our way along the wide passageway. There were doors to bedrooms on either side, each of the closed.

'Are you sure she'll be in a bedroom, if she's being kept prisoner?' Midir whispered as he carefully opened the first door, and peered inside and closed it again.

I did the same on the other side of the passageway. Inside all the furniture was covered with dustsheets and looked like it hadn't been used in a long while.

'I told you,' I sighed. Midir had to doubt everything I told him for some reason. He'd always been the same, even as children. 'Taranis has put out the story that he's looking after Sibeal because she's been taken ill.'

Another bedroom, just as empty and unused as the previous one.

'Tighe told me Sibeal was brought here in a coach, she was unconscious. I think Taranis decided to abduct her while Llyr was in the human realm. He had the same idea as me.'

Midir didn't react to that fact and I wondered if I was being spectacularly paranoid. Sibeal's refusal to develop Llyr's dragon-breeding programme had led to her imprisonment, I couldn't see why Taranis would interfere. I checked inside another bedroom, it was empty. Something in the back of my mind niggled like an itch, Taranis and Llyr weren't close, certainly not allies, which meant there had to be another reason for spiriting Sibeal away at the opportunity Llyr's absence offered. I couldn't work what it might be and I didn't like not having answers, especially when I was risking so much.

We heard the boggart guards long before we saw them, their heavy-footed march hammered on the wooden floor. We hid in a linen closet half way along the passageway and kept the door ajar. Half minute later we heard the snorted conversation of two boggarts as they drew closer, to stop directly outside our door. My pounding heart almost skipped a beat. They sniffed the air, boggarts are known for their keen sense of smell and I tensed. In the dim light I saw Midir's hand reach for his knife, I shook my head to discourage him, his knife wasn't that big and boggarts could inflict serious damage with their huge tusks. He shook his head in return and glared at me, he wanted to be the hero. This was why I'd hesitated about bringing him along but then I doubted I'd be able to escape if they did open the door, they'd block it easily.

There was more sniffing but then I relaxed. Their interests lay in the smells from the kitchen downstairs, they were more preoccupied in working out how they could get there before the rest of their comrades. They marched towards the staircase with purpose.

Back in the passageway again I felt a slight movement of air, which told me Clodagh had done her job. I turned to Midir, busy opening another bedroom door.

'The ventilation system has been turned on,' I said.

He nodded and reached inside his shirt to pull out his mask and placed it carefully over his mouth and nose.

'Hardly seems worth it, knocking out a handful of boggarts , I could have done that easily.'

He didn't see my ironic smile behind my own mask. How typical of a man to want to use violence to solve our problem.

'And that would have made this look like an attack.' I'd explained all this but it represented another example of not listening to your sister. 'We have to avoid any connection between the Light Court and Sibeal's disappearance. By using the sleeping gas no one will know who was involved. This is the subtle method.'

'Still say my way is faster.'

It was typical of my brother to refuse to listen. From the stories that reached me, his seduction of women lacked any subtlety too.

Downstairs I heard a couple of heavy thumps, I guessed our guards were finding sleep irresistible. We hurriedly peeked into each bedroom, aware we had little time before our Clodagh's chemical concoction wore off. I opened the door of the last bedroom at the end of the passage and gasped through my mask. Our rescue mission had just turned a lot more complicated. It explained why Sibeal's arrival had required a coach and a stretcher.

The woman lay on a bed, surrounded by medical equipment, there were tubes connected to her wrists and a mask over her mouth, like the one we wore. It meant when we drew closer her eyes were still open, though a little unfocused. A nurse lay on the floor, unconscious, a notepad next to her. I picked it up and read it. I didn't understand everything but I didn't need to be a doctor to know what they were doing.

They were experimenting on this woman.

Midir stood over her, held her hand in his and spoke softly, telling her she was going to be all right, he was going to rescue her.

'I don't think she'll understand you,' I said, 'the things they're pumping into her...'

Midir shook his head. 'She can. She's looking at me now and she's just squeezed my hand. I think she's trying to speak.'

He went to lift her mask.

'Don't! She'll inhale the sleeping gas.'

He nodded, taking his free hand away quickly. He bent down, placed an ear close to the mask then shook his head.

'Can't tell what she's saying. We need to get her out of here.'

He started to pull the pipes out of her arm then noticed the woman wince, I pushed him out of the way.

'Midir! Stop! We don't know if it's safe to move her.'

He looked at me, big blue eyes widening in concern over his mask, then at the woman on the bed. He shook his head.

'We can't leave her here, Filidea. It isn't right. Whatever they're doing, it's wrong.'

Neither of us knew that for certain but in every normal way, the woman looked healthy. There were no apparent injuries, she had a good colour, a check of her pulse showed it was slow but nothing to worry about. Clodagh, breathlessly, ran into the room and halted instantly, just as we'd done.

'What have they done to the poor woman?'

She performed similar checks to mine. The only difference this time was in Sibeal's eyes, they held ours as we bent over her and I could see her jaw working. I leaned over to hear what she said. Her voice was little more than a whisper but her message was clear enough. She wanted to escape. It was reason enough. I pointed at the notepad by the side of the nurse's sleeping form

'Bring it with us Clodagh, it will help us find out what they've been doing.'

Delicately, carefully, I removed the pipes connected to Sibeal's veins. Midir picked her up and cradled her in his arms, with ease. He'd proved useful after all, in her condition I had no idea how we'd have escaped with her otherwise. He looked into her face with a huge, beaming smile that conveyed assurance but I knew my brother, despite her condition, he saw something more. Sibeal was an attractive woman, blonde curls and cornflower blue eyes, just like Oisin. I'd never seen my brother so chivalrous and I knew why.

We hurried along the corridor and down the staircase, out the front door after checking there were no more guards patrolling the perimeter of the house. Midir didn't appear to struggle as we ran through the gardens, along the narrow track where we'd hidden the horses. We'd anticipated Sibeal would be able to ride and I looked at my brother anxiously. He shrugged his impressive shoulders.

'I'll hold her in place on my horse, you take the reins of the spare one.'

'Will you be able to hold her and ride?' I asked.

I got a withering look and decided not to underestimate my brother's skill where horses and women were concerned. We trotted along the track until it brought us to the junction with the road to the manor house. Our plan had been to appear as though we were four people out for a casual ride, Sibeal's nightwear and semi-conscious state in wrecked that idea.

'We can't go to my rooms at the palace,' I said.

Anxiety was making my heart rate increase again, this time the adrenalin was caused by the unravelling of our plans. I felt proud of my detailed plans and preparations, I thought I'd considered every possibility. Rescuing a semi-conscious woman hadn't been one of them. I liked to be in control, I didn't cope with unpredictability and suddenly that was what confronted me.

Midir was the opposite, he shrugged and grinned at me. 'Don't worry little sister. Your big brother has the answer. Good thing you brought me along eh?'

I didn't like his patronising tone but he was right and we both knew it. I swallowed my pride and waited for his solution.

'I have a small cottage not too far away, we'll go there.'

This was new to me. 'What cottage?'

He gave me a wolfish grin. 'Just a place I keep to entertain certain guests.'

I rolled my eyes, I should have known. 'Women.'

'Married ones usually. It's more discreet that way.'

We took off. I'd started to invent stories to explain our situation when we met other travellers but none of them sounded credible so I was glad when we didn't stay on the road for very long. Midir took us through a rickety farm gate and across a couple of meadows, through a wood filled with the sounds of birds and then along a cart track that took us into a valley where a narrow stream gurgled through it. It was a rural idyll, complete with rustic cottage which I realised was an old, sadly neglected mill as we got closer. Its wheel was rotten and didn't move, the guttering was filled with grass and the roof looked like a strong wind would dislodge it. I glanced at my brother in mild derision. As usual he gave a shrug and grinned.

'It serves its purpose,' he said.

We offered to help Sibeal into the cottage but Midir was having none of it, somehow he slid gracefully down from his horse without disturbing the woman in his arms and strode through its doorway. He placed her on a chaise lounge, the main item in what was otherwise a sparsely furnished room, I was in no doubt about its usual purpose.

Despite the journey our patient looked more alert and healthier. Clodagh brought her a glass of water and we sat on the floor and waited for her to speak, Midir sat close to her, still holding her hand.

'Thank you,' she said a little hoarsely after we'd introduced ourselves. 'I thought my life was coming to an end.'

Gradually, she found it easier to string sentences together and to concentrate, so she could explain. She told us how she'd argued with Llyr after discovering the real purpose of his dragon breeding programme, how he'd tried to steal her research. When she released her wyverns, animals that had been her particular favourites, he'd lost his temper and had her hauled off to a room in the Dark Court's palace. She'd remained there for some time, she wasn't sure how long but then she ate food which, she realised afterwards, had a drug in it that made her sleep. She'd woken up in the manor house with Taranis sat in front of her. He'd questioned her repeatedly about her findings from her programme, something which confused her, he'd never been interested in her research. Not directly at least. His interests turned out to be like mine.

'He's investigating genetics, the same as me,' I said.

The woman looked at me, those piercing blue eyes were full of intelligence I could tell, despite the drugs. She'd come to a swift conclusion.

'Is that why you rescued me?'

I nodded, without realising why she'd asked. She became more guarded suddenly, glancing at Clodagh and then Midir, her eyes remaining on him for a few seconds longer than was necessary. My brother grinned at her and she blushed.

Suddenly her concerns made sense.

'Don't worry, I'm not trying to steal your research, I'm not like Llyr and Taranis. Clodagh and I have our own findings, we think we can achieve more by working alongside you.'

I outlined some of the conclusions we'd formed, I wanted her to trust us, as I spoke her eyes widened considerably.

189

'Are you scientists?'

I chuckled at the compliment. 'No. We're enjoy researching in the palace library and came across some theories we thought had merit. But we needed an expert to take us beyond the amalgamation of theories.'

She grinned before stifling a yawn.

'Taranis was experimenting on you, wasn't he?' I asked.

She gave a heavy sigh, it was obvious she was tiring quickly. 'Yes.' She was struggling. 'He violated me.'

Clodagh and I both clamped our hands over our mouths to stop ourselves from reacting the way our hearts and minds demanded. She spoke the words objectively, as a declaration of fact and without emotion. It gave her strength. She marshalled her energy.

'I am not his first such victim. He has experimented others. He considers himself a scientist. He is not. He is a monster.'

Whatever strength she had vanished with that declaration, she flopped backwards and her eyes rolled into the back of her head.

The three of us looked at each other as the implications sunk in. Midir was still holding her hand but his eyes held a fire in them, I think if Taranis had been in the room at that moment, he'd have killed him. I stared at the notebook, it could contain evidence of the man's crimes, not just what he'd been doing to Sibeal. That made it even more valuable to us. It also made it valuable to Taranis as well. I could see the trepidation on Clodagh's face as I looked up. Her voice quivered.

'Taranis will be furious it's been taken, it contains information he will want kept secret. We may be in great danger now Filidea.'

I'd begun to think the same thing but it wasn't something we could change. Midir picked up the woman with considerable ease and carried her up to the bedroom, the familiarity of the process told me he'd obviously done this many times in the past. He came downstairs later, having made sure she'd fallen asleep, and told us he planned on staying there with her. I insisted that Clodagh remained as well, to ensure Sibeal's reputation stayed intact. He wasn't happy about that but he agreed.

There was another reason why I wanted to Clodagh to stay. I hurried to my horse, took out my riding outfit from a bag strapped to my saddle and changed out of my smelly disguise.

'You need to get Sibeal to talk you through the notebook, we need to understand its contents. That's going to mean keeping Midir's passion under control.'

'How do I do that? The man is a raging mass of testosterone.'

Clodagh looked wide-eyed at the thought of controlling my brother's ardour. I had suspicions she felt attracted to his muscular form, he was the type she usually fantasised about after all.

'Don't leave her alone, keep working and studying with her, remind her how important our work is and the danger we face possessing that notebook. Midir will get bored eventually.'

'What are you going to do?' It was obvious she wasn't happy being left alone.

I heaved a sigh. 'We've just committed a crime Clodagh, against one of the most powerful men in the whole of Tir na nÓg. I need to keep my ear to the ground to find out what he does next and that means staying close to my grandmother. Plus, now we know he's competing with our research, we need to find out what he's actually doing, especially if it's immoral or illegal.'

She gave me the look I knew well. I smiled at her.

'Don't worry. I'll be careful.'

Chapter 15

I rode back to the palace genuinely frightened, I think I'd hidden it from Clodagh quite well, but now I was on my own, the implications of my little adventure were penetrating my shaky self-confidence.

Rescuing Sibeal had been risky. When it involved helping another woman to escape the crazed clutches of Llyr, I'd been driven by a moral imperative. I hadn't worried very much because my reasoning told me the man's interests lay in waging war against the humans. Losing Sibeal would have been an irritation, it wouldn't have distracted him from his greater purpose though.

Taranis' involvement changed the dynamic and raised the stakes.

He valued her for some reason. Enough to have openly flouted Llyr's intentions. At least I'd been subtle, Taranis had openly abducted her from the Dark Palace. If he dared do something like that to the High Lord of the Dark Court, he wouldn't hesitate in seeking vengeance against me. No matter what way I looked at it, and I tried very hard to do that as I rode back to the palace, Taranis posed a significantly greater threat. The plain fact of the matter was that he frightened me. Stories of this man's cruelty were the stuff of legend. He'd been a commander in the armed forces and even his training regime had been brutal. While some reports might have been apocryphal, others had triggered investigations and his eventual removal. Even in the Light Palace, everyone knew Lord Taranis to be a ruthless, sadistic, cruel-hearted bastard and I'd just stolen one of his valuable assets, as well as having established myself as a professional rival.

More than once I found myself wishing I'd not behaved so rashly, but what was done, was done. I had to deal with the consequences as best I could. It didn't stop me from feeling sick with fright though.

The palace represented some security. I breathed a sigh of relief as I rode into the stables courtyard and handed my horse over to a waiting groom. No sooner had I arrived than a servant sprinted towards me from the tack room. The young man was sweating, panic stricken, his urgency even caused him to call to me across the yard. Servants didn't yell at royalty, the groom looked astonished as he waited to see how I'd respond. The young man shouted that he had been looking for me for a long time, he'd only just discovered I'd gone riding, he was sorry for his poor behaviour but his mission was an urgent one. Highly important, he gasped.

By the time he reached me the poor fellow was panting and leaned against the astonished groom to get his breath. The drama fed my insecurities. What had happened while I'd been away? I couldn't help but wonder if it was linked to the crime I'd just committed. Waiting for the servant to regain enough breath to pass on his message was torture.

Finally, with enough air in his lungs to speak, the young man told me I was to report to the Silver Reception Room immediately, Lady Nimue waited for me there.

Trepidation turned to dread when the servant told me there wouldn't be time to change out of my riding breeches, my presence was urgently commanded. Grandmother never tolerated such impropriety, except in extreme circumstances, it couldn't be coincidence that I'd just committed a crime which could set the two Courts against one another.

The servant accompanied me, urging me on as politely as he knew how. I ran through explanations and excuses the entire way back, none of them convincing. Now I knew Taranis was involved, my actions appeared rash, impetuous and grandmother wouldn't be interested in any misunderstandings of Sibeal's abductor.

I arrived sweating, with a dry throat, my hair a mess, my clothes mud-spattered and with a distinctly equine aroma.

Dread turned to outright terror when the huge doors to the room of rainbows swung open to reveal my grandmother. And Taranis. They faced each other like two powerful pieces on a chess board. They turned to look at me, each face taking a couple of seconds to compose itself before reacting to the sight before them. My grandmother's expression lowered the temperature to frosty.

'Filidea, where have you been?'

Each word was delivered with a tone that meant, 'why have you come looking like that?' Each gap between the words contained the implication, 'why are you humiliating me?'

In comparison Taranis was all smiles and warmth.

'Well, I may be wrong, I so often am where ladies' fashions are concerned, but I would guess your granddaughter has been riding, my lady.'

The chilly expression didn't thaw as it turned on him. He bit his lip playfully.

'I'm sorry grandmother, I wasn't aware you wanted to see me. If I'd known...'

I let the sentence hang. If she didn't want to be embarrassed she ought to have warned me about such meetings, this was not my fault. I had to keep reminding myself of that. Taranis looked as distinguished as usual and his appearance made me feel more like a servant than a princess. Impeccable hair, with flashes of grey amidst the brown, was styled in a modern cut and the suit he wore was expensive and designed to show off his powerful physique. For a man who was starting to age, he looked quite dashing. Anyone who didn't know him might have been charmed by his smile, handsome features and good clothes. He bowed, perhaps a little lower than was necessary, and that worried me.

'It is my fault, my dear. My visit was unannounced.'

There was a cold look in his eyes that didn't match the warmth of the smile. It was those eyes that betrayed the kind of man he really was. Grandmother watched him greet me with an expression I couldn't read but then turned back to glare at me.

'You're normally in the library Filidea. You lack numerous useful qualities, knowing where to find you is one of your most valuable.'

The old witch. I smiled my apology, making sure I mirrored the political expression worn by the bastard in the perfectly tailored suit.

'Sometimes I like to get some fresh air,' I said, waving a hand around me as though to demonstrate where to find it.

Grandmother wasn't interested in my excuse and dismissed as if she was fanning away a gnat. I would have given anything to be such an insect, so I could fly out of the huge windows that wafted their lace curtains towards us. They allowed in a cool breeze and it made me shiver, though fear was a more likely cause.

'Well, this is hardly the ideal situation to discuss such matters, I had hoped you would have been dressed more appropriately.'

'For what?' I asked before she'd finished her last word.

I didn't like not knowing what to expect and I had the impression I was being manipulated. Taranis kept glancing at me out of the corner of his eye, the kind of look I recognised in courtly politics, one which prefaced an act of vengeance or aggression. I also didn't like the way my grandmother flicked her eyes in his direction before speaking, that spoke of indecision and such a word didn't appear in her vocabulary.

The moment stalled as grandmother's ancient secretary, Vevina, strutted into the room, glasses perched on the end of her beak of a nose. She always reminded me of one of those long-legged birds that hunt fish, their back hunched in the constant search for food. Vevina's search meant staring down at the notebook she carried with her, something which never left her claws; I imagined if those records fell into the wrong hands it could bring down the Light Court in seconds. She ignored me, even Lord Taranis, which shocked me, but her expression conveyed urgency.

A quick glance in his direction, at his narrowed eyes as he watched the old bird, told me he was just as intrigued. The two old crones whispered intently for several seconds, I was near enough to hear the name Oisin mentioned and I felt my heart rate increase. I wondered if word had arrived of my crime. My anxiety didn't decrease when my grandmother did something I'd never seen before.

'My dear Taranis, something has occurred that requires my immediate attention. I do apologise for inconveniencing you so but I'm afraid I have no choice but to attend to this matter. We will reschedule this meeting as soon as possible. Once again, my apologies.'

With that she was gone. No opportunity for replies, reprimands or farewells. Both of us stood like statues, mouths open a little. The professional politician was inevitably the one to recover first, he gave me that same smile as before, one a shark gives its prey.

'Your grandmother's hasty departure gives us an opportunity to get to know one another, doesn't it, my dear?'

I didn't like being called 'my dear'. I didn't belong to him, I never would.

'Erm... Yes.'

He didn't move, neither did I. We remained at right angles to one another and some distance apart, we'd formed a triangle when my grandmother was present, now our positions felt awkward. He retained the smile though sustaining it looked like it caused him pain.

'We share an interest I believe. I think you have a passing interest in scientific matters, am I correct?'

The smug bastard. It was more than a passing interest.

'That's right,' I said sweetly. 'Why, do you?'

The slightest of shrugs. 'I believe our race should develop greater curiosity, we've allowed our long lives to stagnate. I think such a factor may be at the root of many of our problems. Would you agree?'

That's why you abduct women and conduct experiments on them, you bastard.

'I would, yes.'

Now he moved, he took a step towards me then halted as though he didn't want to appear too friendly. I was glad of that.

'Good. I'm so pleased. It will give us something in common.'

Ice ran through my veins and I almost choked.

'Something in common?'

The smile grew. He'd worked out I was ignorant of whatever was happening here. Everyone knew grandmother's machinations were disseminated amongst her family on a strictly need-to-know basis and that most of us in the Light Court were kept in the dark. It was the source of a good many obvious jokes. This bastard was savouring the moment. That was why he chose to wrap up the news as he pretended to be coy.

'I shouldn't say anything I suppose. It is rather jumping the gun. Court protocols and the like, but, well, I've never been one to beat about the bush.'

He took a dramatic breath.

'But as we're to be married, I think having common interests is important. I'm sure you'd agree?'

The witch had gone behind my back, I should have guessed. This meeting was to be a formal betrothal introduction. She'd assumed I wouldn't make a fuss when the man stood in front of me. She'd counted on my in-built need to avoid such an embarrassing situation, royalty didn't indulge in such impropriety. If she thought that, then she didn't know me at all. No wonder she was furious that I'd turned up looking such a mess. My mind reeled with the implications.

My suiter, this ruthless, scheming, sadistic bastard, watched me as he waited for my reply. I had no idea what to say, except I wasn't going to play along. My grandmother might have her plans but I had no intention of cooperating with them. I opened my mouth to reply and hoped words would appear, my only hope lie in the formalities we would need to go through.

'Court protocols, my lord, are the backbone of the Light Court.' My brain clicked into gear. 'And if we were to behave in a way which contravened them, my grandmother would be furious. I'm sure you can appreciate why I don't want to upset her. There are members of this Court who have ignored those protocols and suffered the consequences.'

I gave a polite little laugh. He smiled back at me but it was just as hollow.

'As my grandmother explained, we will need to reschedule. And next time I shall ensure I am suitably dressed.'

'Of course.' He gave me another bow, this time it was no more than a lowering of the head. 'Tell me, where do you go riding? Perhaps we could ride together some time? I'd been informed you didn't ride.'

Behind my smile I gritted my teeth at that comment.

'But no doubt you like to get fresh air after spending so much time amongst dusty books in that dark library of yours, it has left your complexion rather pale.'

I let my smile slip deliberately but his slur was equally as deliberate, the gloves were off.

'It is the penalty of being a serious researcher, my lord, one who is intent on finding the truth, no matter in what dark corners it hides.'

Our eyes met and, even though my heart was beating like a battle drum, I didn't look away. The smile on his face remained but his grey eyes turned predatory.

'Indeed, my dear. I would only say that a lady should always be careful where you search for the truth. Sometimes, danger lurks in darkness and the truth can be an expensive commodity.'

'Whilst that may be true, a good scientist does not allow fear to limit their investigations. As you have just said, our race lacks curiosity. Surely you don't suggest we should only explore those places where we can tread with certainty?'

I wasn't going to let this man think he could better me. With luck I might display enough truculence to make him doubt my suitability as a wife. He was the type to expect a woman to remain quiet and unobtrusive, that was not me. His smile looked like it had been set in dried mud.

'Investigations can be unpredictable, my dear.'

There was that phrase again and I bristled.

'I've learned that careful planning, thorough research, well-informed knowledge are the vital elements of the professional scientist.'

The implication being that I didn't qualify. But those qualities were the ones I'd overlooked in rescuing Sibeal, I realised.

'What you must always ensure, my dear, is not to rush into doing something and then find out your dealing with an entirely different situation. That can lead to embarrassment as well as grave problems.'

My heart stopped. Was he aware of what I'd done? Surely not. It was coincidence. Nothing more. The trouble was, he'd unbalanced me and his smile broadened at my hesitant reaction.

'You see what I mean, my dear?'

He knew how that phrase annoyed me and he used it deliberately now.

'I'm sure our relationship will be full of such fascinating philosophical debate. Just imagine the conversations we'll have over the breakfast each morning.'

That thought made me want to vomit. All the same, our verbal fencing helped me realise I had an opportunity to get the measure of this man. He'd abducted Sibeal and I had assumed his reasons to be malevolent and perverted, I was allowing his reputation to dictate my reactions. I had a chance to watch his reactions first hand. I steeled myself to rattle the cage of this predator.

'I must admit, I do enjoy discussing scientific matters. I was saying as much to my friend Sibeal, very recently. She is the most accomplished scientist that I know.'

His expression betrayed him for the briefest of seconds, but it was enough. The cold stare he gave me caused the smile to vanish, there was no pretence now.

'Yes, she has developed some interesting theories, I agree. But I confess to having no interest in the mating habits of dragons.' He gave a silly little chuckle. 'My interests are far more profound.'

'Really?' My throat was dry and my heart pounded so loudly he was bound to hear it. 'Yet she is acknowledged as an expert in the field of genetics. It was why High Lord Llyr employed her. Are you suggesting that he was mistaken?'

Those dark grey eyes of his bore into mine, there was no smile now. I had got under his skin, I hoped his plans for our impending nuptials might get cancelled as a result. He didn't reply immediately but kept looking at me, even though it was uncomfortable, I didn't avert my eyes. I kept smiling too. He realised he was giving away too much, he sighed and leaned his head to one side in a casual manner.

'You are clearly unaware of recent events, my dear.' The final two words delivered with sugary sweetness. 'The High Lord imprisoned the lady because her aims did not match his. Hardly the behaviour of a gentleman. The High Lord appears more interested in waging war than in science and civilised behaviour, which is why I took it upon myself to provide the lady in question with more suitable accommodation, as my guest.'

I feigned surprise.

'I was unaware of these events, my lord. I commend your chivalry. I would like to visit Sibeal at the earliest opportunity to give her my assurances that she will remain safe from such behaviour in the future.'

'I'm afraid that will not be possible, my dear. At least for the time being. The poor woman's health deteriorated as a result of her incarceration. I've employed a nurse to help her recover but it is going to take some time.'

'I'm sure she will appreciate even a brief visit from a friend though.'

'Sadly no. She is very weak, it would only impede her recovery.'

He gave a deep sigh. He was making ready to depart.

'Where are my manners? You will want to change out of your riding habit, no doubt bathe as well. Don't let me delay you. We can continue our conversation another day.'

He lowered his head in a cursory bow, turned on his heels and strode out of the room, I listened until I could no longer hear his heels clicking on the floor. If I had held any doubts about the man, he's confirmed them for me. He was a reptile.

I took a deep breath to stifle the vomit that threatened to make a terrible mess on the polished floor and hurried to my rooms. I had no intention of marrying such an odious creature. My grandmother might have a different opinion and I needed to find a way to change it, without telling her what I'd done.

Chapter 16

I woke from a dream where I'd been pursued by something dark and deadly. Outside the shack the world had turned white; a thin topping of snow, like icing on a cake, lay on the sleeping wyvern. Oisin lay huddled up next to the smouldering remains of the fire.

I peered into the centre of the demolished ramshackle community, now shrouded in white.

Something was wrong.

I stood, picked up my sword from my backpack and stepped outside warily. For a moment or two I wondered if I was spooking myself with the thought of dead bodies lying beneath the snow but my instincts were seldom wrong. I'd learned long ago the body is amazing, it senses things without the conscious mind realising it. Alec had once explained how his body did the same but to a higher degree; where his ability was a genetic abnormality, mine was borne of rigorous and painful training.

I stepped carefully so as not to tread on bodies or anything else that could cause me to lose my footing, any distraction would trigger an attack by an assailant. Derelict and burned out remains of wooden shacks, their timbers leaning against each other like drunken comrades, offered limited cover. I scanned each one. Nothing. Yet the feeling was growing stronger with every step I took.

The jumble of stone blocks which formed the portal archway remained where they were the night before, snow partly covering the blackened blast marks. No one had rebuilt it overnight. Then, there, on the opposite side of the pile. Fresh footprints.

I followed them as they circled the settlement. On the edge of the escarpment, where a cold wind scoured the ground and pushed snow into drifts the size of a man, the footsteps vanished. I looked around but the clay was frozen solid and left no clues.

Too late I realised I'd been taken for a fool.

I rushed back to the shack. The wyvern remained inert, oblivious of Oisin kneeling in front of the dying fire with a sword held to his throat.

My jaw must have dropped because it made the figure holding him smile.

'I thought you were dead,' I said as I struggled to process what my eyes told me.

The smile widened. The parchment skin creased, wrinkling into ugly yellow folds.

'Hello Robin. I see the two of you couldn't stay apart. Foolish to abandon him.'

I focused my concentration, the next few seconds were critical, I couldn't behave like Death had come to visit. He had, but I couldn't allow myself to be distracted, that was what he wanted.

'The last time we met, you abandoned me to go swimming in the Thames.'

The smile on the face of Death vanished for a second but then returned, though the bloodshot eyes with enormous black irises, like dark mirrors, held no humour. Ankou stood upright, forcing Oisin to follow him as the sword dug into his throat, the black cloak he wore hung over them both.

'An event for which I still harbour considerable resentment. It was to lead to hardship which I continue to suffer.'

I smiled at him. 'I can tell. You really need to use more moisturiser.'

'Still the mischief-maker I see. I wonder if you'll find it amusing when I slit your lover's throat.'

I nodded at the immobile wyvern praying that any minute it would leap into action.

'I don't recommend it. She's possessive where Oisin is concerned.'

Oisin's eyes rolled. The decrepit figure of death sniggered.

'You know little about reptiles Robin. In extreme cold their metabolism slows down so they become sleepy and sluggish, this wyvern poses no threat at all.'

Shit.

'So you're here to pay me back because I encouraged you to go bathing?'

Fiery embers and lengths of charred wood lay between us, the fire was still too large and hot to move through, circling it wasn't an option. His arm moved sideways, ready for a slicing action.

'Partly. But Llyr wants you returned to him and I accepted his commission.'

With all my strength, I kicked two of the longer pieces of wood in his direction, they lifted about six inches, turned end over end and landed on the trailing edges of his cloak. Flames instantly licked at the cloth forcing Ankou backwards, in the process lowering his blade sufficiently for Oisin to fall to the ground and slither onto the snow to extinguish the hot embers on his trousers. Robbed of his hostage Ankou ripped off his cloak with one flick of his wrist, while readying himself for my attack with his other hand, swinging his sword into a defensive position. Not one to disappoint, I attacked.

He looked decrepit, ancient beyond belief, his body almost skeletal but he fought like the young man I'd known so long ago; he'd lost none of his agility, speed of reflexes or his skill with a blade. The last time we'd fought, on London bridge, I'd resorted to conjuring Puck into the battle, not something I wanted to repeat if I could help it. I was never certain if I'd get that psychotic genie back into its bottle.

Our blades clashed in a sequence of blurred images as we positioned ourselves knowing what was coming next, the stage where you test each other to see if anything's changed. It hadn't. We were equally matched.

The fight took us outside, onto ground made slippery by wet snow. It was a tight exchange, we didn't dare travel, the ground beneath our feet was too unpredictable, it left our blades and wrists to do the work. He'd know, as well as I did, that losing your footing meant death. In fights like this your attention is focused on where his blade will be in the next millisecond, he on yours, it's not a fight to entertain audiences because all they see is a blur of blades, until that last second.

It was when he changed position slightly, his attack coming from an acute angle rather than head on that I realised he was about to shift the rhythm of the fight. I'd been thinking of doing the same, when you're so equally matched all you can expect is for exhaustion to become the critical factor and we both knew that wasn't imminent.

He burst forwards, his sword like rotor blades, pushing me backwards against the wall of the shack. It was a risky strategy, getting that close, it left him open to attack from my foot or spare hand. I chose to kick his knee as I shifted my balance. He staggered slightly, lost his rhythm sufficiently to allow me to push him backwards, without any obstacle to stop me.

What you don't want in speedy exchanges like this is to retreat, you don't know what's behind you. Trouble is when the fight is so evenly balanced you have little choice, if I hadn't had the shack to stop my retreat I'd have been in the same situation but a lesson you quickly learn in training is to find something to cover your back. There's risks in that approach, you get trapped if your opponent is better than you.

It was a strategy which hadn't worked for my opponent and now I had him taking half steps backwards, with half an eye on what was around him. He increased his speed, I didn't think it was possible our swordplay could get any faster and it started to worry me, this was exactly what had happened on the bridge. The difference this time meant there was no gap in the bridge for either of us to fall through. Deep in my brain Puck stirred, eager for slaughter.

I was so intent on my opponent's blade and where it was going to be microseconds before it entered that space, I didn't see Oisin. My surprise must have reflected Ankou's. Knowing he faced danger behind him caused him to lose focus for a second as he half-turned. Oisin brought a tree branch down hard on the grey skull, Ankou dropped to his knees. In that split second I plunged my blade so hard into his chest it pushed him backwards onto the snowy ground. He lay there panting, staring up at me. I twisted the sword, he grimaced though he didn't take his eyes off me.

Oisin stood with the tree branch in his hand, heaving for breath. He looked at his victim, blinked, shook his head as though he couldn't believe what he'd done. He dropped the branch and swallowed hard.

'Thanks,' I said. He shrugged and kept shaking his head.

My blade lay buried in the chest now moving only slightly as death approached. I couldn't help but think how ironic it was that the man who was known to so many humans as the epitome of Death should now be dying at my feet. I yanked the blade out hard, dragging it past ribs in the process, lifting the chest cavity slightly, I pushed it back down with my boot. A quick glance at my blade showed there was hardly any blood on it.

That didn't bother me, it was the smile on the bastard's desiccated lips that worried me. Dying men don't usually look happy about their situation.

It remained there as yellow eye lids, like shreds of old leather, closed and the sinewy strands of the throat relaxed and rattled their announcement of death.

I looked about the camp, half expecting a troop of spriggans to appear out of nowhere. Nothing, only the silence of the snow and the corpses beneath it.

'Let's get going.'

The fight had delayed us, Purdey would already be on the road and heading for Burrow Mump. As I led the horses out of the ramshackle stable where they'd spent the night I wondered if Ankou had been sacrificed for that reason. Something still didn't feel right but I couldn't tell what. It irritated me.

The wyvern stirred but only because Oisin brushed it with our blankets like he was polishing its scales.

'Leave the bloody thing if it can't wake up.'

He looked at me as though I'd suggested killing it and serving it up for dinner. I didn't say any more, he had helped me deal with Ankou after all. It took him five minutes of rigorous scale polishing to get the wyvern moving and alert, by then the bloody thing decided it was hungry and more time was wasted feeding it.

The clock was against us and, to try to limit volcanic levels of anger building up in me, I tried to work out the role played by the man whose body I'd left lying in the snow. The fact Llyr was conscripting more help to capture me wasn't good news, it proved we were being hunted. Ankou had to have come through the portal with the spriggans, avoided discovery by Brea, and hidden until he thought the time was right to attack. With the wyvern around he must have decided to wait until it fell asleep. It wouldn't have been wise to attack in the darkness so he'd waited until dawn. If my battle senses hadn't kicked in, he could have captured us.

It certainly meant my good friend, Trevor Ratner, had gone back to Llyr and told him where Purdey was taking the kids. With a larger contingent of troops, the crazy bastard would have them by now, a good thing Brea had fought them off. I felt proud of her. When the few survivors of her fury got back to Llyr he'd relied on Ankou to capture me, no doubt use me as bait too.

We set off finally, made our way to the wooden gates of the compound. I needed to get to Burrow Mump quickly. There could be a portal there too and if there was, Llyr would know to send through more troops, more than Brea could handle. And if that wasn't enough pressure, even if there was no portal, Purdey would be taking the kids there to sell them as slaves.

Artic blasts met our faces as we passed through the huge gates, the sky looked heavy with more snow, we couldn't afford for it to slow us down.

I sat on my horse feeling like all sorts of wrongs were being visited on me, despite my urge to begin our journey, something jarred in my head so that I couldn't bring myself to leave Hamdon Hill. Oisin looked at me, uncertain whether to risk saying anything. I couldn't waste time but my battle sense was telling me something and I knew not to ignore it.

I turned the horse's head and galloped back into the camp, regardless of the corpses beneath the hooves of my mount. They were dead, they didn't care. That's what death did, it ended your connection to the living. You stopped any involvement with other people, death made you focus only on yourself. Except that smile on that leather-bound face was different, there was something in that smile that worried me.

I reached the shack, where snow lay trampled, where the wyvern's outline remained and where the fire was now just charred remains.

Where there was no body.

Ankou had gone. Disappeared. Resurrected like the Christian's saviour. Except I doubted this was the work of any god.

I cantered back to the entrance where Oisin and the wyvern waited.

'He's gone.'

It took a few seconds of puzzled expressions for Oisin to work out what I meant while I searched the fort to make sure he wasn't going to attack us again. I thought back to what he'd said about the hardship he continued to suffer, he'd survived drowning in the deadly currents and poisonous waters of the Thames and now he'd survived my blade.

'This is fucking Oberon's work!' I screamed at the icy wind as I returned to the compound's gates and Oisin's expectant face. I'd been delayed still further and now I was being hunted by an assassin that couldn't be killed. Fucking great.

I set off down the hill screaming my fury at the flooded landscape. Oisin eventually caught up as I slowed my horse, realising only a fool rides an animal into the ground because of his temper. I wouldn't get the twins back that way.

'There were stories of Oberon's shady work with blood chemistry. You know how it fascinated him.'

'What stories?'

Oisin glanced over at me, his expression anxious. 'Rumours that Oberon used a ceremonial device, a cauldron of some kind, that could instil life. I heard he took creatures through this reanimation process and then used their blood to stop entropy.'

'I heard those stories before I left Tir na nÓg. They were tales to scare children.'

With a shake of his head Oisin's expression told me otherwise.

'The creatures were called the *dreach-fhuola*. "The ones with tainted blood".'

I'd heard of the term. It had even penetrated Celtic culture centuries ago. The Irish author Bram Stoker had used it to name his famous character Dracula, the undead creature that couldn't be slayed. In Celtic mythology the monster had to be buried upside down with a heavy rock to weigh down its corpse and stop it escaping.

Oisin was watching me. 'You think Ankou is one of these creatures.'

I rode on. That smile on his face as he gasped his last breath declared Ankou wasn't finished with me. I could kill him repeatedly but he'd still pursue me until he caught and returned me to Llyr. Or until he ended my life more easily than I could his, after all, I had no idea how to finish this creature.

We rode in silence towards another lump on the horizon.

Our route lay like a silver thread in the weak December sunlight, amidst the shimmering grey water that reflected the threat contained in the clouds above.

We followed the route of what had once run parallel to the River Parrett, now more of a lake dissected by the raised causeway on which we travelled, to a bridge that brought us into the small market town of Langport. We needed food for the horses and I gambled on Purdey needing the same thing.

Our diversion took us along deserted streets where houses watched our progress through the hollow sockets of smashed windows. The place had been systematically looted and what was left burned and destroyed so it offered no support for anyone else. The place spooked the horses and for a while I couldn't understand why, not until I realised it was the absence of any noise, not even the sound of birds. I'd expected to find the occasional dog or cat but there was nothing, just the echoes of horses' hooves on the crumbling tarmac road.

'I don't like this place,' Oisin declared, head turning from side to side nervously.

I felt the same but any other settlement was out of our way, Purdey would have stopped here for the same reason and probably disregarded the unease we felt. If Ankou hadn't delayed us I'd planned on ambushing him here, its narrow streets made it ideal but that worked both ways. Nonetheless we trotted through the town without finding anywhere that offered help. Eventually, on its furthest edge, we stopped at a farm whose fields ran up to dense woodland. It commanded a good vantage point on a small hill, its buildings didn't look damaged and I reasoned its owner might have repelled assaults until the need to find food moved him on. Perhaps there was at least something for the animals.

In its relatively new barn, amidst the rusting remains of a combine harvester, seed drills and two tractors was a small pile of hay bales. The horses tucked in hungrily though the wyvern hesitated, distracted by scents it pursued like a bloodhound. It found the bodies of two sheep behind the barn, newly killed. It tucked in to its feast with gusto.

The farmhouse had been rifled but with not with any serious intent. We'd followed a trail of tinned foods into the kitchen and found more food which hadn't gone bad.

'Someone's been living here until very recently,' Oisin said as he opened the door to a large cupboard and helped himself to its contents.

'And left it hurriedly too by the look of it. See if you can make something for us, while I check outside.'

He nodded and I returned to the farmyard. No one left food behind these days. People didn't leave well defended locations like this farmhouse either. I vaguely wondered if it was a place where the twins could live for that reason.

I found the farmer laid out on the lawn behind the house. His shotgun lay at his side, so did his head. He didn't have any legs and a chunk of his belly was missing, intestines lay spread out around his body like spaghetti. His corpse showed unmistakeable teeth marks. Big ones.

A trail of blood, more intestines and the farmer's lower leg provided a trail I really didn't want to follow but I had to find out what had happened.

Beyond the lawn I hurried through an orchard devastated by the passage of something big. Ancient apple trees leaned at crazy angles, branches lay broken on the floor and a muddy patch provided a footprint of something with huge hooves.

A wooden stile marked the boundary of the orchard as well as the last resting place of what I assumed was probably the farmer's son, a young man in his late teens. His shotgun lay on the ground; he must have tried to climb over the stile hurriedly and even held on to it as whatever attacked him, grabbed his legs. His arms still clung on to the stile. His legs had been ripped from his hips.

Near to where his legs should have been was a pool of blood. By the stile were two spent cartridges. I assumed he'd shot and wounded the animal before it caught him. The poor kid had fought until the very end.

I ran back to the farmhouse.

Oisin was cooking soup, bread lay in big chunks on the table.

'We're leaving. Now!' I yelled at him.

There was no hesitation or complaint. We ran.

We didn't get very far. The creature, slightly taller than a man, strode along the drive from the main road, just as we'd done and spotted us instantly. It lifted its broad reptilian head and gave out a sound like a rutting stag, only higher pitched. Next to me Oisin gasped.

'What is it doing here?' he said.

We stood perfectly still, both of us reacting instinctively.

'The Fae released them when they invaded. Calculated to sow fear and chaos amongst the population,' I said.

'What are we going to do?'

The creature was still over fifty yards away and it slowed down as it tried to maintain its attention on us. Poor eyesight was its weakness but, for this monster, that was as far as vulnerabilities went. It sniffed the air, a huge forked tongue flicked out of a wide jaw filled with sharp teeth. Its scaly head and muscular neck merged into a powerful body covered in brown fur and it moved on four powerful legs. From its rear a thin tail lashed from side to side like an angry cat's. It looked, to previous generations of human beings, to be a creature made up of lots of other animals, so much so it had become something of a myth. The humans featured it as the antagonist in one of Arthur's legends, where King Pellinore had fought the monster and named it the Questing Beast, as heroes of yore liked to do. In the story he'd described it as an amalgamation of lizard, leopard, deer and lion. I was happier describing it as a fucking vicious monster.

'It's recently eaten. It may not be too bothered with us,' I whispered.

The thing gave a second half roar, half belching noise.

Oisin gently shook his head and whispered, 'I don't think it agrees. What are we going to do?'

'We're not going to run, that's the worst thing to do. The owners of this farm found that out. We keep still and gradually lower ourselves to the ground to confuse it.'

'And if that doesn't work? We'll be sitting ducks.'

'That thing is too swift to avoid. Hiding is a better option.'

We squatted on the pathway to the farm like hens hatching eggs. The animal swayed its head from side to side as though looking for us. I could see, on its flank, just above its foreleg, a bloody wound, the final act of vengeance from the farmer's son.

It took several strides in our direction with alarming speed, despite limping on its injured leg, when it spotted us it let out a high-pitched wail of pleasure. Another roar followed, louder, deeper. It came from the wyvern positioned at the end of drive, head up, teeth bared as it pored at the ground like a bull that's spotted the matador.

They raced towards each other, juggernauts of muscle. Oisin let out a half scream of concern for his pet and grabbed my arm tightly.

As they prepared to collide, the Questing Beast opened it huge jaws to bite whatever flesh it found but, just as those jaws went to clamp on its prey, the wyvern chose a very different approach. It leapt. There was no attempt to use its pathetic wings, instead it used its powerful hind legs and soared over the head of its opponent. It landed on the creature's back and raked the fur with sharp claws and sank its jaws into the base of the neck. The Questing Beast reared up like a stallion, hooves pawing the air as it howled its protest, twisted its neck to bite the wyvern but the red menace was already off its back, it landed like an athlete on the ground, facing its foe yet again.

'She's amazing,' Oisin gasped. 'The intelligence needed to attack that way!'

The Questing Beast approached slower and with greater care this time, the wyvern roared its defiance but remained where it was, watching its enemy's every move. Suddenly and with startling speed the Questing Beast leapt at the wyvern just as it started to turn thereby exposing its flank.

They collided and rolled over and over each other, both pairs of jaws snapping at whatever part of the other could be reached. The Questing Beast was first on its feet, the wyvern shook its head like a punch-drunk boxer and tried to stand but found itself pinned to the ground by one powerful hoof placed on its snake-like neck. It screeched alarm.

Oisin was on his feet instantly and I had to hold him back from dashing to the rescue.

The Questing Beast roared its supremacy, swishing its tail furiously.

But the instant it roared, the red-scaled snake-like neck twisted and jerked, freeing itself from the other animal's foot. It caused the Questing Beast to lose its balance for a few seconds, it tottered and as it did so the wyvern twisted it neck so that its jaws could close around the lower part of its enemy's fore leg, making it howl in pain.

It didn't stop the Questing Beast from reaching out to grab the wyvern by its exposed neck but the wyvern was out of range in seconds. The Questing Beast let out another howl, a mixture of pain and frustration, judging by its pitch. I realised the bitten foreleg was the same one already injured by the farmer's son. I wondered if that had been deliberate or if I was crediting the wyvern with too much intelligence.

The wyvern's position was only just out of reach but it did the strangest thing, it turned to present its backside to the other creature, as though it was going to run away. The Questing Beast paused, uncertain how to react to this unexpected behaviour but the temptation of the exposed flank was too good a target to resist. It reached forwards, stretching its neck and head to bite the tempting hide. At the same time the wyvern's tail flicked like a whip, striking its opponent hard in the face, or rather, its eye. Red liquid spurted in all directions and the Questing Beast squealed like a pig.

Blinded on one side the Questing Beast turned its head so it could still see its opponent, but the wyvern anticipated the movement and lashed the tail again, it missed the other eye by inches but struck the muzzle and drew more blood. Like dancers they circled each other, tails lashing at each other but the wyvern was an expert, its tail raked the flesh along the Questing Beast's side and even on its already injured foreleg.

Each time the injured leg was struck the Questing Beast howled even louder, blood poured from the bite marks and the shot gun injury a little higher up. Like a warrior, the wyvern assessed where to strike its enemy so as to capitalise on the injuries. I'd watched men fight with less strategy than this animal, it was like watching a champion in a melee deal with a less experienced and weaker assailant. It kept tipping its head from one side to the other as it always did when it was working something out. I turned and grinned at Oisin who was too preoccupied with his pet's safety to be interested in its battle strategy.

They moved around each other like they were performing a dance and, at just the right moment, the wyvern's tail lashed out to target the same place each time. It meant the Questing Beast, which was starting to limp badly now, didn't dare attack, it kept circling in the hope the other animal would lose its concentration so it could strike. Occasionally it resorted to using its jaws to bite but, with one eye this was a risky strategy, it left itself open to another attack on its neck and head.

Finally, with blood pouring from its leg and head, it staggered and dropped to its knee briefly but with an effort managed to right itself.

The wyvern broke the circle they'd been making, turned to face its foe but didn't move, just watched with disdain as though it knew it had won and wanted to give its opponent the opportunity to withdraw.

The Questing Beast stood, unable to put much weight on its injured foreleg, at right angles to the wyvern. It snapped and snarled impotently. The wyvern roared once, and rushed at its enemy, head down. Like a bulldozer, it pushed the Questing Beast over on to its side. The wyvern rammed its head up against the Questing Beat's belly then yanked it upwards, ripping flesh with its jagged crest in the process.

The Questing Beast squealed and spasmed but the wyvern thrust its head against the thing's belly, ripping the hole wider. Squeals of agony ended in a throaty gurgle.

The wyvern's head disappeared into the beast's stomach briefly, only to return with a jaw full of blue-white intestines which it chomped on and returned for more.

'I recommend you leave it alone for a while Oisin,' I said as he took tentative steps towards his pet. 'Leave our red warrior to savour her victory.'

As if in answer it lifted its head up and bellowed loudly then yanked out more offal.

'I think you're right.'

His wide-eyed horror was almost comical.

'We need to get something to eat too.'

Oisin looked at me aghast. 'After that sight?'

I shrugged. I was hungry.

Chapter 17

The cave was damp and smelled of urine.

As my entry into the human realm, it wasn't the most auspicious of places. The opposite of the luxury of the Dark Palace, even its servants' quarters. I moved the crystals from the base of the archway and the primrose yellow light vanished, leaving me in a world of darkness and foul smells. A narrow shaft of light drew me upwards where the temperature threatened to freeze me. I'd been warned of the low temperatures and to recognise snow but no one had prepared me for the intense cold that went with the fluffy flakes that dropped from the sky. It penetrated my clothes, quickly chilled me through to the bone so that I started to shiver uncontrollably.

At the mouth of the cave, I looked out over a watery landscape that stretched for miles. It was a world without colour, warmth or any welcoming features and it made me wonder why my race was intent on winning it back. As far as I was concerned, they could keep its bleak misery.

Outside the cave, behind me, was a hill. Atop it I could make out a rectangular stone building surrounded by a camp of fragile constructions. Some were made from sheets of heavy material that billowed like flags when the wind caught them. Others were more solid, made from wood or metal. None of them looked hospitable, even habitable. It confirmed what we'd been told, these people were savages.

It was certainly a place to avoid.

Except now, with this new location, I had no idea where I was or where Cochrann might be. My quest felt enormous, unsurmountable and as the snow blew in my face, briefly robbing me of my breath, for the first time I felt real despair. I had little time and I was lost.

A narrow path, just above the water line, led me upwards. It wasn't the route I wanted to follow because it took me nearer to the settlement, but unless I chose to swim, I had no other choice. As swimming wasn't something slaves were taught, I decided to risk following the path, it was safer than drowning.

I trudged upwards in the hope the path might circle the camp but luck was not on my side. The camp got nearer. Close enough to hear the everyday chatter of people going about their daily jobs. I began practising the greetings Master Darragh had taught me.

The muddy path, no more than a rarely-used track animals might use, turned a corner and I came face to face with two young girls, carrying buckets. They were pathetic creatures, dressed in thin rags, exactly what I'd imagined savages wore. The path divided at this point, downhill to a small beach, up to the camp. They were so busy talking they didn't see me, not until we almost collided. That was when they screamed.

'I give you good morning, my ladies,' I said as warmly and welcoming as I could.

They screamed a second time, dropped their buckets and fled up the hill, still screaming.

Panic gripped me. I might have enough time to hurry back to the cave and activate the portal to return home, empty-handed. Or I could meet these people and hope someone had seen Cochrann. Master Sidwell had said there were others with my skin colour in this realm, perhaps there were some in this settlement. Or they could be savages who would kill me. I dithered, turning one way then the other, wishing someone would give me instructions. I was a servant, I didn't think for myself.

Indecision stalled me, I hadn't moved when five men that looked like bears, with long hair flying behind them, ran towards me. They carried an assortment of weapons I didn't recognise, their shouts and curses helped me conclude these people would not be welcoming hosts. I raised trembling hands in surrender, something I'd been told to do in such circumstances, and did my best to smile.

The savages wore furs and beards that hid most of their faces so it was impossible to see if my smile had any effect, I could only go by their eyes and they looked angry.

'Greetings fine sirs!' I said as calmly as my quaking stomach allowed.

They surrounded me, the pungent smell of body odour was overpowering, and looked confused by my welcome. One of them, with a scar across his face that made him the ugliest in a tough competition, shrugged, raised a heavy looking weapon and brought it down on my head.

A firework spectacle, like the ones we have on Samhain Eve, burst in my head until darkness granted me peace from the pain that went with it.

Pain followed regularly after that.

I woke in a small metal cage, one of several lined against the stone wall of the big building. Its size only allowed me to kneel, squat or sit, I assumed it was meant for animals and I worried they might treat me as such. I was also naked. I suppose I should have felt self-conscious but my greater concern was that I felt very, very cold. I'd been told by Lady Mab that the low temperatures in this world meant we couldn't survive very long, my fingers and toes were losing sensation and I guessed that wasn't a good sign.

The stone building was at one end of the camp so it was quite isolated. I called for help on the few occasions when a handful of women hurried by, intent on their work, but they ignored me. I assumed they were women, it was difficult to tell, they looked nothing like the women in the palace. Where the men wore thick clothes made from animal skins mostly, the women wore rags, they were stick-thin with heads shaved or covered in stubble. I noticed one of them wore my coat and I called out to give it back but she shouted something that I assumed was a curse, judging by her expression and tone.

I don't know how long I remained in the cage, without any sun to track across the sky, time drifted. Eventually the men returned, they didn't speak but roughly dragged me out of my cage and tried to make me walk. The problem was I'd been penned up so long the cold and stiffness in my joints made it difficult to move, I had trouble walking but the men weren't prepared to wait. One took a stick out of the folds of his animal skin coat and brought it down hard on my back, I screamed. When my legs buckled under me as I tried to stand, he struck me a second time, even harder. I screamed again. Beatings were normal for me but this method was new, it was applied with such force and in line with my spine so it struck bone rather than flesh and muscle. I struggled to my feet and managed to stand upright but he beat me with his stick again, this time against my buttocks. All the men laughed. An even bigger man with a face hidden by hair, and with shoulders like a bull, nudged the other man.

'Careful with that arse, Jack, we'll want to use that later!'

They all laughed even louder. One of them, he was younger with less facial hair, grabbed hold of my hips and dragged me against his crotch and in a pantomime of exaggerated thrusting gasped and gurgled loudly.

'Ooh, nice and tight, lads!

The one they called Jack pushed him away from me.

'Fucking hell, Rimmer, you'd fuck a brown skinned one?'

The younger man wrenched me back and threw an arm around my chest and held me tight.

'Who cares about that? He'll be tighter than the women you fuck!'

He looked around at the other men who sniggered.

'He's better looking too. He'll keep me warm at night!'

The lad turned back just in time for the other man's huge fist to connect with his jaw, it sent him reeling backwards, carrying me with him. We collapsed on the ground, me still on top of him. He quickly pushed me off him, onto the muddy ground and jumped up quickly, fists presented to the big man.

The one like a bull, stepped between them, arms outstretched to keep them apart.

'Save it for the fucking fairies. We don't fight each other here.'

The man's words seemed to have a calming effect and the man he'd called Jack placed his stick back into the folds of his coat and stomped off, most of the others followed. I struggled to my feet, which felt so cold I hardly felt the ground beneath them. The wet mud that now covered my body only made me shiver even more. The big man grabbed Rimmer around the shoulder roughly.

'If I were you, I'd keep your mouth shut. He's a sly bastard, he'll slice your throat in the dark without a second thought. Now, grab this prisoner and bring him along. You never know, you might get to keep this one.'

The young guy nodded and rubbed his chin. 'Thanks Gunner.'

Rimmer snatched my arm as he started walking, with frozen feet that had little feeling and slippery mud I stumbled and fell against his slim body.

'Looks like he can't wait, don't it Gunner?'

I was roughly made to stand upright and the big man took my other arm and they dragged me between them. We didn't travel far. It was obvious this was a very small settlement. We passed groups of men, women and a few hollow-eyed children, all of them looked like they were only days away from dying of starvation. The children wore little, some of the younger ones had bare feet and I marvelled at how they coped. All of them watched me with blank expressions as though they'd been drained of emotion. They were all filthy and the stench of unwashed bodies turned the air rank.

Irvyn, whether he knew it or not, had led me into a world inhabited by savages where terror and torment ruled. I suspected these men were taking me to somewhere where things were going to get worse, knowing my luck.

Rimmer flung me down on the muddy earth close to a large, metal cylinder in which fire burned and radiated warmth. It appeared to be the only source in the whole camp. I looked up, scanned the crowd hovering around the fire until I saw an old woman. It must be a slave's instincts that alerts you to the source of power, it was obvious to me she was the one who dictated events. The huge men, including the cut-throat Jack, all deferred to her.

She leaned heavily on a wooden pole, one of her feet turned inward in a way that wasn't natural. She spoke to the man with a scar, who'd brought me in to the camp earlier.

'You found him where?'

It was obvious they didn't understand what was in the cave beneath their feet, to them it was just a hole in the ground.

'I don't understand how he got there,' she said, looking around the men for an answer and getting none. Without anything more to go on she shrugged.

'Oh well, one for the slavers when they next come a-calling.'

Jack shuffled his feet awkwardly.

'Do you think they'll be wanting him, with his dark skin an' all?'

The old woman sniffed and wiped her nose with the back of her hand, she jerked her head upwards to show she wanted me upright. Rimmer was quick to oblige. She hobbled close and jabbed my stomach with the top of her wooden pole.

'He's scrawny too. No muscle. We won't get much for him, you're right, but anything is better than nothing. Jake Bayle will be around in a couple of days, he'll take him.'

That got a snort of derision from everyone.

'A miser and a skinflint be he!' said someone in the crowd.

The old woman held up a twig-like arm and got silence instantly.

'As we paid nothing for him, whatever we get is profit. Stop your moaning!'

In the silence that followed her reprimand I decided to try my luck. I couldn't wait two days, only to be sold into slavery then. I had to take a risk. I hoped Master Darragh's lessons would pay off.

'Excuse me, my good lady,' I said to the old woman and bowed low. I got a gasp of surprise from the crowd which I hoped was a good thing. 'But I visit your home to search for a red dragon. Have you seen such a beast?'

Mouths opened like fish stranded on a shoreline.

The old woman was the first to reply. Her gaze reminded me a little of Lady Mab, the way her eyes drilled into mine.

'You're not a local boy.'

I smiled as innocently as I could, the worst thing to happen would be for them to work out my origins.

'Where are you from?'

Her tone sharpened and her gaze hardened.

'I look for a red dragon. Have you seen such a beast?'

I repeated the same thing in the hope they'd think I didn't understand anything else. As it was I found their accent hard to penetrate anyway.

'P'raps he don't speak English good?'

'He ain't from around here's, like.'

'Bloody foreigners, thought we'd got rid of 'em all.'

The old woman raised her hand and silence was restored.

'Why is he searching for a dragon?' she said. She turned to the man with the scar. 'You don't think he's a fairy do you?'

Scarface snorted laughter. 'With that colour skin? They're all fair-skinned bastards ain't they? Besides, how would he get here?'

The old woman continued staring at me. I continued smiling.

'That's my point. What if there's one of them gateway things they use, in that little cave? Go have a look now.'

The mood had changed. The dozens of pairs of eyes studied me with suspicion.

Rimmer stepped forward. 'Chief? I could get some answers out of him if you give me an hour or so. I'll tell you what he is then.'

She looked at him as if he was something she'd scraped off her boots.

'He doesn't sound like he speaks much of our language? How do you get answers then? Besides, judging by the condition of the last one I gave you, we wouldn't get anything for the little bastard.'

She gestured for the young man to move back into the crowd with a wave of a hand.

'Take him back, I've got more important things to do.'

With that the crowd dispersed. Gunner moved closer to me and kicked my backside hard, sending me sprawling face down onto the mud.

'You know where to go. Get going.'

I got up as quickly as I could and we made our way back to the stone building. The thought of being trapped in my cage, where they'd ignore me again, perhaps let me die during the night, was more than I could bear. I looked about me, for somewhere to run or to hide. Everywhere tents and tin shacks and people filled every little bit of space, squeezed together in their desperate need to stay alive. It was a need I shared.

It was obvious to me now Cochrann hadn't come through this portal, there was nowhere for her to go that these people couldn't have seen, they clearly had no knowledge of her. Irvyn had finally got his revenge. By sending me on this wild goose chase he had guaranteed I'd never return. I was going to be trapped here, a slave again, but in another world. My heart sank and I felt tears well up, my stomach churned and I wanted to vomit.

Rimmer joined us.

'I'll take him Gunner.'

The big man giggled deep in his chest. 'I bet you will, you horny fucker.'

There was a hoarse quality in the younger man's voice I noticed, the predatory way he looked at me fed my terror. I turned to the big man with eyes that pleaded for him to refuse the request.

'Come on Gunner. Let me. Please?'

The big man shook his head slowly. 'If we had one of those religious types that threaten you with Hell all the time, you'd have been roasted by now Rimmer. You know that, don't you?'

The young man nodded, still grinning. 'Why do you think I stay here. It's not for the scenery.'

The man he'd called Gunner shook his head again but was grinning now. 'You heard what the Chief said. She'll have your balls this time.'

Rimmer held up his hands in surrender but I could see something else in his eyes, I didn't like what I saw.

'Nothing like that this time. Just a man's need for satisfaction. You understand that.'

Suddenly, shouts and loud commands were everywhere, the camp dissolved into chaos. The big man looked around the camp urgently then shoved me at Rimmer.

'Put him back in a cage and get yourself to the main entrance. Quick!'

It may have been the slightest of pushes from the big man but I slammed against the young man's narrow chest. He caught me easily and grinned. He grabbed my hair and ran while I did everything I could to keep up with him. People were running in the opposite direction to us, knocking me aside in their hurry, yelling things, picking up weapons and looking worried.

The area around the derelict stone building was deserted. Rimmer let go of my hair and pushed me up against its wall, pressed one powerful arm against my neck. I could feel the weight of his body trapping me in position. He kicked one of my feet to one side and I yelped at the sudden pain in my ankle.

'Please do not hurt me.' It was a gasp, I could hardly breathe, the pressure he exerted was pushing the air out of my lungs.

His mouth was against my ear now, his breath hot, it smelled foul.

'I fucking knew it!' He breathed the words hoarsely. 'I knew you fucking spoke English. All that foreigner shit you were trying on them. I fucking saw through it.'

This man was going to do unspeakable things to me and there was nothing I could do to stop him. If I said too much he'd guess I wasn't human then his torment would be nothing compared to what the others would do. Tears burned my eyes and the growing lump in my throat made speech, even breathing, even more difficult.

'Who are you?' It was a whisper in my ear.

I could only sob.

He eased his pressure against me slightly and I hoped he might relent until I felt his hand push between our bodies and caress my buttocks. I sobbed harder. His hand reached further, parting my cheeks to explore between them.

'Who are you?' An insistent whisper. 'Tell me and I'll be gentle.'

'Please don't hurt me. Please.'

His voice, thick, hoarse and rasping now. 'Only if you tell me who you are. I prefer it rough you see. But if you tell me...'

His hand withdrew and I dared hope for a reprieve until I felt him tugging at his clothes.

'All right.' I sobbed. 'Please, don't hurt me. I'm no one really.'

He chuckled, it was not a nice sound. Then I felt his manhood, hot and stiff against my buttocks, his hand returned to parting them. I tried to scream but he pressed my body hard against the wall and all the air escaped in a strangled gasp.

'So who are you, pretty boy?'

My throat and lungs burned and speech felt almost impossible.

'I'm...'

'Fucking hell Rimmer, what did I tell you to do, you horny little shit!'

The weight pressing me against the stone wall vanished. I turned my head to see my abuser stagger backwards and fall on his backside in the mud, exposing himself as his fur coat flew open. Gunner and another man laughed.

'Fucking bastard Gunner! I had the little bastard about to tell me who he is. He understands English. I was just...'

Gunner went to kick him between the legs and the younger man rolled away quickly, covering himself in mud. The other man laughed wildly.

'We know what you was just about to do!' Gunner said.

The other man bundled me in a cage roughly and locked its door, hung the key on a peg on the stone wall. Gunner in the meantime helped Rimmer to his feet, still laughing. They positioned themselves either side of him.

'Come on. We've got visitors. The Chief wants all the Watch present.'

As the three of them ambled off Rimmer turned to look over his shoulder and pursed his lips before giving me a wide grin.

I knelt in the cage and trembled uncontrollably, every muscle shook and left me begging unknown powers to help me get home. Fear gripped me tightly so I couldn't breathe except in short gasps that never quite filled my lungs. Every sound made me jump. He would be back, he would wait until dark, he would satisfy himself on me and I would not be able to call myself a man from that moment. There were stories of what the High Lord had done to men who had tried to stop him from ascending to the throne, stories that meant other men pointed at them and laughed and women kept their distance.

I cried. I only stopped when two children were marched towards me. They were guarded by the men I'd encountered, what Gunner had called the Watch. The children were identical, a muscular girl whose face was covered in blood from a recent beating, she was manacled at the wrists. The boy, slight and hunted, had obviously had a beating from Jack. Both of them were half-naked.

Rimmer was there, holding the boy tightly to his body, grinning.

He bundled the kid into the cage next to mine, tying him up so he couldn't move. He leaned over to me, the grin still there.

'You can watch me fuck this one first. Then it'll be you.'

The threat, spoken loud enough for the boy to hear, scared him so much he started to cry. I'd been doing the same thing only moments before but now I held his eyes and tried to convey reassurance. It must have worked because he took deep breaths and stopped weeping. The girl fought like an animal as she was pushed into her cage, her hands were buried in the dirt and tied into position there. She continued to spit and hurl curses, despite her injuries.

It was only after they'd gone and as night fell, that she gave in to the tears that we all shared as we tried hard not to think of what the morning would hold for us all.

Chapter 18

'She's certainly proven her worth, hasn't she?'

There was no need to glance in Oisin's direction to know he'd be looking over his shoulder, with the expression of a proud father, at the wyvern trotting behind us. I'd lost count of the times he'd said the same thing. I wasn't sure he even realised he was repeating himself. I'd stopped replying in the hope he'd get the message. Apparently, he hadn't.

He must have ignored the dried blood around the animal's mouth, still preferring to think of it as a pet. Even so, after such an intelligent display of battle tactics, I had to admit she was an asset, one we might need in any conflict with Llyr's forces.

The road to Burrow Mump had been empty and without any further delays or threats and we'd made good time. Just like we had with Hamdon Hill, we'd aimed for the bump on the horizon and hoped, this time, we didn't find more slaughter. As we approached we could see movement in the small settlement at the top of the hill, centred around a derelict church, it had to be a relatively positive sign. Of course no community these days welcomed visitors, we still ran the considerable risk of attack, I made the point as clearly as possible.

'We need to be careful now, they'll see us coming and there's bound to be a welcoming party. Remember, we only use your pet if everything goes to shit.'

Oisin didn't like me referring to the wyvern as his pet so he frowned but nodded all the same.

Burrow Mump was a smaller fortification than Hamdon Hill. At its base a small shanty town had developed, over which two wooden towers stretched into the sky that threatened much.

As we approached a loud, course voice reached us. 'Stay where you are.'

I kept riding and called back. 'See my red friend behind us? Try telling it to stop and see what happens to those wooden towers.'

There was no reply. Inside its wooden walls there'd be panic and confusion. We needed to arrive before it turned into anything strategically planned so I stirred my horse to a gallop. Behind me the wyvern's paws beat a heavy rhythmic thump like a war drum.

An avenue of the same pathetic shacks we'd seen the day before stretched in front of us and led to a closed wooden gate. I felt dozens of nervous pairs of eyes watch us but no one was visible. I called up to the tower above me where I could see movement.

'Do you want the wyvern to demolish the gate or are you going to open it?'

With a lot of creaking the gate opened and we rode inside.

The place was a down-market version of Hamdon Hill, the kind of place estate agents would have called 'up and coming' a long time ago. It was a dump in every sense of the word. Its inhabitants were the dregs of humanity, though not from their own choosing. Too many of them lived in too small a space with too few resources, and these were the lucky ones with a high wall to hide behind. Men shambled into a large group, dressed in furs supplemented with the remains of clothes which had survived the years since they'd been bought in shops. The women looked oppressed and mistreated, several bore fresh bruises and wore rags and repeatedly-mended clothes that hung off their emaciated bodies. A handful of kids hung back to see the monster, fearful and bare-footed. Their desperate lives reminded me of the boy I'd invited into my kitchen so long ago.

'Where's that bastard Joe Purdey!' I yelled at the assembled mass of humanity.

I got blank-eyed stares. I couldn't tell if it was a sign of their demoralised plight or a sullen resentment that didn't have the energy to boil into anger. At the rear of the mob, movement, a narrow gap opened. Out of it limped a woman holding a wooden pole she clung to with determination. She didn't look any different to the other women, her hair had been shaved to the scalp and she was filthy but her expression told me she was their leader.

She stopped in front of my horse.

'You wouldn't be so fucking high and mighty if you didn't have that four-legged corruption.' She nodded at the wyvern.

'Perhaps not. But as I have, I'm going to ask you one more time before I order it to turn this shithole into matchwood. Where's that bastard Purdey?'

She glared at me with a hatred that could ignite tinder. My quarry ambled through the same gap in the crowd and stood behind the woman.

'It's all right Chief. I'm used to dealing with this arrogant bastard.' Purdey turned his one eye on me and applied the same level of hatred as the old woman. His two henchmen arrived at his side, just as they had outside the cottage. I felt my anger boil.

'You left the party early Purdey. You didn't see what happened to the last lot of people who made me fucking angry. Such as that religious maniac who you left us with, the one who tried to burn us alive. He had great fun riding the wyvern, we left his flock picking up bits of him.'

Expressions of fear mixed with hostility spread around the crowd like a virus.

Purdey flexed his shoulders and took a deep breath, his ruin of a face was set into determined rebellion. When he spoke it was loud enough for everyone to hear.

'There are two of you and that creature. I'm betting we could all teach you a lesson.'

I snorted my contempt loud enough for everyone to hear. I'd come across men like him before, ones with military training who assumed they commanded the respect and cooperation needed for others to carry out their orders. Often they fooled themselves. But not always.

'True. I wonder how many of your friends are willing to die to win that bet?'

A quick glance around the assembled wretches and refugees suggested little enthusiasm, they might not like me but life was a daily battle, it made no sense to go searching for death.

'Especially when I'm here to collect the two kids who might end this war with the fairies.'

That turned the tide. Dozens of pairs of eyes turned to Purdey and he knew it.

'You're not still telling that tale are you?'

'You see, Purdey, if you weren't so eager to make money by selling them as slaves, you'd have realised by their special skills they're not normal kids. They're built to fight the fairies. You know that, don't you? You saw the girl kill the fairies that butchered the Taunton Gang on Hamdon Hill.'

That brought a loud gasp from the assembled populace.

'But you've put your greed ahead of your desire to help your own race.'

Hostility shifted. Now the crowd glared at Purdey and mumbled their discontent.

'I didn't. I just wanted...'

The woman at his side turned to him. 'You didn't tell me about this.'

I let my voice dominate the dissention.

'I want those kids now. We've got an appointment in Glastonbury to defeat the fairy king and we haven't got time to waste.'

Before anyone said another word I got off my horse, signalled to Oisin to stay with the wyvern, and walked towards the narrow gap where Purdey had come from. The crowd parted without a word. I didn't trust these people as I walked the gamut of hard stares, through the mass of stinking humanity.

There were metal cages against the wall of the derelict church. These weren't prisons with beds or chairs or even a basin for a toilet. They were animal cages just big enough to accommodate a human being; they showed the value these people placed on human life. Slavery was a common feature of life in this land now and it angered me that humans should have returned to the same immoral society as the one where I'd grown up.

The twins were in two of the cages. I looked at the denizens around me as their eyes waited for my reaction.

241

They expected me to erupt, do something irrational and perhaps overextend myself and so become vulnerable. I took a breath and tried to rein in the fury that threatened to consume me.

As I got closer I saw thick ropes binding Finn by his ankles and wrists to the cage. The few clothes he wore were covered in muck and blood. The milk white skin on his back had fresh whip marks across it.

Brea knelt on all fours, like a dog with a collar around her neck. Her hands were buried in the mud, manacles around her wrist held her hands in place. She wore few clothes, her shirt barely covered her bare backside. Her face was a mass of bruises and her bottom lip was badly swollen.

These were kids I'd made a solemn vow to their father to protect and I'd failed, failed beyond all belief. The erupting anger that rose in me wasn't only directed at the men running towards me now. I was to blame but I'd deal with that issue later. The men following me must have sensed my fury and chose to pre-empt my reaction, so they attacked. Wrong choice. The self-control I'd hoped to preserve snapped. Veins in my head throbbed, my heart beat a loud tattoo in my chest and the world turned red as fury overwhelmed me and the need to shed blood became an obsession.

An obsession Puck happily obliged. When he arrives I remember little, just a few images. They are always indelibly etched into my memory.

Joe Purdey raising a sword against me, my own blade slicing across his ruin of a face, bearing bones and the grey matter in his head to the world. Yanking my blade out to deal with his burly sergeant major lunging at me with an axe, easily swatting it aside and slicing off his arm in the process, his friend raising a gun to take aim and me scything off his hand and a leg. Another man, also badly scarred, wielding another sword, letting it sweep downward to slice through his leg, dropping him to the ground, stamping on his chest and shattering ribs in the process. Another man, huge and hairy, rushing me with a fiery branch taken from an oil cylinder, opening up his belly as he twists to swing it at me. A younger man, eyes wild with lunacy, rushing at me with a long metal pole as though it's a lance. Stepping aside, lopping off his head as he draws level. Others watching me with the wariness of cowardice, unwilling to attack because they understand the inevitable outcome.

I'm left with a terrible weakness seeping through my body, like every drop of blood has being drained, it announces the return of Puck to his dark dungeon.

It was always this way, for as long as I wish I couldn't remember.

It's like waking from a nightmare.

Joe Purdey's body lay hunched at my feet, his head split in two. There was carnage everywhere, bodies with blood pooled around them and my sword daubed with gore. Men screamed, writhed in agony and howled for help or death. They got the latter when those around them got sick of the noise.

If the local population had been scared of the red-scaled wyvern at the entrance, they looked even more fearful of the red-spattered monster in front of them now, Puck certainly knew how to get respect. When I gave the command for the twins to be freed there was a free-for-all to oblige. The leader continued to watch me.

'They were like this when they arrived,' she said. There was no apology, no regret just the assertion that they couldn't be blamed and suffer a similar fate. I didn't care.

The twins stumbled towards me, holding each other like children left to face abject terror, with only each other for comfort. They said nothing but looked at me with a mixture of relief, exhaustion and horror on their faces. I had no idea what to say, everything sounded trite so I let silence speak for me.

Finn gestured with a shaking hand behind him.

'There's another one.' His voice a dry croak.

Along the wall were more cages, all of them empty save for one. I walked towards it, found an equally pathetic creature, a young man, completely naked, with skin the colour of chocolate. His eyes were also filled with terror and his injuries explained why. The last thing I needed was another responsibility but I couldn't leave the lad. The darkness of his skin labelled him a victim, someone different who, like me, humanity held responsible for their current mess.

'Let him out,' I called.

'Wait!' the woman said, holding up her wooden pole in some sort of gesture of authority. 'He isn't yours! He belongs to us!'

I was in front of her in a second, knocked her pole away so she lost her balance and only remained standing because those around her held her upright.

'He isn't yours. He isn't something to be owned. He's a human being. A fucking human being.'

Despite my weakness rage bubbled up and threatened to explode again. I think my impending rage was visible on my face because the old woman and the whole crowd froze.

'You're as bad as the Fae! If they conquer you, they'll make slaves of you all. They'll treat you as commodities, to be bought and sold. You need to be better than that. If you lose your humanity they will defeat you, then this life will be paradise in comparison.'

I stood in their midst, my tempest exhausted by the look of incomprehension on their stupid faces.

'Take him!' the woman spat. 'And leave us.'

I glared at her. 'You'll clean them up and give them clothes to wear or so help me, I will wreak havoc on this place, without the help of that fucking dragon!'

They obliged.

I waited, sword at the ready in case they needed extra motivation. A little while later, washed clean of muck, wearing clothes that were covered in it, the three returned. They each looked around at the stern and resentful faces as though there was a risk their good fortune might come to an abrupt and brutal end. We walked the length of the fort with me like a drum major in a marching band with my sword held aloft as a threat.

The moment we arrived at the entrance to the fort the dark-skinned lad let out a squeal of surprise, looked abashed at his behaviour and slammed both hands over his mouth as though he regretted his action. At which point all hell broke loose.

The wyvern went berserk.

At least that's what the mob thought was happening. They ran screaming for safety.

I had no option but to dive out of its way and hoped the others would do the same but the lad stood his ground. I was vaguely aware of a grin on his face as I watched from my position on the muddy ground as the animal thundered to greet the lad. I thought it was about to kill him as it placed its crested head against his body, vivid memories of how it used the position to disembowel the Questing Beast came to mind. Except now it did it with such delicacy and care.

The young man stroked its head, spoke softly to the animal, its reply sounded like a purr from deep in its chest. They stayed like that, like lovers, for several moments. The locals gradually gained the courage to step out from the places of safety to marvel at the sight.

'We need to leave,' I said with as much authority as I could muster, though if the wyvern wanted to disobey, I knew I couldn't do anything about it.

The young man said something to the animal and it walked alongside him as he passed through the gate, beyond the shanty town and into the field beyond. The rest of us followed, astonished by their partnership. Oisin treated the animal like a pet but this was something else and he watched the two of them with poorly-concealed resentment.

We took shelter in a copse of beech trees, far enough away from the settlement and hidden from view. Small flakes of snow began to fall. The twins huddled together, they were a pathetic portrait of exhaustion with their normally pale skin now a sickly pallor, their jade-green eyes surrounded by black circles. I needed to find a place where they could recover.

When I said as much they looked at me empty of expression, drained of any emotion or reaction. They still hadn't spoken.

Oisin beckoned me over, we moved to the edge of the copse and pretended to watch the wyvern and the young man display their affection for one another.

'Perhaps we should go back to that farm in Langport, give these kids chance to recover. They're useless to us at the moment,' I whispered.

Oisin shook his head, placed a hand on my arm, looked at me with an expression I couldn't read.

'I found out there is a portal here, though they don't know it as anything other than an ancient artefact. There's no sign of any spriggans either.'

'Where?'

'It's not in the settlement. It's in the hill itself, in a small cave.'

I frowned. 'Why are you telling me this?'

Oisin nodded his head towards the twins, their heads resting against each other, eyes closed, holding hands.

'You're right, they need somewhere to recover. But they're too exhausted and traumatised to travel.'

'What are you suggesting?'

He looked at me, reading my expression carefully, weighing up what to say.

'This place is so small, so insignificant, I don't think anyone knows about it. We might be able to use the portal to return to Glastonbury.'

He kept watching me as I processed the idea. It was risky and he knew it. He also knew if anything went wrong, I'd blame him. We could meet Llyr and his army who might be travelling in the opposite direction. But Oisin knew I had to accept our limitations, the twins couldn't travel. If we met any more opposition they'd be no use defending us, I needed to get them somewhere safe where they could rest. Plus, in Glastonbury we'd have help.

'If we travelled through the portal to the Tor, we'd be near to Amelie's cottage.'

It was Oisin's turn to nod. He jerked a thumb at the young man.

'What about him?'

I sighed. He was an enigma but Oisin summed it up better than me.

'He can't be human, not to have such an affinity with the wyvern.'

He didn't give the animal its name I noticed.

'Yeah. I'd reached that conclusion too. There's something about him, his skin colour particularly, that is nudging my memory. Let me talk to him.'

Oisin held my arm again.

'You know Llyr could have sent him here, as a spy.'

I nodded and ambled over to where the lad sat on a tree stump and stroked the wyvern that lay curled at his feet now.

'You've got quite a friend there, haven't you?'

I sat next to him. He turned his head and smiled shyly. I noticed how he glanced at me for a second too long, as though expecting me to do something.

'You don't recognise me, do you Mister Goodfellow?'

I smiled a knowing smile, as though I'd been about to declare his identity, while hiding my surprise at the lad using my real name.

'Of course I do.' I whispered softly. 'I didn't want to say anything in front of the others.'

He grinned then grimaced as he rubbed the dark bruise on his cheek. The kid had clearly suffered, if he was a spy he was a very frightened one. The more I looked at him now, the more my memory itched at a vague recollection.

'No, you don't. Why should you. It was a long time ago and I'm a nobody.'

I pointed at the wyvern. 'She doesn't think that.'

'No.' He stroked the top of the animal's head, fingers lightly caressing the red crest. 'She's the only one though. They are tremendous loyal animals, Mister Goodfellow, I had to return that loyalty. It's why I came looking for her.'

This young man was certainly an enigma. I looked closely at the curtains of black hair dangling over his face that he kept brushing out of the way, at the intense black eyes and the fine bone structure of his face. He knew I was looking at him and kept smiling as I tried to place him.

'Still can't place me?'

I shook my head.

He sighed heavily. 'Let me help. Imagine my voice belongs to the High Lord.' He took a breath and curled his lip and spoke with the same oily derision. 'Shit stain!'

And recollection dawned. The young man, eyes saddened by the slur, smiled but there was huge sadness behind it.

'You're a kitchen slave aren't you. Kai? Kane?'

'Keir sir.'

'Keir!' I remembered the occasions when Llyr's spoilt-brat behaviour used to embarrass me when I was climbing the social ladder of the Dark Court and wasn't prepared to challenge his moronic conduct. The lad had suffered terribly.

Another mind worm suddenly began to burrow deep in my memory. I stared at the lad and saw in those eyes something else. I knew then that I wasn't dealing with a spy.

'Tell me Keir, is Master Sidwell still running the palace single-handedly?'

The lad nodded and smiled. 'Yes sir. He helped prepare me to visit this realm.'

'He still keeps watch over you does he?'

Another nod. 'I let him down badly a little while ago.' He patted the wyvern absently. 'I kept her secret for a time and it meant lying to people, including Master Sidwell.'

The lad fiddled with a ring on this finger nervously. He noticed me looking and immediately stopped it.

'But he's forgiven you no doubt?' I said.

A hesitant nod this time, there was tension there suddenly.

'What? I can't imagine Master Sidwell doing anything cruel to you.'

The lad turned and looked at me, there was uncertainty in his eyes suddenly but it passed.

'Yes, mostly. We found out we had... more important things to talk about.'

'And you came here to look for your wyvern. A servant. Who wouldn't be allowed to leave the palace without permission, never mind travel through the forbidden portals. I think it's about time you were completely honest with me Keir.'

He went back to fidgeting with his ring, even when I continued to watch him. I gave the lad my best reassuring smile.

'It's because, if I return with Cochrann, my wyvern, I can be a dragon trainer.'

'I see, that sounds exciting.'

He'd lost some of his nervousness, the lad wasn't lying. It told me what I needed to know. I smiled at him again. This young man didn't know what he was. Master Sidwell did, it was why he'd watched over him. There was also that ring on his finger.

For the first time since Llyr had attacked my home, I began to see a way in which I might solve a lot of people's problems, including mine. I ruffled the guy's hair affectionately and he looked at me, baffled.

Chapter 19

Master Goodfellow frightened me.

I was in awe of him as well, perhaps that was the same thing. I've watched lots of fights in the lists during Lughnasa celebrations but never anything like the way he killed all those men. His sword was a blur and he moved like water, every action flowed into the next so you couldn't tell in advance what he was going to do. It was like a dance, a bloody and violent dance. What scared me most was his face, it was without any expression, it was completely blank. Everyone has some kind of expression on their face, to see someone without any emotion at all, I think that's what frightened me most, that he could kill and not be affected by it.

Then, when it was over, he looked at the bodies and his face started to change slowly, like it was made of ice and had started to thaw. He stood there, not moving for at least a minute, while everyone stared at him like he was a monster. We all looked at him as though there was someone, or something, inhabiting his body and it had left him.

He was different to the man I'd known in the palace so long ago. He had been a clown, a mischief-maker, the sort of person everyone liked to be around. I hardly recognised him. Not because he'd changed physically, there were a few more lines on his face and he still had the body of an athlete, the kind women like, though I know he isn't interested in women. He'd changed because all that mischief and humour had gone. He looked so serious and angry and... scary.

When he came to sit next to me I was so frightened I'd have runaway if Cochrann hadn't been there, I knew she'd protect me. But I was excited at the same time. He was Robin Goodfellow. I'd once dreamed of being as popular as him. It's the thing about being a slave, you're no one; then someone like him wants to talk to you like you're their equal, well, it makes you feel special.

I got worried when he started to look at me strangely, he stared for a few seconds and then gave me this weird smile. That was when he started asking lots of questions; about why I'd come to the human realm. I told him about being a dragon trainer but he kind of saw through that, he knew I couldn't have got here without powerful help. I didn't want to tell him about Lady Mab but he got it out of me. Like I said, I was afraid.

He got excited then. His eyes sparkled, just like they did when he played a prank on someone. I always liked it when the prank was on Prince Llyr. He used to make him look really foolish.

Then everything turned serious. He explained what I had to do. He said it with so much speed I didn't understand all of it and he had to explain a second time, he slowed down that time. I didn't understand why he was so excited.

I was to go home and give Lady Mab a message and I had to hurry.

When I asked him why I was doing these things he wouldn't say, just that the lives of a huge number of people depended on it. Then he said something that scared me even more. He said that if I could bring Lady Mab here it would start a chain of events that would change my life forever. He must have realised how much that scared me because he patted my shoulder and told me I was braver than I realised.

He looked at me, straight into my eyes, then asked me if I was happy in the palace. Obviously I told him I wasn't. I was a hybrid and didn't have any choice about my life so I didn't understand how I could ever be happy.

He laughed then. Actually laughed. The others turned to look at him. Master Oisin, looked astonished when he heard the sound.

The next words Master Goodfellow spoke took my breath away.

'If you return with Mab quickly enough, you will become more important than you can imagine.'

I wasn't certain if that made me feel scared or excited. I pointed out that I couldn't make Lady Mab do anything she didn't want to do, she might not even listen to me. He grinned, he had this strange expression on his face by now. He sighed, very deeply, it was such a sad sound and proved how much he'd changed.

'Tell her that you've spoken with Robin Goodfellow; he knows about her plan and he won't cooperate unless she's there to watch it.'

He said she'd understand what he meant.

We waited until dark before I showed everyone where the portal was located so the local people weren't worried by our return with Cochrann. Apparently Master Oisin had called her Scathach but admitted Red Girl was better. I didn't mention that he'd used a name of a very frightening woman in the palace who'd be angry at him for calling a wyvern after her.

We returned to the cave. Its entrance was a squeeze for Cochrann but she followed me inside readily enough, I think she thought we were going home. I wanted to take her but Master Goodfellow said he needed her. When I asked him why, he didn't hear. It was terrible, leaving her again after such a short time together. I massaged the spot by her ear and kept repeating that I'd come back for her. I was glad it was dark, so the others didn't see me cry.

The front of the cave was partly hidden by a heavy curtain of ivy and long grass, beneath it a little stream tumbled down the hill, which was why it smelled so damp.

In the centre of the cave was the archway. I could tell no one looked after it because the stone blocks were crumbling and the mortar holding them together had all but disappeared, it was covered by mould and lichens now. Master Goodfellow said the humans didn't understand how to use the portals, it didn't surprise me, my injuries proved what savages they were. I wanted to leave this realm as quickly as possible.

The Knight children were unwilling to travel though the portal. The girl thought it was a trap and argued with Master Goodfellow that either Master Oisin or I was a spy and we'd betray everyone. Neither of them had spoken until that point and it surprised me, I thought they'd be glad he'd rescued them, even risked his life.

The girl was so angry. We'd all suffered at the hands of the men who'd locked us in the cages, the girl perhaps most of all, but that was because she had fought like an animal. I tried to explain what life was like as a slave, if you behaved like an animal you got treated like one, that it was better to do as you were told. She called me names and said I wasn't a proper man if I thought that.

The boy was different, I think he understood that I was trying to help them. Once or twice he'd smiled at me, though only when the girl wasn't looking. In the end Master Goodfellow said we were travelling through the portal and that was the end of it. The girl didn't look happy at all.

I put the crystal onto its plates at the base of the archway to activate the portal. It made Cochrann uneasy when the energy formed but I stroked her nose, that calmed her.

Master Goodfellow watched the curtain for a few seconds and when he didn't move I thought something was wrong. He smiled at me and said he hadn't used a portal for a very long time and had forgotten how beautiful they were. I hadn't seen many, and even though this one was old and poorly maintained, I knew what he meant. It lacked the quantity of energy that makes the big ones fizz like sparkling wine, this one looked like a waterfall of lemonade. It poured out of the keystone and tumbled to the cave floor where it grounded itself.

Cochrann remained uneasy so Master Goodfellow went through first, followed by the others to reassure her everything was all right. Except it wasn't. Even as I led Cochrann though the yellow cascade of light that made our skin tingle, on the other side something was wrong. We stepped out of the curtain into the ante-chamber with its three archways, it had been dimly lit when I'd used it before, now there was only darkness. It was impossible to see anything. The other two portals weren't activated but on the walls large crystals should have illuminated the room.

'It's an ambush,' the male Knight called out.

Then everything was chaos.

Clashing swords echoed off the wooden walls, Master Goodfellow yelled at us to stand behind him but it was too dark to see where he was. Suddenly there was a loud cracking sound and white light stabbed the darkness, blinding us briefly. In that split second I saw things moving, dark shapes but what they were, I couldn't tell.

A few seconds later an arc of light flashed across the room, like sheet lightning, branching in all directions. It hung there long enough to see a small group of boggarts shield their eyes and someone in their midst wearing a dark cloak and hood. I watched Master Goodfellow run his sword through the round belly of one of the creatures as it tried to recover from the light. It snorted and fell, its enormous tusks smashed the floor. The other boggarts reacted, raising swords quickly but blindly staggering into each other in the process. Boggarts are not very clever, the tusks that jut upwards from the lower jaws can be lethal but on the slippery wooden floor their hooves had little purchase and it made them snort their frustration through their narrow snouts.

The girl's energies flickered out and I heard her gasp with exhaustion but it had given me enough time to notice one of the light crystals was askew. Our attackers must have moved them so we were forced to fight in darkness. Boggarts' eyes are small and beady so they don't like light, they prefer darkness for that reason.

I shuffled towards the light, fumbled around trying to find the crystal and became aware of a boggart nearby, purely because of its horrible smell. I froze, expecting to feel its blade cut me down. Instead there was a high-pitched squeal, a loud thump and Cochrann's distinctive snort of satisfaction, she must have been next to me, providing protection.

I shifted the crystal in its cradle and pale yellow light pooled around me. All eyes turned in my direction but the boggarts' focus was not on me but on the hulking shape of the wyvern at my side. The ante-chamber wasn't built for creatures her size, she had little room for manoeuvre but it was enough to snap at the nearest boggart. She bit its legs with one snap of her powerful jaws and the pig-like creature fell forward to writhe and scream until she stomped it into silence.

It was enough to make the rest retreat to the far corner of the chamber where a couple frantically fought each other to activate the portal.

In the confusion and semi-darkness it took us a moment to notice Master Goodfellow fighting with the man in the black cloak. It was a fight like none I'd seen before. The cloaked figure was as skilful with his blade as Master Goodfellow, if not better. We all watched anxiously and ignored the escaping boggarts who'd opened one of the portals. It filled the room with a pale green light and created long shadows as the two warriors fought.

The thing worrying me most was the expression on Master Goodfellow's face. When he'd killed the men in the camp he wore no expression, his face was a mask. Now there was intense concentration, I could see his shock at realising no matter what he did with his sword, the cloaked man had prepared for it. What was worse, some attacks came with such force or from an unexpected angle it left Master Goodfellow reeling, fending off a blade so close it had us gasping and holding our breath. The attack was so relentless it caused Master Goodfellow to make mistakes and lose ground or his balance, when that happened the assault by the cloaked figure intensified.

No one spoke. We daren't in case it distracted him.

Master Oisin turned to me, he looked very pale as he nodded at the wyvern; I knew what he was thinking, she could attack the cloaked figure. Trouble was, she had so little room to move around that she would be more of a distraction than an asset, I knew the skilled swordsman needed less than a second to land the fatal blow. I shook my head while Master Oisin looked like he was about to cry.

The man in the cloak, though he looked to be more of a skeleton than a man, lunged forward and Master Goodfellow staggered backwards towards the open portal. I realised what was happening, what strategy the cloaked figure had in mind. He was going to take the fight through the portal, that was why the boggarts had left it open, the whole thing was a trap.

Master Goodfellow must have realised it too because his face started to change, his expressions drained away, to be replaced by a fierceness in his eyes and in his swordplay. Even then, their battle didn't ease, it just got quicker so that blades were lost in a blur, where heavy breathing was the only sound as they got nearer and nearer to the pale green light.

The girl, who'd been getting more and impatient, broke loose from her brother's grip, he'd been holding her arm I realised. She stepped forward and with a loud grunt fired a bolt of energy into the back of the cloaked attacker. The girl staggered, her brother caught her and lowered her to the ground. The cloaked man staggered as a thin wisp of smoke rose out of his back, Master Goodfellow lunged forward, ran the man though and almost collapsed with exhaustion.

Master Oisin rushed forward to help his friend who leaned against the wall and slowly slid down it. Distracted for that second the skeletal attacker staggered through the portal, leaving a trail of blood, and disappeared as the portal closed.

It plunged us into near darkness again so I hurried to straighten the rest of crooked crystals so we could see clearly.

Master Goodfellow sat on the floor, his face white and covered in sweat. The girl lay on the floor, I think she had passed out when she'd blasted the cloaked man. Her brother looked concerned and scared in equal amounts. There was little I could do but stroke Cochrann and keep her calm.

It took several minutes for everyone to recover, the boy urged everyone to leave the room in case their attacker returned with more boggarts, I reassured him Cochrann would deal with them. The girl woke up and screamed at Master Goodfellow.

'I told you! I told you it wasn't safe to use the portal! One of them set us up!'

She waved a hand at Master Oisin and me then glared at Master Goodfellow with such vehemence it shocked me. He'd just risked his life to protect us and this was how she thanked him! The boy tried to calm her but she brushed his hand away impatiently.

No one replied, which was probably best and we waited in tense silence for Master Goodfellow to say something.

He stood up, a little unsteadily, looked at me.

'You know what to do Keir. And be quick.'

The two Knights and Master Oisin looked at me suspiciously. I felt my face turn red.

The others asked what he meant but all they received was an exhausted shake of the head.

'You know where to return with her, don't you?'

260

I nodded. That wasn't the difficult part. Persuading one of the most powerful people in the Dark Court to follow the instructions of a servant was a different matter. I knew better than to say anything though.

Cochrann watched me closely, she knew I was leaving her again and she whined softly. I stroked her nose and told her I'd come back for her. Everyone else looked impatient, they didn't understand how badly I felt about leaving her. I knew they'd use her as a weapon and it made me worry for her.

Mister Goodfellow jerked his head towards the portal that had just closed, my signal to leave obviously. I hoped the boggarts and the cloaked figure weren't waiting on the other side. I re-activated the portal so that its green energy cascaded to the floor once more. On the other side I could see the vague outlines of a field and a couple of trees but no boggarts and cloaked figures. I looked at the downcast head of my wyvern for the last time and stepped into the light, wiping tears from my eyes.

Chapter 20

Exhaustion does strange things to you. It turns certainty into doubt, affection to distrust and belief into blame. All those things registered on the exhaustion meter for me. I sat quietly in Amelie's kitchen with a hot cup of lavender tea, inhaling its sweet scent as I tried to reassure myself. Everyone had left me alone. I wasn't handling my present situation well. Amelie had packed the twins off to bed and told Oisin to feed and stable the wyvern, she had gone to help; her diplomatic way of avoiding my irritable behaviour.

Ankou had almost beaten me. Brea's intervention had made the difference. I was a soldier, pain was a familiar friend but now that pain was in a part of me that had never felt its hurt before. In my pride. I was the one to bring an end to a fight normally, not a traumatised and exhausted teenage girl.

Brea didn't care about that, as far as she was concerned I'd led them into trouble, despite the warnings I'd chosen to ignore. Then the most hurtful thing of all; she'd learned that the only person to keep her and her brother safe, was her.

She was right and it led to me blame myself, to doubt my ability to protect not only the twins but anyone I loved. A conclusion that pitched me deeper into that dark pit than I'd ever fallen before. It was so deep I was still falling.

When you have one doubt, it summons others and they swarm. You distrust everything you think you know, reality unravels like a cheap sweater. You distrust people and it slowly turns into paranoia. I no longer knew who to believe any longer.

I doubted Oisin most of all. I'd started to think the impossible; he and Ankou were connected in some way. I'd been sent on a wild goose chase so Ankou could hold him hostage at Hamdon Hill. His suggestion to use the portal had allowed Ankou to lay in wait with his band of boggarts? Apart from Brea, we'd been saved by the wyvern, I couldn't escape that irony. I'd been the one who'd constantly wanted to leave her behind. Now I trusted her because she couldn't be manipulated.

One thing eluded me. Who might be pulling Oisin's strings. He wouldn't be the one initiating the treachery, I knew him better than that. But he might be the means.

The same thing was true for Keir. He'd led us to the portal but my doubts went beyond that simple coincidence. The lad was following Mab's orders. It made no sense for her to use a kitchen slave to do her dirty work, unless she knew his secret, though placing him in such danger didn't make sense either. She was a strategic thinker, ambitious, a woman in a man's world forced to abandon her sexuality to achieve respect whilst also being one of the fiercest warriors I'd ever known. I'd respected Mab when she'd been my commanding officer but I couldn't work out how her ambitions connected with someone as honest as Keir unless he was oblivious of her motives. Something about his hesitation, whenever I'd mentioned Mab, hinted at this but I couldn't see him being complicit. Perhaps I was wrong.

Questions buzzed around my head like insistent flies and failed to produce answers. As I plummeted to the bottom of the pit I thought back on everything that had happened.

I'd left my cottage to protect the Knights and fulfil my obligation to Alec, yet I'd put their lives in danger. I'd pledged to kill Llyr, when I had the opportunity Oisin persuaded me otherwise which led to me being hunted. Now, the political machinations in Tir na nÓg threatened everything.

I'd been ready to sacrifice my life to fulfil my obligations, my final attempt to carry out a noble act, having been guilty of so many ignoble ones. Yet Brea and the wyvern had prevented my body from littering an ante-chamber in an obscure portal between the two realms. It would have been a fitting irony, as someone who didn't fit in to either.

I appreciated Ankou's bitterness. I suppose he wanted to die too. Oberon and Llyr were the ones who forced him to continue living a life of violence. I couldn't escape the similarity of our situations. We'd both been Trooping Fairies, we'd been told repeatedly we served no other purpose than to slaughter our enemies. It was probably inevitable we'd end our days trying to kill each other, as murderers steeped in violence and blood. In the last few hours alone, I'd slain men out of pure hatred, adding to my ever-expanding body count. I'd exiled myself to a life of misery to avoid such casual butchery but here I was still doing it, just in a different place and for slightly different reasons.

The handle of my mug snapped off in my hand, to tumble to the floor and smash into a thousand pieces. I stared at the mess, uncertain how it had happened. Light from a lantern appeared suddenly to illuminate the bits of broken crockery and Amelie stood at my side.

'You need to get some sleep.'

I tried to object and met a face as stern as her voice.

'Go to bed. You look like Death.'

I snorted. 'I hope not. I'd like his skill with a sword though.'

Amelie's hand cuffed the side of my head sharply and made me yelp.

'You were probably seen on your journey from the Tor portal, that fucking red wyvern isn't exactly inconspicuous. My friends are keeping a look out but I'm not sacrificing them a third time, Robin. I want you out of here, first thing in the morning.'

I glanced up at the old woman, at her arm bound up in a sling. The cottage was quiet without Major to growl at me when I stepped out of line and his pack to bark and howl. I smiled sadly at her. I hadn't apologised for the trouble I'd caused and now was too late. She wiped her nose with the back of her hand.

'You can have my bed.' She jerked her head at Oisin standing timidly behind her. 'But only to sleep in.'

He rolled his eyes, and when I tried to object a second time, he took hold of my arm and led me upstairs. I collapsed on the bed, he sat in a large but uncomfortable chair until I told him I was too tired to be a threat and he should sleep on the bed. He did as he was told.

I stared up at the ceiling, savouring the mattress' comfort, aware of Oisin's body and reprimanded the urges that fought their way to my bloodstream. reminded myself that I was probably lying next to a liar and a spy, someone who had put us all in mortal danger. Thoughts buzzed in my head again and drove sleep away. Until that point I hadn't considered how my feelings for him coloured my decisions but now, as I listened to his gentle breathing and inhaled his scent, the buzzing focused on that possibility.

Like a dying man, life flashed past me as I relived the moments since he'd entered my life, the buzzing turned into a low hum as some of my doubts turned into real possibilities.

I turned on my side to look at his dark outline. The full moon peeked through thin curtains to shed silvery light across his handsome features. He turned in my direction.

'You're too tired. Remember?'

I smiled. 'We've spent several nights together haven't we? Like old times.'

It was his turn to smile.

I threw myself on top of his body, grabbed him by the throat, it was so sudden he didn't have time to fight me, knew he couldn't anyway.

'Was that why Mab sent you?'

His expression froze as he stared into my eyes, as he calculated the value of lying. My heart sank at his betrayal, I'd hoped the paranoia was a product of my exhaustion but it only confirmed I shouldn't trust anyone. Regardless of my feelings.

'Partly.' A throaty whisper through a gripped windpipe.

'The portal was your way to lead me into Ankou's trap.'

'No!' He tried to shout but all he did was choke. I eased my grip. 'No. That was a terrible coincidence. You must believe me Robin. I didn't know he'd be there.'

'At Hamdon Hill, when he held you hostage. That wasn't real, was it?'

He hadn't taken his eyes off me. 'No. At least not after I told him who I was working for. All he wanted was you at that point. I agreed to cooperate.'

'Why?'

Oisin wasn't a threat, I'd achieved my goal of frightening him so I released him and hurled myself back on to the bed, angry at myself more than him.

'You'd told me you were ready to die, to stop Llyr. I couldn't let that happen.'

How typical of a poet, making grand gestures from the heart. I snorted my derision.

'Even though it meant he would capture the Knights and potentially win his war with humanity?'

He gave a heavy sigh.

'They're not as important.' I heard him turn, felt his eyes on me. 'I'm sorry Robin.'

I ignored his simpering excuses. 'Why is Mab involved? Why are you spying for her?'

Oisin took a deep breath, as though he was unburdening a great weight he'd carried. 'Llyr's grip on power is tenuous, his invasion has stalled. Everything I told you in your kitchen is true. Mab told me to accompany him so I could report back what he was doing. She offered to help me free Sibeal if I cooperated. I haven't sent Mab a single report since we left your home. Honestly Robin.'

'But why does Mab want reports from you? Why not ask Llyr?'

Another deep breath, he took my arm and tried to turn me to face him. I obliged for no other reason than to see if I was getting all the truth this time.

'There is a plot to oust him. Mab and others can't do it themselves, not openly, that's not how they work. You know that.'

'Who's they?'

I felt him shrug. 'I don't know. Mab is secretive. But there are powerful players involved Robin. Very powerful. I think they have ambitions for the Light Court too.'

'Depose Nimue? Impossible.'

'She's old, tired. She's lost much of the fire that you'll remember.'

I remembered it vividly. I'd suffered its heat on several occasions when my mouth had got the better of my brain. Even so, I'd always had the impression she liked me. Probably the way fire likes kindling wood.

'Does she know about the Dark Court plans? Has anyone told her?'

Oisin snorted loudly. 'And risk getting caught, tortured and executed? Don't you remember what I told you about life there now?'

'But why bring the fight into the human realm?'

He laughed, it was a bitter sound. 'You don't see it, do you?'

'See what?' Exhaustion made my brain sluggish.

He reached down and took my hand then squeezed it.

'To remove Llyr from the throne, someone has to kill him. They can't move against him, not openly.'

Exhaustion was claiming me and Oisin was spinning out his explanation as if it was one of his heroic ballads. 'Get to the point, I'm tired.'

'Llyr is Oberon's only son, the rightful heir to the Dark Throne. He rules like his father. He's so paranoid he kills anyone who presents a threat. He's hated Robin, by everyone. Mab was the one who suggested if he captured the Knights it would help him regain his popularity and strengthen his hold on the throne.'

Oisin paused in the way he used to do when performing a dramatic tale.

'She knew there was one man who would protect the Knights at all costs, even if it meant killing the High Lord of the Dark Court in the process.'

I didn't have the energy to react. For much of my life in Tir na nÓg, I had been a political pawn. I thought I'd escaped, instead I'd been hauled into a game being played across two worlds. At any other time I would have been angry, shouted and bemoaned my lot, broken furniture and people's heads. I was too exhausted for any of that. These people had even succeeded in souring the one relationship I'd hoped might stand apart from the darkness surrounding me. I glanced at the anxious eyes of the other man, still gripping my hand, he saw something in my eyes and let go immediately.

'So I'm Mab's puppet.'

'We both are Robin.'

I awoke to Amelie's strident voice calling my name. It broke me out of a dream where I was a prisoner in a glass cell where I could see Oisin, the twins, Amelie and Keir but they couldn't see me. Each one was in danger but I couldn't intervene, no matter how hard I screamed and hammered on my transparent prison wall.

I turned my head to find the bed next to me empty.

'Where's Oisin?'

Amelie held out a scrap of paper, I was on my feet and in front of her in seconds. Her expression was as bleak and uncompromising as the message.

I'm sorry Robin.

I screwed up the piece of paper and threw it away. Amelie took hold of my arm.

'They're coming. You need to leave now.'

It wasn't an orderly departure. Waking two exhausted teenagers from their sleep and marshalling them into action I left up to Amelie. I hurried to the stable where I had similar problems with the wyvern, sluggish from the cold and disorientated without either of its masters. She gave me a look that spoke openly of her dissatisfaction but she stirred and stretched all the same. I found myself thinking how Oisin would be grinning at my acceptance of the animal as a valuable asset. If the bastard hadn't deserted me.

I stomped into the cottage and bellowed at the twins to hurry up.

An early morning sun, no more than a hazy orange ball in a dull, grey sky hung just above the line of trees behind the cottage. Everywhere was damp from melting snow and a light mist hovered in the air to decorate clothes with a pearly sheen of cold moisture that froze you to the bone.

The twins stood on either side of me as I surveyed the roadway at the foot of Amelie's drive, their jade-green eyes watching me resentfully. Behind us the wyvern grumbled.

'Where are you taking us now?' It was Brea who asked and she did it with that tone I knew teenagers used when they'd rather be in bed, or anywhere other than where they were at that moment.

'I don't know,' I snapped.

'Great.' Brea again, no doubt rolling her eyes.

'If you haven't noticed, I'm running out of places to hide you. I'd hoped to have had more time to make plans.'

'Too busy fucking your boyfriend were you?'

I clenched my fist as I whirled around, to glare at the girl whose fierce expression met mine. Her brother stirred, his voice, like his face, filled with stoic dejection. His entire body sagged.

'Pack it up sis. It's not helping.'

She sniffed and returned to resentful silence. I glanced at the lad.

'Can you sense them yet?'

My question was met with a frown. 'Nothing.'

'This way then,' I said and pointed into the centre of the town.

'Why?' Brea asked, 'that is if I'm allowed to ask questions?'

That girl had turned resentment into an art form.

'We might get lucky and reach the Abbey. There's a portal there. We could leave Glastonbury and find somewhere else in this country. The portal at Stonehenge might still be working.'

'Another portal?' Her question dripped sarcasm. 'Won't the walking skeleton be waiting for you again?'

I smiled, just to annoy her. 'If he is you and wyvern can deal with him.' Then, because they deserved to know my motives, 'Using the portals gets us to places faster and avoids meeting any more gangs. We might avoid Llyr too.'

Finn nodded his agreement, Brea sniffed her indifference.

A wind off the Bristol Channel stirred, whipping up the mist into a cold sheet we trudged through as we made our way towards the recreation ground where Oisin and I had met the gang of boys. It was deserted now. Often, when Finn was about to say something he thought was important, he cleared his throat first. He did it now.

'The skeleton man can't be killed, can he?'

'How did you know that?'

The kid could look a little awkward when he had to describe his psychic abilities, as though he was embarrassed by them. I remember his father being the same, he'd once told me a teenager's need to conform is compromised with such a talent. You can't fit in with everyone else, no matter how hard you try. Worse still, you know they think you're a freak.

'All the time he was fighting you he kept thinking how he'd kill you eventually, no matter how many times you killed him.'

'That's encouraging. Thanks.'

The lad flushed and I regretted the sarcasm. He wasn't his sister. I'd never known how to deal with his sensitivity. A thought struck me.

'Could you sense what can kill him?'

From some distance away dogs started barking. I picked up the pace as we hurried along Benedict Street. I hadn't had a reply to my question but I knew the lad would be monitoring the area as well as reviewing what he'd found in Ankou's head. He'd once described it as like searching through a filing cabinet with hundreds of folders filled with thousands of documents.

He cleared his throat.

'Nothing definite. His body can heal given enough time, he hates that it can do that, but knows it gives him the edge in any fight, especially against you. He really loathes you, doesn't he?'

'What about his head?'

I'd once come across a character with similar abilities. I'd decapitated him in the end.

Finn's eyes lost focus and we kept walking. As we reached St Mary's church and the dog barking resumed in earnest and much closer, I got my answer.

'It's different. You swung your sword near his head on one occasion, didn't you?'

I had. I think, deep in the recesses of my memory, that thought had been knocking on the door of my conscious mind at that point.

'It was the only time I sensed real fear from him.'

The wyvern behind us stopped and raised its head at the same time Finn tensed and looked about him with urgency. The noise from the dogs ended abruptly, mid bark.

'What?' I asked.

The lad's head snapped one way and then another, panic growing on his face.

'I don't know. I don't know.'

'That doesn't help!' I yelled. 'You must sense something, tell me, anything.'

He kept shaking his head as he looked up and down the empty street. The wyvern made a noise deep in its chest but it stared towards Magdalene Street.

'Get ready,' I yelled at Brea who rolled her eyes and sighed loudly. She'd already raised her arms, fingers straight out ready to fire, she watched her brother avidly.

I withdrew my sword from its permanent position, strapped on my back. I held it ready. We weren't in a good position to defend; St Mary's church sat at a T junction, we needed a strong wall at our backs. The entry into Magdalene Street was partly blocked by a wooden cart with a broken wheel but there was just enough space for the wyvern to get through. I reasoned we stood the best chance against the wall of the Abbey so I gestured towards the narrow gap.

'Through there!'

At the same instant dark figures at the far end of Benedict Street appeared, running towards us with real speed.

'Hurry'! I yelled.

I didn't remember the abandoned cart from earlier and I certainly wasn't going to squeeze past it at the same time as the wyvern, so I held the twins back. As the animal drew level with the cart it stopped suddenly, blocking the junction completely, I swore at its cantankerous nature and gestured for the twins to crawl under the cart.

The animal snorted and shuffled its body. That was the moment I realised it couldn't move its legs.

'Stop!' I yelled at the twins.

Too late. On hands and knees they looked over their shoulders at me in bewilderment, unable to move either. Brea screamed her protests as she tried to pull her hands from the ground. Finn froze and turned his head to look beyond the cart, two seconds later the unmistakeably stylishly dressed figure of Llyr appeared on top of the cart, smiling broadly in my direction.

'Hello again Robin.'

From around the corners of St Mary's church swarmed soldiers of all kinds, spriggans, boggarts and even a bunch of Nemean lion-men with their powerful bodies, mane-like hair and their distinctive double-headed battle axes. I considered trying to take on the spriggans and boggarts but the Nemeans were a different threat and there were too many of them. Llyr knew what I was thinking as he surveyed the scene from the top of the cart. I flashed the inevitable grin. The wyvern lashed her long neck and tail against the cart, making it wobble and thereby robbing Llyr of his big moment, he leapt down to stand in front of me as though he'd meant to do it. He gave the animal a withering look, she responded by thrashing from side to side until the cart shook. He nodded at my weapon.

I made a point of dropping my sword to the ground, it's metallic clang echoed around the buildings.

'Get the kids free before that animal kills them,' I yelled.

They'd come prepared. Before freeing the kids, they manacled Brea's hands and placed leather collars around their necks so they could lead them to stand in front of Llyr like pet dogs. A bunch of boggarts nervously pushed the cart out of the way, doing the best to avoid the wyvern who continued to snort and smash her tail against the buildings on either side of the road while staring in bewilderment at her immobile feet.

'You've been elusive Robin,' Llyr's voice was like thick oil. 'Trying to catch you involved fighting a rear-guard action in this shithole. Considering you claim to care for the humans, you're responsible for so many deaths.'

'But you've got me now.'

We were surrounded, there had to be over a hundred of them. We'd been corralled, like farm animals, into a pen. I couldn't understand how it had happened and when I glanced at Finn I could see he was trying to find a similar answer. We held eye contact for a second and he discreetly shook his head.

Llyr spotted it too. The inevitable smile widened.

'Don't blame the boy, Robin. I came prepared.'

He turned and, without a word of command, his soldiers parted to allow Ankou to amble through their midst. There was no smile on those wizened features, I doubted his parched skin was capable of it, instead his eyes focused on me. They had the satisfaction in them. In his hands, which were little more than bones covered in leathery parchment, he held a device which he carried with great care.

It was shaped like a large wooden goblet with runes etched on its outer edge, on its top surface was a glass sphere in which two crystals sat in indentations carved so their multi-faceted surfaces connected at one corner. They emitted a bright, vaguely purple energy, even from this distance I could hear it fizzing like the portal curtains. I suddenly realised what it was. I'd seen much bigger versions, never one that could be carried so easily. They carried lodestone which reacted to whatever crystal was positioned next to it; large, powerful ones generated enough electro-magnetic energy to wipe out an entire regiment's technology. These things, in the early days, gave the Fae an edge over human military power they should have capitalised on. This object must have a different purpose.

Finn moaned quietly, closed his eyes and sagged.

'What are you doing to him?'

'Don't worry.' Llyr moved towards Ankou and stared at the object with an expression full of pride, like a father for a son. This was another of his creations.

Ankou carefully handed the object over and Llyr stared with fascination into the glass sphere. I guessed the purple glow lighting up his face came from an amethyst. I'd rarely paid attention to my physics lessons but I vaguely remembered something about the amethyst affecting the wavelengths of the brain. Llyr was watching me, I tried to look nonchalant but I must have failed.

'It interferes with the boy's psychic signals, it stopped him sensing us.'

'Clever.'

An assured nod. 'You've caused me to expend more resources than I intended Robin. It's a price I did not want to pay. But don't worry, I'm going to exact an even greater one from you.'

'As high as the price Mab's demanding of you?'

He froze.

Ankou flicked a glance at his leader's face, realised too late I'd spotted it. I didn't know what edge it had given me or what I was going to do with it, all I knew was that I had one. I needed to throw these bastards off balance somehow long enough to work out a plan.

Llyr watched me though eyes with irises the colour of dark chocolate, the bitter kind.

'Oisin should learn to keep his mouth shut. Where is he by the way? Surely you've not driven him away again?'

'Oh, it wasn't just Oisin.'

That hooked him. He glanced at Ankou briefly who replied with a wide-eyed look of innocence that almost made me smile, so there was no trust there either.

'But don't worry Llyr. I'll be interested to see what Mab has to say about this situation when she arrives.'

I was gambling on Keir's mission being a success, and timely. All eyes turned to Llyr. Fury built in him rapidly but I think it was fuelled by urgency, the need to escape.

'Bring them!' Llyr roared as he started to edge his way past the frustrated wyvern. He flung a pointed finger at me. 'And if he causes any trouble, kill him.'

Chapter 21

'You're pregnant?'

The pitch and volume of my voice rose unnecessarily high but I couldn't stop myself.

Sibeal gave the slightest of nods. She sat on her bed, still pale and fragile and looked nervously at Clodagh then Midir, her eyes met his and stayed there.

'But how?'

I managed to modulate my voice this time and added a sharpness directed towards my brother as I glared at him.

'It wasn't me!' he replied, holding his hands up defensively. 'I'm infertile, every woman in the land knows that!'

I took a breath and composed myself, it had come as such a shock. Women did not get pregnant, it was as simple as that. Normally such events met with jubilation because they were so rare but there was no pride in this woman's announcement, quite the opposite. I couldn't imagine how poor Sibeal felt. She had tears in her eyes now, it was enough for my brother to hold her hands and squeeze them affectionately, smiling at her while glaring at me almost simultaneously. The small bedroom felt oppressive.

'It's a sunny day outside. Why don't we sit in the sunshine and talk? Are you up to it Sibeal?'

It took a while for us to navigate the staircase. Midir wanted to carry her downstairs but his offer was refused, Sibeal wanted to test her strength. It had been two weeks since we'd rescued her and her recovery had been slow. Despite her refusal of help, her progress down the staircase, through the dark sitting room of the cottage and onto its veranda involved my brother watching her every step. He sat her down in a wicker armchair and placed a woollen rug over her legs and knelt at her feet like a loyal dog. Clodagh brought out two stools and we sat on either side of her, she held the notebook stolen from Taranis too.

The identity of the baby's father was no great mystery, I'd been naïve to overlook what she'd meant by her violation by Taranis, unsurprisingly Sibeal struggled to recount the details. In the end we resorted to carefully worded questions which received reluctant nods or emotional shakes of the head. Midir's fury, which had festered since we'd first realised what had happened, now exploded into a vigilante's need for justice. It was only my reasoning and Sibeal's pleas that stopped him from riding off to kill Taranis.

'He raped her,' Midir kept repeating as I led him into the sunshine where we could speak openly. 'The bastard needs to be punished. You know as well as I do that will never happen. She's not strong enough to testify against him in court. No, he needs to face a more direct punishment.'

I grabbed his arm as he reached for his horse. I'd never seen Midir so angry before, usually he was the relaxed one and I was the one who got worked up about everything.

'Listen to me. You may be a prince of the Light Court but he has powerful friends in the Dark Court. Anything you do could flare into war if we're not careful, especially if you killed him.'

Like me, he'd grown up amidst the tension that existed between the two Courts, we both remembered the last war and the bloodshed it brought. No one wanted that. Thankfully sense prevailed, not something I associated with my brother normally. He released the reins of his horse and looked at me. I could see the resentment burn in his eyes, it worried me he could still do something stupid, perhaps less directly.

Clodagh joined us, she'd waited for me to calm things.

'I've been going through Taranis's notes. Sibeal was an experiment.' She glanced at Midir before continuing. 'After he... did what he did... he treated her with drugs which seem to have increased her fertility. Increased it enormously.'

She looked at me intensely, it had been one of the issues we'd researched for years. When she spoke again it was with astonishment, there was a tinge of something else though I couldn't tell what it was.

'Filidea, he's made a significant breakthrough.'

My brother's rage reignited.

'And that gives him the right to rape women, does it?'

Clodagh shook her head, reached out like I'd done and held his arm. It calmed him.

'Of course not. But can you imagine how people will react to this news? He has potentially solved our race's greatest curse.'

We stared at each other in silence. Even Midir's anger subsided. He knew any court would consider Taranis's actions to be immoral but they would be outweighed by the benefits to society. What was one rape in such a context? I was certain even my grandmother wouldn't see anything wrong in what he'd done. It was a means to an end.

Even though she clung to Midir's arm, Clodagh's eyes hadn't left mine.

'What is it?' I asked.

Clodagh took a deep breath. 'I don't know enough about this. I'm not a physician. But by suddenly ending the treatment, I don't know what effect that will have on the baby. Or the mother.'

Midir's eyes widened. I suppose mine too.

'What are you going to do?'

My brother looked at me, then at Clodagh and back at me again, his eyes demanding answers we didn't have.

'Is Sibeal aware of any of this?' he asked eventually.

Clodagh shrugged. 'She's a scientist. She isn't stupid.'

He turned and raced back to the cottage. Clodagh's lengthy sigh told me she was thinking the same as me, I was the first to say it.

'She can't stay here, she's going to need a physician.'

We looked at each other, we both understood the implications. It would mean taking her back to the palace, admitting what we'd done so we could get her medical help. Inevitably, Taranis would find out.

So would my grandmother. I didn't know whose reaction I dreaded most.

We walked back to the cottage in silence, lost in thought. Our act of chivalry had triggered terrible consequences, as each one formed in my head it felt worse than the one before.

'I'm going back to the palace before I'm missed. I'll visit tomorrow and hopefully have some answers.'

I received a hesitant smile and as I turned to get my horse, Clodagh held my arm.

'Things will turn out all right, won't they?'

I made sure my smile exuded more confidence than I possessed, I patted her hand.

'Taranis won't make a fuss. He's a rapist. He may have succeeded in his experiment with one woman but he's still committed a crime. He will need to keep quiet, no matter how furious he might be in private.'

Clodagh's smile had more belief in it as she nodded her agreement. I only wished I felt the same. It was likely Taranis's private reactions would be far worse than any public display, something that scared me beyond belief, as the woman scheduled to marry the bastard.

I rode back home as I tried to find ways to conceal Sibeal in a place that was quiet and out of the way. It wasn't going to be easy. The Light Palace would be consumed by gossip regarding the mysterious woman in my care, at the same time as another had mysteriously disappeared from Taranis' protection. I began concocting a fanciful incident where I'd discovered the woman, lost and wandering alone in the countryside. It wasn't going to hold up to close scrutiny but it was a start.

For the second time I arrived at the stables and found the same servant waiting for me with the inevitable message from my grandmother. This time I insisted on changing my clothes. It allowed me time to compose myself for whatever horror waited for me. The worst possibility was that Taranis waited for me, like last time, I couldn't face him now, knowing what he'd done. The thought made me want to vomit.

I stared into the mirror in my bathroom as I splashed cold water on to my face. I was supposed to marry this man. A rapist. Someone who experimented on people. How could I face him on a daily basis knowing that? Worse, the thought of him touching me made me feel sick. As for sex... that did cause me to vomit.

The girl staring back at me in the mirror looked ghastly. Red-eyed from crying, pale-faced from being sick, she had a hunted look about her I'd never seen before. My impetuous good intentions had back-fired on me in ways I had never imagined.

The young man who'd brought the message waited for me outside my rooms. My journey to meet my grandmother felt like I walked towards my execution. I wasn't going to marry Taranis. I would sooner die. The consequence of my decision meant I would have to explain why and events would then unfold in ways I couldn't begin to imagine.

I was so wrapped up in my thoughts that it took me a moment to realise we weren't going to the Silver Reception Room. We were outside. The fear that threatened to overwhelm me amplified when I saw my grandmother waiting for me at the entrance to the orchard.

It was her private space.

No one was allowed in its walled grounds. When times were difficult she could be found trimming branches, pollinating flowers or just walking amongst trees as ancient and crooked as her. She beckoned me inside and shut the wooden door in the high orchard wall. We walked in silence to a bench where we sat, it was probably the most peaceful location in the palace but it didn't feel like it to me. My heart raced.

'I'm leaving shortly. But I wanted to speak to you before I left.'

I swallowed to lubricate my dry throat. Grandmother never left the palace these days. Something was wrong. I turned to her.

'What's happened?'

She gave me a weak smile. That wasn't her either, she was actually worried. Perhaps even frightened.

'Let me come to that in a moment, my dear.'

My dear? She hadn't used an affectionate term with me since I was a little girl. My anxiety increased, panic stirred. Her smile strengthened, she must have realised what effect this was having on me, she patted my knee.

'You and I are very similar Filidea. It's why we fight. I see a great deal of me in you. I would get involved in activities I didn't know how to resolve, purely because I knew they were the right things to do from the outset. I used to assume I'd find a solution to the problem eventually. And I always did. But that kind of thinking isn't how you rule, you cannot jump from one crisis to another. You have to see the problem coming before it strikes you.'

She patted my knee again.

'But that comes with age and experience. I have too much of it. I think it makes me rather cautious and conventional these days.'

She was still smiling at me. I tried to reciprocate but failed.

'I know about the woman at Midir's cottage.'

I think my jaw dropped. It made her grin.

'How? When did…? Why haven't you…?'

The old woman locked eyes with me though the smile remained.

'Filidea, dear, cover your tracks more carefully next time. Going riding so frequently, for someone who hasn't shown any interest in even being outside, draws attention. I think it would have been wiser to have brought Oisin's sister nearer to the palace, to make her more accessible. Of course, your brother's motives would be very different. It was wise of you to leave your friend as chaperone.'

I blinked repeatedly and nodded dumbly. My mind tried to find answers to the inevitable interrogation but every synapse felt sluggish and numb.

'However, your actions are commendable. You have successfully sabotaged Taranis and his callous activities. You need to bring the woman here, quietly. I'll make arrangements. We will need to be careful only those we trust know what we're doing.'

'You're not angry grandmother?'

Another pat on the knee.

'I'd considered doing the same thing when I found out what the bastard was up to. But, like I said, age has made me cautious. It's why I'm pleased you're following in my footsteps. When I've gone, I expect you to assume my role. For a while, I thought your decision to shut yourself away in the library was going to define you. I see I needn't have worried.'

My head was in turmoil. Everything I thought I knew was getting turned upside down.

'But why are you marrying me to that bastard?'

'I'm not my dear. We are going to appear as though you are.'

'We are?'

'Politics, my dear, is like sleight-of-hand. You make sure your audience is focused on one hand while the other does something else. You and I are going to perform a sequence of conjuration that will bring about some changes. You've shown yourself capable of deviousness, we need to make it more subtle now.'

'I see.'

Except I didn't.

'The only way we can find out what Taranis is doing, is to get close to him. What better way than to be his fiancé?'

'You want me to spy on him?'

'How do you think I've maintained control all these years? It's because I have eyes and ears everywhere, it's a skill I learned from a very good friend of mine, when I was a young girl. You need to become a spy so that you learn how to manage them effectively.'

The door in the wall creaked open. Vevina, my grandmother's ancient secretary, stood in the gap but said nothing. The atmosphere became brisk and business-like suddenly, an imperious, arthritic finger was raised to signal Vevina to wait. She must have noticed my increased anxiety, grandmother smiled again.

'Events are afoot, Filidea. Events that will have far-reaching consequences for our people. I am genuinely worried where they will take us. Something is about to happen which will be the first chapter of a story that's ending could spell the destruction of our race.'

My grandmother never spoke in such dark terms, it frightened me.

'I blame myself. Old age has made me cautious. My inaction has led to events unfolding which are connected to mistakes from the past. There's an old human saying, the birds have come home to roost. Except these birds are not welcome. I once put measures in place to counter the conflict they will provoke.' She sighed. 'There are powerful forces determined to destroy that peace, Filidea. They operate in the shadows. They manipulate others. They have been performing their own sleight-of-hand and I allowed myself to be fooled.

Vevina tapped her wrist. Grandmother flexed her shoulders and stood up slowly, brushed invisible creases out of her clothes.

'We will talk more about this when I return. I have a pressing matter to address.'

'Where are you going?'

Grandmother looked at me through rheumy eyes that looked tired and old suddenly. I had never seen her like this. Whatever had happened had shaken her, perhaps even upset her and she was still recovering.

'I am needed elsewhere. Those roosting birds I mentioned are about to instigate an action which could destabilise our world. If they succeed the implications are grave for all of us, including Taranis. It goes beyond his raping of women. Much further. I will need your intelligence and cunning to help me deal with the consequences.'

My grandmother turned and took a couple of steps towards the doorway, she hobbled, clearly in considerable pain then stopped. When she turned her head, there was an expression of granite-like determination on her face. For the first time in as long as I could remember, I felt sorry for her. I wanted to help her, though I knew she'd dismiss my assistance with a couple of sharp words.

'Filidea, dear, I don't know how much longer I've got. You need to be ready to take my place. Think about what I said. Look for the problems before they arrive, that politics is all about sleight-of-hand but remember others will be performing their own conjuring act too. I missed this one completely and now we're going to suffer the consequences.'

I watched her shuffle to the door which Vevina opened wider, behind her, in the shadows, I could just make out the outline of someone else, a man. She placed an arm through his as Vevina closed the door behind them, leaving me alone with my thoughts in the orchard.

I had no idea what she'd meant when she talked about roosting birds and the dire consequences of the conflict they brought, the woman talked in riddles. I sat in the peace and quiet of her orchard, aware that the levels of anxiety I felt now were even greater than when we'd met.

She was Nimue, Lady of the Lake, she didn't get frightened. Yet fear was etched into the lines on her face. In all the time I'd known her, she'd never shown even the slightest nervousness about anything, she was always so self-assured. I'd assumed fear was beyond her.

She didn't leave the palace either. Any form of travel was painful for her, it exhausted her easily. Everyone came to her, it was a sign of her authority. Who could demand that an old woman should travel to them? Whatever was happening had to be serious.

I stared up into the branches of the apple trees around me, at the clear sky and the gentle breeze that wafted the branches lost in thought, until one of those thoughts struck me with the intensity of a thunderbolt.

It had been said in such a casual, offhand manner that I'd missed it. I'd been so surprised by her knowledge of my activities that I hadn't been listening.

"When I've gone, I expect you to assume my role."

Grandmother wanted me to be First Minister of the Light Court. Me.

If I'd been anxious and frightened before, it was nothing compared to the ice that filled my veins now. I wasn't capable of such a lofty position; my father would never agree. More importantly, if there were dire events unfolding that meant the possible destruction of our race, I didn't want to be First Minister.

Until I thought of the scale of ignorance, complacency and rank stupidity of the rest of my family. Midir was the brightest and the best in comparison. I certainly couldn't rely on my father to provide the leadership, he was only interested in drinking ale with his friends.

Still, I had to deal with more immediate problems. I had to find somewhere to hide Sibeal and decide who I could trust with that knowledge. Plus, play political match-making with Taranis while discovering his secrets. That would be enough for now. Everything else I'd deal with as it came along.

I sat and stared at the branches of the apple trees and savoured the peace this place provided. Something told me I wasn't going to get much of it in the future.

Chapter 22

Nothing prepared me for the sight we faced as we reached the junction with Magdalene Street.

In happier times, before the floods and the Fae invasion, tourists had visited its new age shops and vegetarian restaurants. It had offered an alternate lifestyle, a place where people smiled, wore ludicrous outfits and felt at peace with the world.

The twins and I arrived in a very different place.

An abattoir.

Magdalene Street had been the location of a battle, though a massacre was more accurate. There were a few spriggan bodies but a lot more human ones; men of all ages but also women, even kids, though I suspected they were unlucky victims. The street ran with blood, its stench hung thickly in the air, it seeped into gutters like red rainwater. You wanted to avoid looking at the carnage, but you had no choice as you searched for places to step, to avoid slipping and falling into the blood and guts. We tiptoed like dancers.

The twins, Finn especially, threw up repeatedly. The Nemean lion-men, our escorts, pushed and prodded the kids forward impatiently. As warriors, this sight meant nothing to a culture that worshipped the perfect warrior. They bathed their offspring in blood within their first month of birth, which was why they showed such contempt for Finn and Brea.

'Please Robin,' the lad mumbled as he wept, 'make them take us somewhere else. I can't do this. I can't.'

When Brea tried to help him she received a swift smack on her legs with the shaft of a battle-axe. She glared at her abuser, swore at him and then turned on me.

'Are you going to let them treat us like this? You know he's making us walk through this shit on purpose, don't you?'

I did. It was the privilege of the victor and the misery of the subjugated.

'What do you suggest we do Brea? Do you want me to fight every spriggan, boggart and Nemean here? Not forgetting Ankou and Llyr.'

'Why not? You got us into this shit.'

I looked at her, jaw set with the rigidity of the deeply resentful.

'It's about picking your moment Brea. This isn't it.'

She sniffed loudly. 'We're going to be at the portal in a few minutes, it'll be too late then. When I get this fucking thing off my hands,' she shook her manacle hard, 'I'm going to blast every bastard I find.'

We rounded a corner and arrived in front of a space that had once been a car park for the Abbey. Both twins gasped as they looked up at the instigator of much of the carnage.

A dragon chewed thoughtfully on body parts, its muzzle and jaws dripped with blood. It was significantly bigger than the wyvern but it lacked its cousin's fine lines, elegance and beauty. If they'd been vehicles, the wyvern was a red sports car built for speed and manoeuvrability whereas the dragon was a bulldozer with solid, powerful leg muscles and enormous jaws that took up most of its head. There was intelligence in the eyes of the wyvern, this creature looked vaguely bovine, like a cow dumbly chewing the cud.

The purpose of the rider on top of the animal was obvious. This thing couldn't be relied on to think for itself.

Like a horse, heavy leather straps around its enormous middle kept a saddle in place and reins were drilled into the sides of his scaly head.

Llyr stood in front of it, radiating manic glee.

'My dragon breeding programme is producing creatures that make victory inevitable. This type is useful for dealing with half-hearted uprisings like this one, but you should see what my battle dragons will achieve.'

'Will?'

My question deflated his pride for a second.

'We're training them still. But once broken-in, they will be unstoppable. Your little wyvern was a mistake, an ill-advised diversion, my dragons represent real power.'

With his lecture completed, Llyr turned to enter the Abbey through what remained of the gateway. Our impatient escorts jabbed at the three of us with their long battles axes and we were marched into the Abbey grounds.

Glastonbury Abbey retained some of its original glory. Its gothic walls still reached up to the heavens, beautiful archways with dog-tooth carvings hinted at the spectacle it once had as the prime religious location in medieval England. Recent features scarred its stone surfaces, like the graffiti that cursed the Fae and described their fates when mankind finally achieved victory. Llyr and his army walked past these affirmations unaware, or indifferent, to such violent and demeaning threats. At my side, two youngsters who represented humanity's opposition to the Fae, trudged along, heads bowed, shoulders slumped. Like every other person in this land, they were emaciated, weakened mentally and physically. Simply finding ways to stay alive preoccupied them these days, any opposition lacked coordination and firepower and ended in the kind of carnage we'd been forced to trudge through.

Ahead of us Llyr marched with the swagger of the conqueror. One thing niggled away in my head that gave me some hope. I'd fought in enough battles to know if someone with the skill and experience of Mab had led the Fae, human beings would already be slaves. I ought to be grateful for Llyr's ineptitude, I told myself. There was still a chance I could use it to my advantage, but I needed the odds against me to change.

Our route took us past the circular building once affectionately known as the Bishop's Kitchen towards the centre of the Abbey. When Thomas Cromwell's hooligans destroyed the Abbey, enough of their respect for religion stopped them desecrating its sacred centre, the Lady Chapel, dedicated to Mary Magdalene. Or perhaps someone understood what power the chapel really contained. Whatever the reason, the infrastructure to one of the most powerful portals in the south of England, remained in good condition. Stories of Glastonbury's doorways to fairyland had existed for centuries, primarily centred on the Tor, Christianity had successfully disguised its other entry.

The one we were about to use, unless something happened soon.

The entry to the Lady Chapel was up a flight of steps to a narrow archway. Llyr stood there, surveying the scene below him with an arrogantly inflated chest.

'How are you going to get that thing through the portal?' I called, jerking a thumb at the grumbling dragon some distance behind us.

'I'm not. I'm leaving it here to wreak havoc. I'm doing that everywhere. Over time they'll breed and humanity will become their fodder.'

At my side I heard Brea grind her teeth and exhale loudly. She twisted her hands repeatedly, they were raw and bloody as they chafed against the metal edges but I could see she was getting somewhere with them. She caught me looking at them and gave me a ferocious smile.

'Well Robin,' Llyr called down at me. 'This is where we say our goodbyes. The Knights will come with me while I leave you to the tender mercies of Ankou.'

The desiccated figure of death climbed half way up the stairs, attempting a smile, while his master giggled.

'He really doesn't like you Robin, did you know that? When my father tampered with his DNA long ago, he found one advantage above all others. He cannot die. Ankou has valued this quality because he's known, no matter what it took, he would eventually destroy you. Looks like that moment has arrived.'

On either side of that shrivelled mouth, parchment-like skin puckered into dark yellow folds as the smile widened. I looked at him and then at Llyr.

'Shame that tinkering with his DNA didn't make him prettier.'

The smiles vanished.

'It doesn't appear Mab is here to stop me Robin. Was that another of your jokes?'

Llyr's smug grin broadened as he turned towards the chapel's crypt where a bright light illuminated the stone walls. They'd opened the portal and time was running out.

'Goodbye Robin.' He turned to the skeletal figure at the foot of the steps. 'Don't make his death quick or painless, will you?'

'No, my lord.'

With a snap of his fingers he beckoned his lion-men escorts who yanked the twins towards the steps.

'Still picking your moment?' Brea screamed at me.

Her brother looked panic-stricken and gasped my name repeatedly.

I shrugged heavy shoulders. It wasn't the ideal moment by any means but I'd run out of choices. I'd hoped Keir might have helped but it looked like I was on my own, which was nothing new. Well, I always wanted to go out in style. Around me a couple of dozen spriggans and boggarts remained behind as the lion-men escorted their High Lord and his prisoners up the steps, through the narrow archway into the chapel. As the last of them vanished from view, Ankou took up position in front of the archway, he'd guessed what I had in mind.

I took a breath, relaxed my muscles and discreetly scrutinised my own escort to see which one lacked concentration, without even a weapon I was useless. A boggart with a broken tusk stood within lunging distance, if I was quick...

The roar bounced from one stone wall to another and made us all turn, including the rider on the dragon that lifted its huge head with interest. The wyvern strode around the corner of the building and roared a second time the moment it saw us. I recognised its tone, it was the same challenge it had made before attacking the Questing Beast. Around its feet were flecks of foam, its jaws were covered in it too, the animal must have used its acidic saliva to melt Llyr's restraining gel. It raised its head, roared again and charged.

Spriggans and boggarts, startled by this unexpected guest, looked at each other with uncertainty and began to edge towards the chapel steps and safety. The dragon rider had other ideas. He yanked the head of the dragon to meet the smaller wyvern, confident in his mount's size and power, he jabbed his heels into its flanks to stir it into action though the animal looked disinterested. It had pigged itself on human remains and probably wasn't in the mood for a fight.

The wyvern picked up speed, weaving one way then abruptly changing direction. The dragon rider yanked his steed's head hard each time, causing the animal considerable pain from the bolted reins in its jaws. It roared but more from pain and irritation than aggression.

The wyvern moved so swiftly it was amongst the retreating soldiers, avoiding the snapping jaws of the dragon easily. It snatched the slower boggarts in its jaws, crunched them in one bite and spat them out in the direction of the dragon. The smell of blood and the instant meal distracted it, until its rider yanked hard on the reins to pursue the wyvern. The wyvern, intent on administering its revenge on the boggarts and spriggans that had immobilised it, herded them towards the chapel steps where Ankou was brushed aside in the rush to reach safety. It ignored me, now pressed against the Abbey wall, as it moved closer to the chapel steps and cornered itself. For an animal I'd credited with so much intelligence, it had made a huge error. The dragon rider spotted his advantage and let out a whoop of excitement as he drove the dragon towards the cornered wyvern. I looked around for a weapon, spotted a sword on the ground and picked it up, I didn't know how I was going to stop a lumbering mass of dragon with a weapon that was toothpick in comparison, but I'd think of something.

The dragon marched forward. I called at its rider, waved my arms to distract the animal but the rider just grinned at me and whooped a second time. The wyvern on the other hand roared its challenge. With its strong hind legs, it powered forwards in a suicidal last-ditch charge. I watched, astonished at its bravery.

The dragon opened its jaws.

It was at that point that I learned not to underestimate the wyvern. It had deliberately goaded the dragon-rider into attacking in that position. It was the same strategy it had used against the Questing Beast.

The wyvern launched. It sprang upwards, like a high jumper. For a moment, I thought it could fly. So did the dragon as it raised its head to watch the red shape soar over it with ease. It lowered its legs, like a plane coming into land, snatching the rider from his saddle and dragged him backwards over the jagged spine of his steed. Blood erupted and the rider's shrieks ended abruptly.

The wyvern landed gracefully just beyond the tail of the dragon, turned ready to attack but the dragon just stood there, dumbly. It looked around as though expecting a command and when nothing happened the smell of its broken jockey drew its attention. It sniffed at the remains and snacked on them before looking around for more. It devoured the wyvern's earlier victims with ease, turned and ambled back to Magdalene Street, no doubt determined to finish its feast.

It completely ignored the wyvern as it sauntered over to me, I swear the animal was smiling as it approached. It stood at my side, eyes intent on the archway where spriggans and boggarts peaked around the stone archway.

I heard a scream and shouts.

'Brea? Finn? Are you all right?'

Nothing.

The wyvern rumbled a sound deep in her chest that I knew meant she was unhappy about something, she was sniffing the air, nostrils flaring.

In the archway consternation turned into pushing and shoving, something was wrong. Now I had an ally I decided my moment had arrived.

I sprinted forwards. Ankou leapt out from the archway, sword ready. I thought the nearby spriggans racing in his direction were going to fight alongside him but they more interested in avoiding the red monster than on me or my black-cloaked nemesis, they blundered past him.

He leapt off the steps to get out of their way to land neatly on the ground.

'My fight isn't with you,' I said watching him closely. 'I want Llyr. If you've got a grudge with me let's settle it later.'

His top lip curled to reveal yellow stumps of teeth.

'I've waited long enough, I will not oblige your requests.'

I gave him a shrug and moved to circle him. If he thought I was getting ready to fight I hoped he might not realise I was moving so I could run up the steps and into the chapel. Whatever was causing the confusion might work in my favour, what I didn't need was any delay. The wyvern watched us, nodding its head from one side to the other in its attempt to understand what the strange creatures were doing.

'I've obviously upset you. I must admit, I can't remember how.'

More a distraction, as I moved towards the steps, than genuine curiosity but it caused the upturned lip to become a tight-lipped snarl.

'How typical of you.'

He lunged at me, sword slashing in an arc in front of my face, forcing me backwards and down a slight dip towards the Abbey wall. For a second I lost my balance and he rushed me with astonishing speed, blade a blur. I could only parry the attack until I regained my balance.

The snarl turned into a smile.

'You've got slow.'

I'd show him fucking slow.

I launched a frenzied attack, causing him to step backwards but he met every move easily, anticipated where I'd go each time and had his sword ready.

'Still the same old plays eh? Nothing original.'

Suddenly his blade wasn't where I expected it to be, he'd stepped much further back than was necessary, like he was retreating. I struck out at thin air and he laughed. In a movement that left me bewildered for a split second, he leapt upwards, far higher than you might expect from someone who looked to be ancient and decrepit. He landed, cloak flapping like the black wings of a huge crow, his blade slicing down vertically, ready to part my skull. I ducked, turned the loss of balance into a forward roll but couldn't get upright in time. He twisted in a way I didn't think was possible, his blade slicing in a diagonal arc, missing my left thigh by a whisker. I rolled over again and again while he laughed.

'Slow. Stiff. Predictable. Yet you were always Mab's favourite. I was the superior swordsman but she preferred you.'

Over at the archway something was happening, there was noise, orders given. It was enough to distract him just long enough for me to get to my feet.

'Perhaps. But that scar on your face was my work.'

The smile disappeared. I'd allowed him to dictate the action long enough.

'That wasn't you.'

He stood motionless. His denial confused me.

'We fought in the Belthane Lists, I gave you that scar in the final tourney.'

He shook a head that was more like the skull of man who'd been dead for six months.

'No. I got it from the crazed maniac you release when your limited swordplay proves insufficient.'

For as long as I could remember, men had insulted me because of what I was. As a boy, Commander Taranis' sneering words would echo across the training ground as he ridiculed me. 'You fight like a girl, no wonder you get fucked like one'. There'd be howls of laughter from the vicious bastards who provided the instruction and much of the fucking at night. He made me train longer, pit me against vicious men rather than kids my own age, so that later they could abuse me as my forfeit for failing to win. The first man I ever killed was one of them and I paid dearly for the privilege, suffered in ways that birthed the creature that would never leave me, no matter how hard I tried to exorcise it. Banishing it to the deep recesses of my brain was my only means of controlling the beast. The creature others had named Puck. Now, my adversary wanted to fight him, rather than me.

So be it.

I exploded into action. My sword arm took over, performed moves embedded in muscle memory and with such speed my weapon was a blur.

Ankou's eyes glanced into mine as he fended off the attack, they reminded me of our fight on London bridge when he'd watched Puck rise to face him there. Those black irises flared with the challenge as he fought the creature he clearly believed he could beat.

I didn't notice any of that, at the time, the monster looks for other things, seconds where decisions get taken, ones that lead to bloodshed and death.

We fought as the things we were; two ancient warriors who didn't care if they died, so long as the other died too. The parlour tricks ended, so did the conversation, this was a silent battle to the death. I've always wondered if Puck feared death, I don't think he does, I think he probably welcomes it. In that respect, we are alike.

Blades clashed, positions shifted to find advantages. I sliced his arm, it drew little blood. His swipe across my chest brought intense pain that blossomed, then vanished, Puck could shut it out with such ease. An arcing slice connected with my cheek, it served to intensify my attack.

I remembered little after that.

One image is branded on my memory, as all of Puck's victories are.

The moment exhaustion stopped him from reacting fast enough, the look of acceptance in his eyes as I raised my sword arm and twisted my wrist to rotate the blade through ninety degrees. He froze and held my eyes, no doubt seeing Puck's glassy stare as the blade severed his spine and his bony skull toppled to the ground.

I watched as the corpse collapsed into a heap at my feet, cold and dispassionate. Puck must have stood there, like a statue, his goal achieved.

Slowly, very slowly, a thaw allowed me back into my body. It always starts with my eyes, I'm made to witness the horror of my actions without the ability to move. To run away screaming. I do that inside my skull.

Feeling returned to my body and brought the full measure of pain with it. Injuries appeared like magic where they'd been ignored before, Puck wore my body like a warrior wears armour, when he left it, the excessive damage remained. Blood poured but my veins were filled with water, I was exhausted beyond belief. I stood atop the body of my victim, staring down at him, empty of emotion and filled with the pain he'd inflicted on me. Remaining upright was a challenge, I wobbled. It crossed my mind I might be mortally wounded, it felt like it, perhaps there was no victory after all. I didn't care.

Darkness enveloped me, I fell into its heart which was as black as the one residing in my chest.

Chapter 23

Urgent hands shook me back to consciousness.

I gazed into the face of an angel, cornflower blue eyes looked down at me and blonde curls surrounded the face like a halo. Finally, I'd died. The relief I felt lasted only seconds, the time it took to remember heaven was a Christian creation and would never be my ultimate destination, according to their belief system I'd be welcomed in a very different place.

'Robin?'

The voice was familiar and I smiled at the memory, though it faded quickly as pain wracked my whole body. That meant either the religious zealots had correctly predicted where I'd go after death or that I still clung on to life.

'Robin? Can you speak?'

I tried and uttered series of garbled groans that made my angel smile. I reached up to touch its face, felt the brush of several days' growth of beard. Angels didn't have beards.

'Oisin?'

I tried to sit up and agony flared in my chest. I looked down, my shirt was sticky with dried blood. I ignored it and preferred to scowl at the man knelt by my side.

I punched him hard and we both yelped.

'What's that for?' he asked.

'For deserting me.'

A voice, wheezing like a pair of punctured bellows, floated towards me.

'He didn't desert you. He came to fetch me.'

Over Oisin's shoulder a stooped figure struggled to come into focus but the voice was enough.

'Nimue?'

Something hard smacked my ankle, I cursed.

'You forgot the honorific, Master Goodfellow.'

She paused sufficiently before using my title and extended the word so it was packed with derision. Perhaps it was the pain, perhaps her presence triggered my deep-seated resentment of aristocracy or it may have been her hitting me with her walking stick that allowed me to sound like my old self.

'Oisin, didn't I tell you to stop grave-robbing?'

Another smack on my shins, harder this time.

The old woman stepped into my line of vision.

'Fuck! And I thought Ankou looked old!'

Her clothes were stylish. Her trousers and smock, partly hidden under a cloak and hood shimmered from millions of shimmering silver crystals, etched in her apple emblem. But it was her grey rheumy eyes that fixed on me, possessed of the colour and strength of cold iron. They were the only part that retained the force of will which made this old harridan the power broker she'd always been. Secretly I'd admired her tenacity. Her children might be the official rulers of the Light Court but they did nothing without her permission, it was an influence which had once extended into this realm.

Despite the pain, I focused my brain on her arrival, Oisin must have listened to me after all and told her what was happening. As its architect, she must think she still had a stake in maintaining the peace between humanity and the Dark Court. I hoped she still had the power and influence to sustain the centuries-long tradition of the

Knights' Protocols. That confidence diminished as I looked more closely, at her stooped back, arthritic hands, a severe limp and her difficulty in breathing. I started to understand why Llyr felt confident enough to wage war again and flout the Protocols.

I shifted my attention rapidly as that thought process sank in.

'Where's Llyr?'

Despite the pain and Oisin's protests I sat upright. A short distance away Keir knelt next to the wyvern, feeding it titbits and stroking its long neck as it curled around him affectionately. If Keir had returned that mean Nimue wasn't the only new arrival.

She leaned against the wall of the Lady Chapel casually, one leg bent at the knee, her boot planted flat against the wall while she cleaned fingernails with a dagger. She wore beautifully crafted, finely cut leather armour across her chest, exposing bare arms with bulging biceps. Sensing my attention, Mab looked over at me but didn't react or speak.

At the foot of the steps to the Lady Chapel stood Llyr, flanked by two of Mab's personal guards, identified by the tightness of their uniforms, their impressive physiques and stern expressions. Llyr knew they wouldn't dare kill him, not even Mab could permit that, but they'd incapacitate him in seconds.

As if she believed Mab's goons weren't enough of a threat, Brea stood a short distance in front of Llyr, hands splayed, ready to blast him if he stepped out of line. Finn stood by her side looking anxious as usual.

Struggling to my feet caught Brea's attention.

'At fucking last!'

'I'm alive, thanks for caring!' I called back. It was meant light-heartedly but it came out as resentment.

Her animosity didn't change, not that I expected it would.

'Well, while you were going sleepy-byes the rest of us subdued this sly bastard. His freaks ran back to fairyland but we didn't give him chance to follow them.'

Mab stirred.

'To be clear, girl,' she spoke the final word with such contempt Brea physically bristled, 'my arrival prevented him from leaving.'

Llyr raised a humbled head, perfect features formed into a portrait of defeat.

'And you will regret that decision Mab. I am ruler of the Dark Court. You were once its Commander-in-Chief, now disgraced and isolated. When I return, your humiliation will drive you from Court, no one will dare speak to you when I'm finished.'

She turned her head towards Llyr with languid indifference, exhaling loudly.

'You imagine yourself returning, do you?'

I caught the quick flick of Nimue's eyes in Mab's direction and her frown, until she noticed me watching her. I noticed Oisin's eyes on mine as well, his way of telling me he'd told the truth about Mab's intentions where I was concerned. Despite my best efforts, I was in the middle of a political battle, equally as brutal and merciless as the one on Magdalene Street. If I wasn't careful I'd be the dragon, dumbly slaying all before me.

In my kitchen, so long ago, I'd vowed to kill Llyr. I hated the bastard. The image of him slicing open the throat of Mickey's brother was burned into my memory.

The trouble was finding vengeance for the kid, and the thousands like him, led me into dangerous territory. So they'd kill me for murdering the bugger. That didn't bother me. I was ready for that fate.

But Nimue's arrival proved this battle had more than one side.

By murdering Llyr, I was aiding Mab and her Machiavellian chums, I would help them prepare the ground for the Dark Court to attack humanity with even greater ruthlessness. Far from ending the war, Oisin may have been right when he'd persuaded me not to kill Llyr, I could be instigating something worse. I glanced at the twins who watched the whole thing in bewilderment, the other side of that debate said that until I did kill Llyr, they would never be safe.

Mab's words had turned the Abbey grounds into the worst moments of Oberon's rule, when everyone watched each other for the slightest sign of indecision and weakness. She'd lit a fuse and I was the dynamite.

Llyr glared at Mab, red-faced now, genuinely furious.

'You wouldn't dare harm me Mab. I'm aware of your ambitions but even you could not defend the killing of the Dark Court's lord and master.' He changed tack, his voice took on more of a wheedling tone as it was obvious his threats had no effect on the woman. 'Kill me Mab and you'd leave the Dark Court without anyone to succeed me, there is no other rightful heir. The Dark Court would dissolve into in-fighting and chaos, the only ones to benefit would be our Light cousins.'

He scowled at Nimue whose face was an expressionless mask. As was Mab's.

I stood up. It hurt like hell but I wasn't going to stir up a hornet's nest of trouble grovelling on the ground. It was time to introduce a third option to this discussion, one that could upset other people's well-made plans. Ever since Llyr had arrived in my kitchen I'd been buffeted around like a leaf in a gale. It was time to change the direction of the wind.

I called Keir to me.

The lad got up, instantly self-conscious and awkward, glancing nervously at everyone that looked at him now. He stood at my side and swallowed hard. I gave him my best winning smile.

'You're wrong Llyr. The Dark Court does have an heir. He's here.'

I waited for the gasps and Llyr's contempt to cease and looked at the shock on each face. Poor Keir looked frightened beyond belief. Nimue, so good at hiding her feelings, couldn't disguise her astonishment. Mab wasn't attempting to hide her fury.

Good.

I directed my next words to her, to twist the knife.

'You didn't know, did you? You thought that by getting me to kill pretty boy over there, you could step in to the vacuum I'd created.'

That got the kind of reaction I wanted from Llyr. He screamed and cursed Mab, straining to get to her while her two minions restrained him.

Mab was the epitome of calm. She didn't pay any attention to Llyr's tantrum but looked at me with cold eyes.

'You can prove his lineage, I assume?'

For the next section of this little drama, I relied on my performance experience. That bastard Shakespeare would have been proud, after all, it was this secret he'd shared with humanity, hundreds of years before when he'd used my name in one of his plays. Apparently my indiscretion hadn't reached the Fae after all.

'Of course. Oberon left papers with Master Sidwell. I don't think even he knows what's in them, though I'm sure he suspects.'

I turned to Keir who looked stupefied.

'Has Master Sidwell watched over you?'

The boy nodded dumbly. I took hold of his right hand, held it up for Mab to see.

'Who gave you this coral ring?' I said as the boy looked at it as though he'd never seen it before.

'Master Sidwell, when I was young. He told me I was never to take it off, no matter what.'

I smiled at the lad. His brown skin had turned significantly paler.

'In your mother's culture, coral was given to children as a form of protection. She'd insisted your father gave it to you. He did so, through Master Sidwell.'

'My mother?'

The lad gasped the words. Now it was time to include Llyr in my performance.

'Describe your father's bedroom for me.'

He scowled at me, without any idea how I intended using his answer to reinforce my story, he couldn't invent any lies.

'A long time ago he decorated it with brightly coloured silks, like he was in a tent.'

I nodded. 'He copied the design of Keir's mother's home.'

They all watched me, an avid audience, one Oisin might appreciate.

'Before the signing of the Knights' Protocols, Oberon's travels took him to many places on Earth after his wife died, giving birth to that bastard.' I nodded at Llyr. 'It was in a land the humans call India, where he met a princess and fathered a child with her. He begged her to return to Tir na nÓg with him but her loyalty was to her own people and she remained behind. When Keir was born, Oberon insisted he return with him.'

Mab stepped closer to Keir to stare at him as though he was a laboratory specimen.

'Then why did he make him a slave? And how do you know all this?'

I gave her my most engaging smile.

'You know as well as I do that before illness ruined his mind, I was Oberon's friend and confidant. One drunken night we shared stories of past loves and conquests. As for why he made the boy a slave, I think there were two reasons: to keep the boy safe, to hide him in plain sight, for one. I think he already suspected what Llyr was turning into, Oberon knew he wouldn't hesitate in killing a rival.'

Mab and I looked over at Llyr who shrugged shoulders nonchalantly.

'Secondly, I assume the old man's paranoia had started to infect his mind. I think he worried the boy might be a threat in the future, keeping him as a slave was insurance. When Oberon drove me out of the Dark Court, I expect he'd decided his second son was best left where he was.'

My story must have convinced everyone because they all stared at the boy, it made him squirm under their scrutiny.

I turned to Mab. I was guessing on this next part and wondered how she'd react.

'You've seen his affinity with the wyvern. Can you imagine how powerful a figurehead he'd be if he could demonstrate that skill to the Dark Court?'

Bullseye!

There was a slight flicker of an eyelid and flushing of her skin but it was the boy's reaction that gave it all away. She glared at him but it was too late.

Llyr noticed it too. His expression changed as he acknowledged the young man's hybrid background and his right to the throne no longer mattered particularly, Mab had a replacement. One she could control.

If I could manipulate Llyr into directing his anger at Mab, they might direct their violence at each other, in front of Nimue as the ultimate witness. I smiled at the legitimacy of it all.

My satisfaction was, inevitably, short-lived.

If I'd thought of myself as a leaf buffeted in a gale then Llyr turned things into a hurricane.

His hunched shoulders spoke of defeat until he suddenly stood upright, pulled his hands from his coat pockets to reveal a device strapped to his knuckles. The instant he formed a fist, a bolt of energy, just like Brea's, arced across the wet grass like an acrobat. We all reacted too slowly, except one person, Llyr's intended victim.

Mab.

She leapt into the air, somersaulting in the process, to land on her feet a short distance from where the bolt of energy drove into the ground, causing turf to explode into the air.

Llyr swung round, blasted one of Mab's guards in the chest. The man was flung backwards, a black hole in his chest and was dead before his body hit the ground. The other was stupefied for an instant, he made the mistake of reaching for the sword strapped on his back and in that instant Llyr smashed a booted foot against the man's leg, dropping him to the ground and blasting his head clean off his shoulders.

Within two seconds he'd created chaos.

The first energy blast had been close enough to Keir make the wyvern think her master was under attack. It roared with fury and galloped towards Llyr, oblivious of everyone else, which included Oisin and me. We dived out of its way.

Brea's reactions were quicker and unaffected by the route of the vengeful wyvern. Incandescent white energy leapt from her fingertips as she yelled something above the crack of thunder that followed. Llyr dived from his position on the steps just in time to avoid the blast that destroyed part of the staircase. Like Mab had done, he leapt into the air and landed gracefully, paused long enough to fire another salvo of energy at Brea who dropped to the ground to avoid its searing force as it flew a short distance over her body.

'Now!' Llyr yelled as he shot a second bolt at the girl, she rolled on her side down a slight incline which offered temporary protection.

From around the far corner of the Abbey ruins a woman stepped out. We all followed the direction of Llyr's eyes and we all reacted with the same degree of shock.

'Surely not!' I heard Nimue gasp.

They hadn't been seen in the longest time, in fact stories maintained the last of their kind had been killed long ago. In Tir na nÓg they were called Bean Sidhe. Celtic legend portrayed them as women whose keening bemoaned the loss of a loved one. The reality was a lot less romantic, they were weapons capable of emitting destructive levels of sound. Over the centuries people distorted the name: they called them banshee.

I'd called her a woman, though gender was meaningless to this creature. She might look human until you saw the huge mouth, under which a throat pouch made her look more like a toad. It inflated swiftly, she opened her mouth to emit a sound so high-pitched, so loud, everything vibrated around us. The Abbey walls shook, loose masonry fell. The ground itself shook like an earthquake. For anyone with ears, the pain was intolerable.

The wyvern stopped its attack and dropped its head to the ground like it was trying to bury it. All the others fell to their knees, held their hands over their ears tightly and grimaced with pain. Mab had been about to attack Llyr with her sword, she tried to maintain the assault but she could do little apart from slowly drop to the ground and assume the same position as everyone else.

Llyr was unaffected, no doubt wearing something that stopped the scream from reaching his eardrums. He marched towards Keir, his readied sword made his intention obvious, that smile back on his lips.

My reactions to the Bean Sidhe were different.

The reason the Trooping Fairies achieved its elite status came down to two factors. The first was training. It meant understanding what to do against any opponent you might expect to face in battle. The body could be trained to react to a variety of threats and the pain they would likely evoke. The second factor came down to your character; the extent to which you were prepared to tolerate whatever pain they threat threw at you. Your training showed you what you could withstand and what you couldn't, it also showed you some useful techniques to deal with the threat and the pain. Withstanding the scream of the Bean Sidhe was one of those moments I'd endured in my training long ago.

The pain was terrible, I felt blood dribble from my ears and down my neck as I ran towards the creature. The high-pitched keening felt like sharp knives slicing through my brain, it would be so easy to curl into a ball and let the pain overwhelm me but instead I'd learned the technique of constantly yawning. It kept the tympanic membrane in the ear from constantly vibrating which would increase the scream's volume and intensity, opening your mouth and blowing through your nose regulated it to some extent.

The creature was ugly beyond belief, long strands of limp grey hair gave the appearance of great age, which fed the banshee legend but the body was still lithe and supple as it stepped backwards to avoid my attack. The banshee can sustain its scream for a long time but it still needs to breathe, the best time to attack was as it took its breath.

I raised my sword as I ran up to it, the creature dodged to its left to run past me, just as an energy bolt blasted the earth to my right. Llyr was trying to stop me, that was good, it meant he'd abandoned trying to kill Keir for the time being. The banshee dodged to run past me but the exercise caused it to use up its remaining breath. I drew level with the creature just as its throat sac deflated and hung limply under its mouth. Out of breath, it staggered, unable to avoid me any longer.

I ran my sword through the sac, the throat and out the other side.

The banshee gave a huge shudder and fell to the ground, dead.

I whirled round. The others were struggling to their feet, they'd suffer for several minutes until their tympanic membranes could adjust and I was too far away to do anything but hurry back. My exertions had opened my wounds again, the slickness of my blood worked its way down my face and chest but I dismissed that irrelevance.

Llyr watched me, grinned as he raised his hand to point his knuckles in my direction.

'I should have done this long ago!' he called.

Orange energy left the device as no more than a trickle that bounced around the wet ground at his feet and quickly fizzled out. He tried again, this time only grey smoke appeared.

'Never rely on technology!' I yelled as I raced towards him, sword raised.

He hurled the mass of wires and crystals to the ground angrily and looked around. The wyvern continued to shake its head in discomfort, everyone else struggled to stand up only to stagger like drunks. Llyr resumed his attack on Keir.

The wyvern saw the danger, tried to intercept but staggered and collapsed in a heap.

Keir, on his knees, raised both hands in a defensive position and called out 'Don't!'.

I was too far away to intervene, Llyr's perfect mouth formed its manic grin and his dark eyes burned with the same malevolence I'd seen in my kitchen before he murdered the boy. Behind him, from the Lady Chapel crypt, spriggans and boggarts poured through the archway.

The Bean Sidhe had been his insurance policy in case something had gone wrong.

Llyr's soldiers piled down the steps towards us. Brea leaned heavily against the Abbey wall, supported by her brother, to blast the ones at the front of the column but it didn't stop the rest from pushing forwards.

Mab raised her hand as a command for them to halt, it slowed them down briefly, she wasn't someone you crossed willingly but she appeared to be drunk as she staggered towards them. Llyr turned to his troops to bellow commands at them. He stood, sword raised, the picture of the leader in battle, authority in his voice and in his body language and the moment of indecision passed. They continued their advance.

Llyr grinned at me as I did my best to run, chest heaving, pain blossoming everywhere and knowing I wasn't going to make it in time to defend the boy. Llyr's oily words were spoken loud enough for all of us to hear as he raised his sword again.

'Time to die, little brother.'

'Stop!'

Nimue's voice rang out as she stepped in front of Keir and held up an imperious hand, it was enough to make Llyr pause. She had her back to me but I knew what he'd see, the force of will that made the most powerful warriors wilt.

'Stop and think Llyr. Consider what you're about to do. If you commit murder you will face execution. You will lose the throne as well as your life. Is that what you want?'

But Llyr wasn't intimidated by the old woman, I don't think he even cared about her threats, he'd burned his bridges and had nothing to lose.

'You're assuming there will be witnesses, you old crow.'

He swung his sword, not at Keir but to decapitate the old woman. The blade flashed as it caught what little sunlight there was, slicing downward towards the old woman, she turned her head defensively, unable to move out of its way. Suddenly Oisin was there, in front of her, pushing her backwards. The sword struck him, a fountain of blood rose into the air and he landed heavily on the ground at her feet and didn't move.

I screamed. I don't know what I said, or even if it was anything intelligible. I screamed something and the world stopped. Everything about my life distilled into one moment of wisdom. I'd suffered untold agonies to be trained to fight those who needed my protection. I'd been pushed beyond normal limits, until a part of my brain had plumbed such depths it released the monster that no doubt lies dormant in us all. Despite those experiences, even though I'd come through the other side of that training, I'd had to leave Tir na nÓg, because I feared what Oberon would do to those I'd loved. Especially Oisin.

Since then, not only had I failed to protect others, I'd put them in danger. Even the wyvern had saved us when I couldn't. I'd risked the lives of the Knights, the kids I'd vowed to their father I'd protect at any cost.

And now Oisin lay dead, or dying, I couldn't even protect the man I loved. All my indecision and uncertainty vanished in that moment, to be replaced by crystal clarity. I'd spent too long thinking what was best for people, trying to do right by them, and all it had brought them was danger and death. I had overlooked the basic premise of my role, to destroy anyone who tries to kill those you've vowed to protect. I was a killing machine and it was time to do what I did best.

The world turned red. A roaring sound filled my ears and the pain in my chest vanished. That's the good thing about adrenalin, it stops you feeling anything. All I wanted to feel was vengeance.

Puck rose within me, normally a reaction I dreaded but this time was different. I welcomed him. I couldn't remember ever doing that before, his arrival usually had the effect of making me shut my eyes to his mayhem, of hiding behind the sofa. Now, like a slumbering leviathan rising from the deep, he made his way to the surface while I savoured the horror that was about to be unleashed.

Puck exploded into action.

Somehow he was already standing over Keir when his blade clashed with Llyr's, who looked shocked at Puck's arrival, an expression that only deepened when he saw the face of the thing standing in front of him, his fear annihilated the shock.

Somewhere beyond Puck's vision, which was centred firmly on his adversary, there were gasps and muffled words of horror. I assume Mab and Nimue had noticed the change.

Puck didn't care. His blade flashed as it sliced the air in aggressively choreographed moves which pushed Llyr backwards. It was a masterclass of swordplay. There were techniques I didn't know I knew, presumably from my training which lay dormant in my synapses, like the monster that used them now.

He was silent, there were no replies to Llyr's teeth-gritted promises of power or his hastily constructed threats. The sword was Puck's response, swift, sharp and severe.

I found myself smiling, an enthusiastic observer to the battle, I felt like cheering as Llyr stumbled or lost his rhythm so that he looked suddenly vulnerable.

Others arrived. Blades swiped and cudgels swung into view, thwarting Puck's attack, forcing him to defend himself. It was like watching an exciting film through my own blinkered eyes, Puck's attention zeroed in on one thing, his victim. Everything else was extraneous. Creatures that got in his way were quickly despatched, though the cost was never clear, weapons appeared out of nowhere, sometimes knocking him to one side or on to the ground. Every time, Puck was on his feet in a second.

Bodies appeared. Blood gushed. Limbs severed.

Until Llyr's face appeared in the diminishing crowd of those who aimed to frustrate Puck from his goal.

A spriggan appeared in front of him, opened its mouth to roar something but Puck's sword slammed into it, hit hard skull on the other side. It fell to the ground as the sword drew back to slice across another's chest that took its place. Puck's boot smashed against the creature's thigh, knocking it out of the way. A slicing action and a head rolled off shoulders. With both hands on the sword's grip a vertical chop opened up a ribcage from sternum to the belly. The whole time Puck's attention remained firmly fixed on his victim who tried to hide behind the dwindling number of defenders.

Something hit Puck from behind, pushing him forwards, almost losing his balance. Except he turned the stumble into a quick-footed dance, turning to attack the tusk-faced boggart that looked astonished at the recovery. An expression that remained on the creature's face as its head fell on to the ground.

Puck whirled around. Fixed his attention on his victim again.

There was something new about his behaviour I noticed. It wasn't just the swiftness of movement in positioning himself in front of the other man, it wasn't the blur of blades as they clashed, echoing around the Abbey walls. It was the focus on his quarry.

This wasn't a fight, it was a hunt.

The sword became a sequence of hypnotic flashes as individual movement was lost so that the eye was drawn into the centre of chaos.

'You'll. Suffer. For. This.'

Llyr gasped his last words as exhaustion claimed him.

His eyes widened and he frowned. Looked down at his chest, at the blade sunk deep into it. Eyes closed. Breath heaved. Stopped short.

He collapsed.

Puck stood over him, hilt of sword in one hand. Stomped hard on the perfect face. Bones crunched. Another stomp. More crunching accompanied by squelching noises. He went to stomp again but the effort was too great.

Puck, his mission complete, receded.

He handed my body back to me. I wasn't grateful for the gift. Pain exploded everywhere, I screamed in agony I had never known before. I looked down at my body where my blood merged with that of my victims.

Just feet away from me lay Oisin's body. I thought I saw his chest rise and fall, just the shallowest of movements. Nimue was examining him; clinical, calm, dispassionate.

'Save him. Please?'

It was no more than a croak but she glanced at me.

'And if I do?'

I wanted to scream at the bitch, he'd saved her life and she demanded reasons. But this was Nimue, she did nothing unless there was gain to made. With my final glimmer of energy, I found the breath to make yet another vow.

'I will serve as your paladin.'

Her gaze intensified, scrutinised me for any signs of mischief. When she found none, she nodded very slightly.

'I will heal him.'

I think I may have smiled. Not just because I'd ensured Oisin would live but because I'd fooled Nimue. Death waited. I reached out a hand, ready to be led to wherever he wanted to take me. I didn't care where. I'd had enough of life. It had taken a long time to find Death but now, at last, I held his hand and I wasn't letting go.

Chapter 24 - Epilogue

There was light.

It filled the room, blinded me with its brilliance. There was comfort too. Plus, there was no pain. If this was Death, I approved. I sighed with satisfaction.

'He's awake.'

I recognised the voice and satisfaction vanished.

Death had forsaken me. With that realisation came a terrible sense of emptiness and loss. I'd felt his cold grasp and been comforted by it, I'd given in to him like a lover, only to be rejected.

Brea's face hovered over me, frowning.

'Finally.' An accusation by someone kept waiting.

Her silver hair was longer. She'd lost the unhealthy pallor and the dark circles around her eyes but none of the hostility.

'Thirsty.'

My voice sounded hoarse, my throat burned.

I got a nod as though she'd expected the request. A glass of water appeared in front of me, I lifted my head towards it and she held it while I drank thirstily. She poured more from a jug on the bedside table and I downed that too and thanked her. She gave me a quick shoulder shrug of indifference.

Her double appeared on the other side of the bed and smiled at me.

'Welcome back to the land of the living.'

I had no interest in being in such a place, it offered me nothing. I'd hoped to escape from it and somehow, at the border crossing, I'd been turned back.

'What happened?'

The twins looked across the bed and held eye contact for a second.

Suddenly Amelie was in front of me, bustling, busy and business-like, re-arranging pillows and tucking in well-ordered sheets.

'I've got soup ready. You must be hungry after all this time.'

I wasn't hungry. With my thirst slaked I wasn't anything. Except alive.

'All this time?' I croaked.

My eyes felt heavy and suddenly the effort of being awake overwhelmed me. My eyelids drooped and I let darkness take me, hoping this time it would be final.

Except it wasn't. The next time I woke the room was dark. I drank from the glass of water positioned ready for me to reach easily. I was alone. For the first time I became aware of my body, of the injuries healing, of the bandages that covered almost every part of me. It surprised me there wasn't any pain.

Instead they brought back memories and the avalanche began.

Memories of Oisin's body, covered in his blood, limbs at awkward angles. Memories of my plea to Nimue to heal him.

Memories of my vow to be her paladin.

Fuck.

I'd made that promise expecting them to be the final words of a dying man.

Fuck. Fuck. Fuck.

My eyes burned and tears formed, they rolled down my cheeks in big salty globules. I couldn't remember the last time I'd cried. It had to have been as a kid. A vague recollection of a beating from Commander Taranis. There had been so many of them, they all merged into one long punishment. They were silent tears, there was no blubbing or heaving of breath, I cried for the unfairness of everything, of the frustration, the knowledge that I had no escape from this life.

Fate had chosen to torture me by re-introducing Oisin, tempting me with him. It was the most exquisite torment, keeping the man I'd come to love again beyond my reach until he was taken from me a second time. Fate hadn't just denied me my dreams, it had dashed them against sharp rocks that left his beautiful body a bloody mess.

I don't know how long I cried but I woke again to light streaming through a window. It felt strange, to have a window that wasn't boarded up.

'How are you feeling?'

Amelie's lined face smiled as she bent over me, wiped my face with a cool cloth.

'Best get rid of those tear stains, eh?'

The mere mention summoned more of the salty bastards. She squeezed my hand and broadened her smile yet it was tinged with sadness.

'I'm sorry Robin. No one deserves what you went through. But, if it helps, you've made such a difference. The war's ended. The Fae have gone.'

I suppose I should have been pleased but I didn't feel anything. Perhaps whatever kept the pain at bay was doing the same to my emotions, that offered an addiction I'd readily adopt.

She watched my reaction and her face clouded at the lack of response but then she said something that showed how much she understood of me.

'I'm sorry Robin. We don't know what happened to Oisin.'

I looked at her and felt a lump in my throat. Words were hard to form.

'But Nimue kept her promise?'

A tight nod.

Before I could interrogate her further the twins entered the room. I felt Amelie's hand tighten around mine as she told them I was feeling better, even though she hadn't asked.

'Does he know?' That was Brea, terse as ever.

'Know what?'

I tried to sit up but was pushed back by Amelie's firm spare hand. She sighed and glared at the girl. Her brother watched me closely, I could feel him in my head, rooting around, it triggered big watery eyes as he looked into mine. He tried to smile but failed. Brea looked at him, then at me and frowned.

'Know what?' I asked again.

Amelie took a breath and smiled like the doctor that's about to tell you bad news. I steeled myself.

'You were very close to dying Robin.'

Just not close enough.

'For a while we thought you weren't going to make it.'

I'd depended on it but there was no point wishing.

'They want me for murdering Llyr, don't they?'

More glances but this time with smiles.

Finn placed a hand on the part of my shoulder that wasn't bandaged.

'Apparently Mab reported Llyr died in battle, honourably. There's been no mention of your involvement at all.'

Brea giggled, I hadn't heard the sound for the longest time. 'She was more concerned about getting that Indian guy back and checking if what you said was true.'

'I felt sorry for him. He looked petrified. What a shock, to go from slave to aristocracy.' Finn turned to me. 'How long had you known about his heritage?'

Now it was Amelie's turn to giggle. 'Oh, he's known about it a very long time, haven't you Robin?' She was trying to distract me, to lighten the mood. She looked at the kids, face beaming with mischief. 'You remember how Oberon and Titania fight over the Indian prince in A Midsummer Night's Dream?'

They both turned to look at me, mouths open. Amelie laughed as she nodded her head in my direction.

'Too much beer one night in a tavern with William Shakespeare.'

The three of them chuckled like school kids. It was good to see them happy again. She might be old but Amelie was the closest these two had to a parent. She was certainly much better than me. It gave me time to think about what Mab had done. If I wasn't facing execution for killing the High Lord of the Dark Court what were they unwilling to tell me?

'What are you not telling me? If it's not Mab..?'

The mood changed and Amelie held up a hand as both the kids started to reply.

'It's about the pledge you made to serve Nimue.'

I was awake enough for realisation to strike me like one of Brea's bolts of energy. The old woman had called my bluff. She'd known I was dying and wouldn't be around to fulfil my obligations. I should have known no one reneged on a deal with the Lady of the Lake.

Fuck.

'She took you and Oisin back to Tir na nÓg and then her people brought you back here to recover, before time ran out.'

Brea shook her head dismissively. 'That was two weeks ago. You've done nothing but sleep all the time.'

'But you don't know what happened to Oisin?'

They shook their heads at the same time.

'The Fae dumped you and left. They were in quite a hurry,' Finn said.

I lowered my head and stared at my hands gripping the bedsheet. At least, I told myself, Nimue was honourable. If she'd healed me to fulfil my pledge, she'd heal Oisin to fulfil hers. He was probably lying in bed like me, in a Light Court bedchamber, recovering.

In another realm. A world apart.

But with Llyr and Oberon gone, there was no longer any need for my self-imposed exile. Amelie and the twins were babbling about the end of the war but I wasn't listening. I could go home.

I could go home.

The thought brought more tears but I didn't care. Brea noticed and sniffed disdainfully as she shook her head.

'What are you crying for? Aren't you pleased the army are destroying them?'

My puzzled look made her frown in confusion.

Finn looked at me closely.

'He didn't hear what we said.' He blinked as he looked at me a little more closely and then swallowed hard. 'Oh. Oh dear.'

His glance at Amelie told me that bad news was on its way.

'He was planning to go back,' the lad mumbled.

All three looked at me, frowned and glanced at each other in the assumption someone else would break the bad news. The long pause was unbearable. Apparently, fate had one more ace to play. Amelie gave a sigh of resignation, she hadn't let go of my hand the whole time and she squeezed it harder now. I held my breath.

'Mab returned hours after your fight with Llyr. She announced the end of the invasion and the withdrawal of all Fae forces. A week later an Army unit arrived in the town and confirmed it. They declared martial law.'

Amelie took a deep breath and tried a smile.

'Remember Robin, you were the one that ended the war. It was your bravery.'

The words she and Finn had used earlier struck me now. The urgent need for the Fae to return meant one thing. The soldiers would have one objective to carry out beyond maintaining order.

Amelie sighed. 'They destroyed the portals. They had to make certain there was no chance of the Fae returning. It's happening all over the country, every historic site is being demolished.'

I nodded. The lump in my throat threatened to choke me but what words were there to say? I was trapped here. My exile was permanent.

The three looked awkwardly at each other and stood up. Amelie reached in the pocket of her pinafore and drew out a piece of brilliantly white paper that shimmered. I held my breath, I knew who it was from and its purpose.

'I was told to give you this,' she said quietly. 'It's from...'

It weighed no more than a bird's feather. 'I know who it's from.'.

The paper was folded twice and sealed with silver wax stamped with the sigil of an apple. I broke the bond and opened it. The message was short and written in a spidery handwriting. It was signed Nimue.

'You know as well as I do this is far from over. Your vow to be my paladin was perfectly judged, even if you didn't intend to fulfil it.

You will be my agent in the human realm, Master Goodfellow.

Mankind will seek vengeance. The Dark Court will use it to retaliate with even greater force. Next time they will not be led by an idiot. There are forces abroad in the Dark Court that have ambitions beyond those of Llyr and I am no longer able to withstand them. The past is never dead, Master Goodfellow, it can return and cause chaos to both our worlds.

You must stop it from happening. That is your obligation to me.'

I refolded the paper, moulding the wax bond together again. Instantly the message evaporated into silver mist.

'What did she say?' Brea asked, suspicious suddenly.

I looked at the girl and her brother and smiled.

'Apparently my obligation to Nimue is to continue to protect the Knights.'

Brea snorted. 'Continue to protect? That's a fucking joke.'

I wasn't sure why I was lying about it, except that I needed to keep the kids safe, they'd suffered enough. Finn watched me, frowning now. I hastily emptied my mind.

'But the war's over. The Fae can't return without the portals. Why do we still need protecting? It doesn't make sense.'

I smiled reassurance. 'We're a long-lived and unforgiving race Finn. I'll be your insurance, just in case.'

Death had rejected me. I was obliged to continue living, and as much as I hated the thought, I had to accept its decision. Part of me was a demon with a dark heart but I was also a soldier, pledged to protect others. I'd made vows to Nimue and to the twins' father and Robin Goodfellow was an honourable man. I'd keeping trying to fulfil my commitments.

Hopefully next time, I wouldn't fuck it up.

Want to know what happens next?

Robin may think things are over for him but they're only just starting! He's upset a lot of people and they want to get their own back. Plus, Keir is about to experience a very different life as High Lord of the Dark Court and Filidea is about to discover what life is like beyond the Light Court.

Read the first chapter of

'The Renegade of Two Realms'

Renegade of Two Realms: Chapter 1

People were trying to kill me.

Technically, they weren't people but that didn't matter, it was their determination that bothered me more. I stared at the kitchen ceiling and waited but the creaky floorboard refused to make another sound. I slammed my mug of tea on the table so that its steaming contents spilled over my hand and cursed.

'Comes to something when you can't enjoy a mug of tea without some bastard trying to kill you.'

The mug didn't reply, none of the inanimate objects did, but it didn't stop me talking to them.

I picked up my sword from its place by the back door, snatched a bag of salt off the kitchen table, stuffed it in a trouser pocket and hefted my sawn-off shotgun over my shoulder. Having weapons to hand was proving to be essential these days. I listened intently, still nothing.

I snuffed the flame in the lantern, plunging the kitchen into near darkness. Shafts of purple June twilight seeped through holes in the boards at my window, they offered all the illumination I'd need. I climbed the stairs on tiptoe, keeping my attention focused on the darkness in front of me.

Doors to the bathroom and spare room on the right remained closed, as I'd left them. Not so the door to my bedroom on the left, over the kitchen, I stepped towards it and listened carefully. Nothing.

Someone dropped on to my shoulders, wrenched the shotgun out of my hand and hurled it to the floor. An arm wrapped around my neck; thick, rigid hairs dug into my skin. My head got yanked back to expose my throat. I threw myself back against the wall before the attacker could finish what he started. It forced air out of his mouth, fetid and hot, I followed through by jerking my head back, smashed it hard into my new friend's face. It was enough for the arm around my neck to release its hold slightly, I dropped my sword so I could perform a tight forward roll along the landing. I reached out, felt the pommel of the sword and stood up.

I wasn't fast enough.

A hairy and very solid head hit my chest, forcing my arms to windmill as I tried to keep my balance at the top of the staircase. I grabbed at the vague shape in front of me, felt his greasy clothing as I lost my footing but held on to him as we tumbled downstairs.

We rolled, head over heels, and not always my own, until we landed in a tangled heap at the foot of the staircase. Somehow, no doubt rigorous training in my youth, helped me land without injury. My sword clattered after us but in the dark and cramped hallway, amongst the snarl of arms and legs, I was trapped with the hairy bugger on top of me. A narrow beam of light from a boarded window fell on a small but deadly looking knife in a hairy hand. I watched it draw back, knew I had a second, no more.

I brought my knee up sharply in the hope of connecting with the bastard's balls, my luck was in, I struck soft tissue and heard a loud gasp of pain. The knife vanished but the gasp told me Mister Hairy's head was directly in front of me. I lashed out with my fist, punched as hard as I could and heard him groan. Rather than give up, hairy hands clawed my face, clutched at my throat. We rolled around on the floor, like passionate lovers, as we both searched for the knife in the darkness while trying to inflict as much damage on the other person.

After failing to find the knife he rolled me onto my back, which gave him the advantage. He pinned me to the floor with his weight and tried to punch my dodging head in the darkness, I hoped it offered enough of a distraction. By raising my knees, I managed to lift him slightly, letting me free one hand just enough so I could reach into my pocket. I grabbed a handful of salt and ground the granules into the bastard's face.

It generated a high-pitched wail, with his attention focused on the pain in his face for an instant I tipped my new wrestling partner sideways. A couple of frantic seconds later I found my sword and thrust it into the darkness, hoping luck was on my side.

The blade point penetrated something fleshy but without any real resistance, so nothing fatal, probably a limb. Mister Hairy grunted something I didn't understand, probably cursing my ancestry or my good luck. Fighting in darkness didn't bother this guy, I needed a change of location. I ran into the kitchen. Heavy breathing followed just behind me, the stumbling sound suggested I'd wounded the bastard's leg, I hoped it would slow him down.

Just as I flung open the back door, my foe pounced. We staggered outside and rolled around in my recently dug vegetable patch.

In the fading light I saw my would-be assassin for the first time; the small beady eyes set deep within a face covered in bristles and above a snout with protruding long whiskers, smeared in blood. The rest of the body was human in appearance and dressed in filthy clothes but now I knew what I was fighting.

A Fir Darrig.

The Light Court called them rat boys, not a name intended as a compliment.

Their ability to move without making a sound, their cruelty and lack of any morality made them perfect assassins. This bastard had deliberately made the floorboard creak to bring me upstairs into the darkness.

With him back on top of me again, I managed to hurl him sideways, to give me time to dig into my pocket and haul another handful of salt. He was so busy trying to stop me getting up he missed my hand as I rubbed the salt into the bloody wound into his leg. He howled, tried to brush away the granules clinging to his wound, which gave me enough time to get up and level my blade at the rat boy's bloody face. Small black eyes followed the blade upwards until they met mine.

'Tell me who sent you, you rat bastard or I'll fucking skewer you!'

The creature said something unintelligible but judging by its snarling mouth and spitting delivery, he wasn't offering to surrender. I doubted it could even speak English, languages were probably low down on the curriculum at rat boy school. Plus, there was an advantage in sending an assassin to do a job when it couldn't give away any secrets, no matter how much torture you applied.

It prompted indecision, taking the rat boy prisoner was pointless but I couldn't bring myself to murder the thing in cold blood, I was trying not to be too psychotic these days. My hesitation was all Mister Hairy needed, it hurled lumps of soil at me, rolled to one side and was on its feet in a blur.

It crouched and sprang, like a real rat, avoiding my blade in the process. It clung on to me, arms wrapped around my neck, legs around my waist so we staggered like drunken dancers, until the rat-boy headbutted me. For a brief second I smelled its putrid stench until my nose stopped working and blood trickled into my mouth.

Rat Boy tried using his body mass to force me up against the cottage wall, thereby restricting my mobility. I had other plans, I dug my heels into the soft ground and roared into his spiky face and pushed towards my garden shed. We grunted and pushed and pummelled each other like rutting stags, I got head-butted a second time but it didn't have the same power. His leg wound made the difference in the end, it left him without the essential leverage so, with every bit of strength I could muster, I pushed him until I slammed him against the side of the wooden shed, forcing air out of its lungs in a loud gasp. The shed, which had withstood storms for years, lurched under the pressure, wood creaked and splintered and we crashed through one wall and landed on the floor, followed by dozens of objects that had sat on shelves. Rat boy glared up at me angrily as he sucked in air, blood trickled out of his mouth and a small pool of blood formed near one armpit. He made no effort to move and the pained expression told me he'd skewered himself on something. I struggled to my knees, leg muscles burning, still not sure what to do with my prisoner.

Somewhere nearby I heard a hissing sound.

I glanced around, wary of another attack until I spotted my hairy friend doing the same thing. We spotted it at the same time. A damaged gas cylinder.

'Shit!'

I jumped up, evading the weak clutches of the rat boy and stood over him as his pool of blood grew bigger.

He gave me a look of burning animosity, said something unintelligible again but didn't try to move.

The roof emitted a loud creaking sound, informing us it was about to surrender to the inevitable, something snapped loudly and the remaining walls and the roof shook. Instinct made me sprint through the hole we'd just created as the shed, like a pack of cards, collapsed inwards, loudly and with a great deal of dust.

I heard the sound, an enormous whoomph, felt the heat and found myself flying through the air, to land heavily on my back in the freshly dug vegetable patch. Billowing flames and intense heat filled the air until darkness swallowed me.

'Keep your head down Puck! Something that size makes an easy target!'

Smoke billowed and worked its way into my lungs, made me cough until my throat burned, it reached into my eyes, filled them with tears so I couldn't see. I stayed like that until I thought I'd die, the need for fresh air became an obsession, one I was deliberately being denied. Suddenly an outline loomed in front of me, greyer than the grey smoke. Its overlong arm reached backwards as it prepared to drive the object in its hand into my chest, leaving its side open for a split second. I held a similar knife in my own hand, drove it between the ribs of the figure above me. The effort dragged in more smoke into my burning lungs. The grey shape coalesced into the hulking weight of a seven-foot spriggan and collapsed on top of me, leaving me unable to breathe. I was going to die and if it brought an end to this torture, I didn't care.

Just as my lungs searched for air that wasn't there and dark blotches appeared at the edges of my vision, a strong breeze cleared away the smoke. With what little

338

strength I had left in my muscles I moved the corpse just enough so I could pull in fresh air. I hacked and heaved as my lungs tried to push out smoke while inhaling clean air, slowly calming myself in the process.

With the smoke gone a shadow loomed over me, I couldn't see beyond the corpse but the painful kick up my arse and the snarling voice told me all I needed to know.

'Useless Puck. Useless. You kill your opponent and let him kill you in return.'

'I'm sorry, my Lord.'

An arm in a leather sleeve with gold embroidery grabbed hold of the corpse and yanked it off me. I staggered to my feet, tears streaming down my cheeks, blurring the towering figure of condemnation so that I didn't see the punch, I felt it strike jaw though. Before I knew what had happened I was laid out on the ground again.

'Sorry? You pathetic little shit. Five minutes and we do this again until you learn to fight in the midst of fire and smoke.'

The figure strode away, turned to where my fellow trainees watched with undisguised resentment. I'd pay for my weaknesses, and not with money either.

Another kick. I gritted my teeth, this one wasn't delivered with the same force. It had to be from one of my so-called peers so I warned him of the consequences in graphic terms. I opened my eyes. There was no smoke, no training ground, I was in my garden and surrounded by soldiers, busy stifling grins.

Except one.

'Get up man! What happened this time?'

The officer stood ramrod straight, hands clasped behind his back to peer down through white eyebrows knitted together like a white caterpillar, cold blue eyes without a trace of humour, compassion or humanity.

My body ached in every muscle, I couldn't breathe properly but realised the congealed blood in my nostrils was to blame. My dream, like the smoke from the garden shed, drifted into the cool twilight air.

'Well! Come on man! Haven't got all day!' the old man snapped.

'Fuck off! I'm not one of your soldiers, you old goat!'

His unit struggled to restrain their laughter until the old man glared them into subservient inscrutability. He gestured to the nearest soldier who reached down, grabbed my arm and yanked me upright, I squealed with pain.

The aptly named Colonel Crabbe looked me up and down with a wrinkled nose and dismissive shake of the head, a gesture like the one I'd received from someone very similar, long, long ago.

'You degenerates are all the same, no discipline, no respect!'

It was said with resignation that brooked no argument.

I gingerly touched my nose to assess the damage. The pain made my eyes water.

'Yeah I know Colonel. I should be punished.' I sniffed and it hurt. 'Why not bend me over a cannon and whip my bare buttocks?'

One of the soldiers snorted but swiftly converted it into a sneeze. The old man glared at him before turning his attention back to me.

'I assume, Mister Goodfellow, there's been another visit from your fairy friends? This is the third time I've had to mobilise my men.'

'They're not my fucking friends.'

My words got waved away.

'These bastards are trying to kill me and the fucking Fir Darrig, in what's left of my shed, came the closest of all of them. I thought you were supposed to be keeping the citizens of Glastonbury safe? Because you're failing in your mission.'

The old man blew disgruntled air out of his mouth, causing his enormous white moustache to ripple like a curtain.

'We protect human citizens. You don't qualify.'

Normally this cantankerous bastard and his bigoty didn't bother me but the pain made me irritable.

'That's where you're fucking wrong, you old bastard. The government need me, they said as much repeatedly when the Fae returned to their own realm. If I'm dead who's going to advise them?'

Blue eyes, without a hint of emotion, levelled with mine.

'The Knight twins now provide that service. After all, they are human.'

I fought down the anger. This was the thanks I got for killing Llyr, stopping the war, leaving the Dark Court temporarily leaderless. Not only had I been branded a traitor by my own race, someone wanted me dead and no one cared.

341

'Do your friends in London think those kids know everything about what's happening in Tir na nÓg? Because news alert, they don't! They've not even been there! How can they advise you?'

A smile peeked out from under the white bush beneath the old man's nose.

'Your advice is no longer needed Mister Goodfellow.'

He spoke with such authority I began to wonder if he knew something I didn't. His smug smile grew.

'Surely, Mister Goodfellow, one fact above all others, must be apparent to you?'

The pendulum in this conversation had swung towards the starchy old man in front of me and I didn't like where it was leading. I kept silent, difficult as that was. That fucking smile widened even more to show yellow teeth.

'I thought not. Let me explain Mister Goodfellow. Do stop me if you get confused.'

The other soldiers shared in the joke with self-satisfied grins.

'When your Fae friends,' and he deliberately emphasized the last word, 'retreated from our world they dismantled the event horizons, it prevented any further travel between their world and ours. Agreed?'

I nodded. I could guess where this was going now and I wished I'd raised the subject earlier to avoid this patronising lecture.

'Yet your three assailants have returned here, unseen, by my men. They have not used the portal in the Abbey or the Tor. Do you know what that means Mister Goodfellow?'

'Yes!' I snarled. 'There's another portal.'

The old bastard nodded his head slowly like an ancient school teacher might praise a dim-witted student for correctly providing the sum of two plus two.

'True. But the military has valuable intelligence, Mister Goodfellow.'

I chose not to make the obvious observation, despite the temptation this arrogant bastard provoked. He continued with his lecture, unaware of his own ambiguity.

'Because the bastards continue to invade our world, we have reason to believe they will attack again. You are a security risk, Mister Goodfellow. Some of my colleagues think you are providing your friends with intelligence and this is just a cover.'

Those blue eyes didn't waver.

'Time to leave Glastonbury, Mister Goodfellow.'

This was not the sentiment from a miserable old bastard, he didn't have the authority. This sentiment was getting handed down the chain of command. How could things change so radically in six months?

'Where should I go, Colonel Crabbe? I'm exiled from Tir na nÓg because I killed a member of their royal family. It was something I did to protect the human race.'

The old man snorted, fluttering the hairy caterpillar beneath his nose. He clicked dismissive fingers at one of the soldiers, when he spoke it was with same disparaging tone.

'Lieutenant Weir, debrief this person and assist him in whatever way will ensure his removal from my town in the shortest possible time.'

The young man, sporting a uniform with sharp creases and such highly polished boots you could see your face in them, glanced at me then turned to his commanding officer with a resigned frown and saluted.

'Yes sir, as you command.'

The old man turned smartly, his unit did the same, casting gloating glances at the young man who remained behind.

'You haven't answered my question Colonel Crabbe. So where should I go?'

The upright figure paused, turned ice-cold eyes on me. 'I don't know Mister Goodfellow. Frankly, I don't fucking care either. Perhaps during the next attack, you will reconsider your situation and allow your assailant to complete their mission successfully. I'm sure that would please everyone on both sides of these fucking portals.'

He turned smartly and marched with stiff-necked precision out of sight. No one else was going to protect me apparently, I wasn't wanted. I might have brought about the end of the war but now I was an embarrassment, a dubious ally. If I was going to survive I'd need to keep my wits about me. Everything I'd fought for, risked my life to achieve, meant nothing.

This was why it paid never to get involved.

I marched into my kitchen to make myself another cup of tea.

30254713R00204

Printed in Poland
by Amazon Fulfillment
Poland Sp. z o.o., Wrocław